Rhyaden

Also By Barbara:

Children's Books:

Badger the Dog
Badger's Busy Day
Badger & Friends
Badger Lost & Found
Badger Grows Up

Novels:

Wait Here, Wait There

Rhyaden

Barbara Tyner

Cover art by CGC Games
Cover layout by Price Johnston
Interior layout by Chuck Barrett
Edited by Jennifer Top and Jamie Smith
Developmental Editor - Laura Johnston

FIRST EDITION

ISBN: 978-0-9985193-8-8 (Print)
ISBN: 978-0-9985193-9-5 (Digital eBook)
Library of Congress Control Number: 2018942907
Tyner, Barbara.
    RHYADEN / Barbara Tyner
    FICTION: Fantasy/Dragons & Mythical Creatures

Published by Switchback Press

www.switchbackpress.com

Dedicated to Rhya, Tynan, Jameson, Juliana, and Ella, who listen to my stories and light up my life.

You have made my heart grow five sizes too big.

ACKNOWLEDGMENTS

No man is an island* cannot be truer than when one is writing a book. There are many to thank, but first and foremost is my developmental editor, Laura Johnston, who pulled me back when I ventured off the grid for middle grade readers, which was quite often. Her help was invaluable, as was Jamie Smith's knack for finding the errata. Chuck Barrett, Greg Hill, and Deb Waldo were invaluable readers, giving advice, encouragement, and that all important ingredient, motivation to keep going. Then there were my Eighth Grade Beta readers, Erica Chen, Gabrielle Scheffing, Cole Spraker, and Devin Ash. Their honest input was delightful and important. Thanks to Jen for editing and input, and to Chuck for putting it all together, and being patient with me. Too numerous to mention, but appreciated just as much, are the friends and family that have stuck with me through the process.

*John Donne

Rhyaden

The trees were not thrilled in the beginning of Niall's archery career. Many of the nicks left behind from the arrows were painful. However, later, it was a source of great pride for the older trunks that the young Niall had started his education in their very own woods, and they had the scars in their deeply furrowed bark to prove it.

You might believe that it is always the wind that causes trees to whisper, but I can assure you, my dears, it is not.

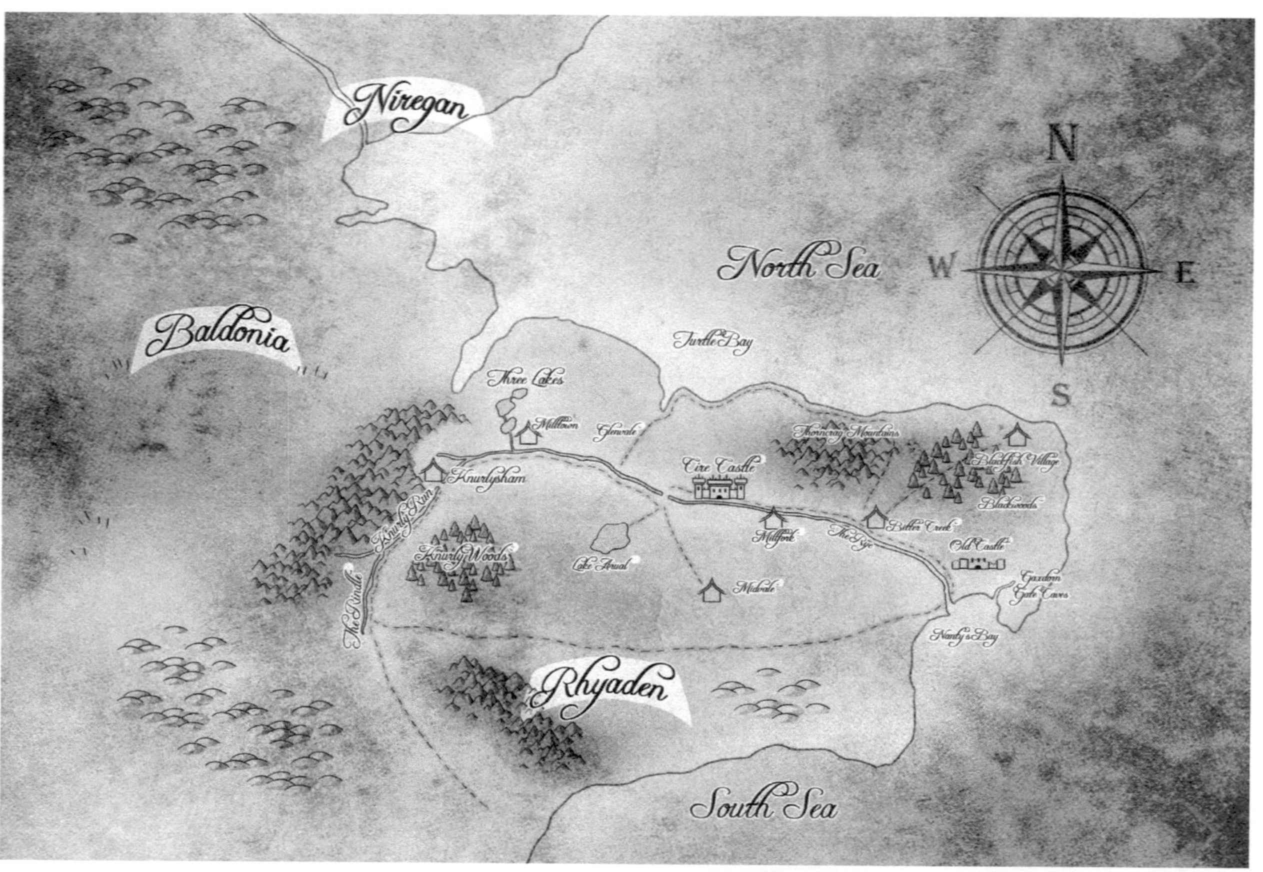

N
W
E
S
Niregan
Baldonia
North Sea
South Sea
Turtle Bay
Three Lakes
Milltown
Glenvale
Thorncrag Mountains
Cire Castle
Blackfish Village
Blackwoods
Bitter Creek
The Eye
Old Castle
Millfork
Midvale
Gaxdown Gate Caves
Nandy's Bay
Knurlysham
Knurly Run
The Rindle
Knurly Woods
Lake Arual
Rhyaden

Chapter One

An hour of chasing each other through the woods brought on the burn of an empty stomach. Niall and his cohorts sat red-faced, catching their breath under great Knurly trees in the woods outside of Knurlysham, a small village on the western side of the kingdom of Rhyaden.

"I'm starving!" Gunder complained.

"You're always hungry," Niall teased. His friend was tall and stout, the fastest runner of all the boys in the village, and the one whose side you wanted to be on come a fight.

"I suppose that's true," Gunder replied, "but that's how I grow these!" He pulled up his sleeve to show off his hard muscles, which were indeed very impressive for a lad of twelve, attributed to long hours working alongside his father at the forge.

"Is THAT where you've been keeping your brains?" Niall asked.

A second later, Gunder was on top of Niall. They rolled through tall ferns, tussling and grunting until Niall was pinned to the forest floor. He hated admitting defeat—again.

During the melee, Ben managed to stay out of harm's way. Younger by a year, he was scrawny but held great promise to grow. He piped up. "Let's go to the bakeshop. I bet I can niggle some biscuits for us." His mop of reddish brown hair and a rash of freckles framed big eyes and an even bigger smile.

"Grand idea," Gunder bellowed. In an instant he was up, dusting himself off. Niall rolled over and got to his knees, shaking debris out of his gold-colored hair and righting his tunic, which had gone decidedly askew in the ruckus.

Ben's parents and two aunts ran the local bakeshop in the village of Knurlysham. His aunts made delicious gingerbread and shortbread biscuits, but nothing topped his mother Gwyn's soft-inside-crusty-outside loaves of warm, golden brown bread. The boys took off at a gallop.

A half mile away, Flin Finwick, Ben's father, pulled the last heavy sack of newly milled flour out of the wagon and carried it through the back door of the bakeshop. He stopped to catch his breath, glancing at the fire in the big oven before returning to put away his horse and wagon. Movement caught his eye as he walked across the cobbled yard, and he couldn't help but smile. Sprinting hard, three figures dipped out of sight in the ravine just this side of the woods. Shortly, one head popped up, then another, and finally a third brought up the rear.

When the three boys burst through the back door into the shop with its tantalizing smells, Aunt Lyn's brown eyes softened and her mouth turned up into a conspiratorial grin. She was Niall's favorite of the three sisters, and he was always glad to see her. His last growth spurt put him slightly above her short stature, so while her affection for him remained unchanged, he had outgrown her reaching out to ruffle his curly locks.

"And just what would you three creatures of the enchanted forest be wanting this fine afternoon?" she asked, dusting flour off her apron and arms.

"Hmm," Niall said, returning the grin, "possibly some of your famous gingerbread biscuits for me, known as they are as the best throughout all of Rhyaden."

"Famous, are they?"

"Oh, yes, I hear they are spoken of most highly at Cire Castle," Niall answered, grinning from ear to ear.

"I'd like some bread if there's any about," Ben added.

"Me too!" Gunder chimed in.

"Oh, you scamps," she said, handing each one a handful of the biscuits and a thick slice of warm bread. "Get on with you now, I've got work to do."

The boys went through a side door into the cozy living quarters. Gunder and Niall sat at the long kitchen table buttering the bread while Ben retrieved a jug of milk and three mugs from the shelves that lined the walls. Dried rosemary, hanging in bunches from hooks in the corners, added to the lovely aroma.

Their hunger momentarily satisfied, they made their way up into the loft of the Finwick barn behind the bakeshop. The heat of the day was waning, and nary a cloud disturbed the soft blue sky. Fat black flies buzzed up from below to investigate the boys idling in the golden straw. The air was heavy, permeated with the smell of livestock, and the heavy pungent oil used to keep the leather tack supple.

"We should make a pact between us," Gunder remarked, settling his long frame against a bale of hay. His hand draped lazily across his satisfied belly. He was working on a belch, but it had yet to ripen fully into something noteworthy.

"A pact? For what?" Ben asked, chewing on a long stalk of straw, watching the light from the high window dance on the inside of his eyelids.

"Loyalty. My father says there's nothing more important," Gunder replied, rolling over to face his comrades.

"What do you mean?" Niall asked, his curiosity piqued.

"Oh, you know, a promise between us, that . . . ," Gunder's eyes narrowed as he thought about exactly how to say what he was thinking, "that we will always be there for each other."

"We would never let each other down," Ben said, his brows bunching into a frown, which only served to make his freckles stand out more. "We don't need a pact for that."

"If war comes, everything will change," Niall said. "Maybe Gunder is right." Silence spread out and filled the loft. The neighboring kingdom, Baldonia, lay directly west of their village with only high rugged mountains between. Baldonia was currently embroiled in a nasty war. Two competing family factions fought for control, first one surging ahead and then the other, and neither side was friendly to Rhyaden. A hundred-year-old rivalry added to a longstanding jealousy between the two kingdoms. On top of that, Rhyaden enjoyed much more fertile land and the resulting commerce. Fortunately, the mountains between the two countries helped to keep a fragile peace.

"A ceremony. We need a ceremony," Niall said, sitting up straight. "Something that makes it real, something we won't ever forget."

"Like what?" Ben asked, his frown turning to interest.

None of the three knew the answer to Ben's question. Ideas were offered up, but nothing suited.

"I'll ask my tutor," Niall said at last.

"Good thinking," Gunder replied. All three settled back against the straw, happy to have found a momentary solution to their dilemma. The quiet was interrupted by Ben's mother calling him to supper. Niall looked out the window.

"Oh, goodness! Look how late it is. I've got to run," Niall gasped.

"Me too!" Gunder bellowed, following hot on his heels.

Niall flew down the loft ladder, skipping the last rungs to land on the wood floor with a thud. He moved quickly out of the way so as not to be crushed by Gunder. Yelling his goodbyes, he ran for home.

Chickens on the hunt for foolhardy bugs squawked and flew out of Niall's way as he dashed through his yard a half hour later. Out of breath when he banged open the door of his cottage, he tripped over the sill and tumbled across the floor. His mother stood stirring an enormous pot of bubbly brown stew. She gave him a look.

"Shed those boots and please wash before you come inside," Moralia admonished.

He picked himself up off the floor, slipped outside and pulled the door shut behind him. He ran to the well and quickly drew water to clean his face and hands. The chickens had disappeared, having settling down on their roosts in the coop. He went over and latched the door tight to keep out predators. Back on the porch, he took off his boots and tried again.

"I think I have come up with a good solution for that very problem," Henry said, motioning toward his son, who was coming in the door for the second time, boots in hand.

"What? Give your son away?" his mother said, her face straight.

Henry laughed heartily, smiling at Niall before answering. "I was thinking of adding a small room on the west side, one with an outside door, a room for our dirty boots and coats."

Moralia and Niall looked at each other, and then back to Henry. Niall's lips pursed as he imagined its uses. Moralia's eyebrows lifted, and then a broad grin crossed her face and she clapped her hands together.

"Henry! What a wonderful idea." She crossed the room in a rush and wrapped her arms around her husband. He nuzzled his face into her silky dark curls, which always smelled of lavender and soap. Niall stared at the floor, his ears red. Parents!

"I shut the chickens in for the night," was all he could think to say.

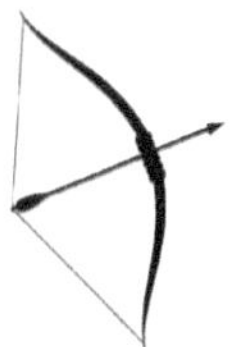

Chapter Two

On their afternoon walk the following day, Niall asked his tutor Lynmeer what made a good ceremony. Lynmeer came once a week for lessons, as he had done for Niall's mother. When the lessons first began, they had concentrated on the many uses for herbs found in the forest. Over time, the lessons had broadened to include healing, history, and science. Most of the rest of Niall's days were spent helping his father.

"Ah," Lynmeer mused, tugging on his graying beard as he stopped to look at his young student. "Good question, Niall. Have you and your friends been contemplating such an event?"

"Well, as a matter of fact, yes, we have."

"And what is the basis of your need for a ceremony, if you don't mind my asking? Is one of you about to be crowned Lord Mayor of Knurlysham?"

Niall laughed. "I rather doubt that. Gunder says we should have a pact among us in regards to our loyalty to each other."

"I can see why it would be important," his tutor said, nodding his head as he began walking again, tapping the ground lightly with the beautifully carved cane he always carried. Niall had asked once why Lynmeer needed a cane, and Lynmeer replied the injury happened many years prior when he was young and foolish. He would say no more on the subject.

They continued through the deep woods at a leisurely pace. Birds scolded in the tree tops above them, squirrels scurried by, their cheeks bulging from the competition to fill their larders. Brilliant crimson leaves fluttered soundlessly to the damp forest floor.

Niall thought for some time before asking Lynmeer why it was more important to Gunder than to him or Ben.

"Think with your head now, not with your heart. Gunder's parents aren't originally from our kingdom. It's understandable they might be worried that others will look at them suspiciously if war comes."

"But they are good people!"

"I know that, Niall, and you know that, but people get funny thoughts in their heads when they feel threatened. Fear often warps one's perspective."

"You mean they can't see the truth?"

"Yes, that's precisely what I mean. In the event of war, people might wonder where their loyalty lies."

"That's ridiculous. They've lived here for years. He's my best friend!"

"And his father is your father's best friend, but what about everyone else? Do they know them as well as you do?"

"I suppose not. What might people do?"

"One never knows what one will do when threatened, even over silly things."

"Even when they know them?"

"Yes, even then. Brothers have been known to kill brothers, Niall."

"Gunder . . . killed because he is different," Niall muttered as he walked. "So, our pact is a good thing?"

"Loyalty to a good cause is always a noble thing," Lynmeer stated, "the qualifier being 'good.' Sometimes, a ruler's most difficult job is gaining perspective and being patient enough to assess a situation fairly to find the truth."

"Hmm."

Leaves crunched beneath Niall's feet. Lynmeer did not chasten him for the noise. Stealth when moving through the forest had been one of their very first, and most constant of subjects. He was improving, but he had yet to fully master the concept.

"As for your original question, there are many types of ceremonies, for instance, awarding someone a prize for their efforts, or placing a crown on their head, but as always, the only thing that really matters is what the recipient does afterward to honor it. I rather imagine you boys are contemplating something simpler, though, just between the three of you. Is that not so?"

"Yes, something we won't forget, though; it has to have significance."

Lynmeer tilted his head to the side. "Perhaps a blood ceremony."

"A blood ceremony?" Niall's eyes grew round.

"Yes, I think that would be very appropriate for you three gallant souls."

The next time all three boys were together, Niall explained the details of the blood ceremony as his tutor had described it to him. The other two hung on every word. Ben swallowed, his eyes as big as saucers. Gunder nodded excitedly. "Yes! That's what we should do."

Niall looked at Ben. "What do you think?"

"If you two think that's what we should do, then that is what we shall do."

✝✝✝

The balance of leaves turned red and gold. The nights grew cold as the days shortened. Niall told Lynmeer the plan, and his teacher nodded approval.

"Sounds like you boys have it all worked out, excepting, of course, how to get out of the house after dark, and then back into the house without waking your parents."

"I've been working on my stealth skills," Niall said.

"That should do the trick," Lynmeer said. He turned away and coughed.

Three weeks passed before they were able to carry out their big plan.

In the waning days of the October moon, the appointed night finally came. Niall could hardly eat supper. He pushed food aimlessly around his plate. His mother's eyes followed his when he glanced out the window. He was sure she had figured out the plan.

"What are you looking for, Niall?" Moralia asked, watching her son's face. His wavy blond hair was so unlike his mother's dark curls or his father's straight brown locks.

"Nothing," Niall replied, returning his eyes to the food in front of him. He stabbed a bite of meat and stuffed it in his mouth.

At the other end of the table, having endured a long day of felling trees, Henry's eyes had given up the fight to stay open. Upon hearing the other two talk, his head jerked up, and he glanced about the table.

"What?"

"Never mind, Henry. Niall and I were just talking. I think you need to go to bed, my dear," she said, laying her hand on his.

"I believe you are right. I was nearly asleep in my plate. Good night, Niall. Good night, Love." And with that, Henry got up, kissed his wife, nodded to his son, and clumped off to the bedroom. Niall listened to the heavy thuds as one boot and then the other hit the wood floor. Nothing but silence followed.

Moralia looked at Niall. "I'm not sure he even undressed."

"He decided today to try and finish the long cut before winter," Niall replied.

"The long cut? It would be impossible to get that large of an area done in one season."

"He said it was the only area without Knurlywood trees, and if we get all the logs hauled in, it will give him plenty of work this winter. Then next year we can work at pulling the stumps, and the following year we could plant a crop there."

"Hmm," Moralia mused, rising to clear the table. "Sounds to me like you better get a good night's sleep, if you are going to be good help tomorrow."

Niall's ears flamed. Moralia carried the plates away. He helped her clear the table before heading up the wooden steps to his bed in the loft. He moved around a bit, as if to undress, then lay down on the bed. There was no danger of his eyes closing as he listened to his mother putter in the room below him. It seemed ages before she put away her sewing and took her candle to the bedroom where Henry now snored soundly. Niall could plainly hear the rumble until she shut the door.

An hour after the partial moon rose, it topped the tallest trees and lit the dense forest with enough light for the boys to find their way. They met at a designated spot where two tall spruce trees arched toward each other along the road between Knurlysham and Niall's cottage. All three had similar stories of getting away undetected, although Gunder complained of a bucket left out where it ought not to have been.

"All right then, let's go," Niall said. He turned and retraced his steps for a short distance before turning off the road. The other two silently followed, stopping eventually in a small clearing Niall had discovered the week before. He had rounded up wood and pine cones for a fire, and piled stones around a shallow pit. It was rudimentary but, most important for this occasion, well off the beaten path.

"When did you find this place?" Ben asked, impressed with what he could see in the dim light.

"Last week when Mother sent me to town for flour. I took a rather long route, you know, scouting for a …"

"Did you hear something?" Gunder interrupted, turning to look behind him. They were surrounded by tall trees and dense undergrowth in this part of the forest, except for the game trail they had followed. All three were gathered around the pit, breaking up bits of tinder to start a fire.

"Just you busting up that wood," Niall scoffed. "Don't be a fraidy. There's nothing in those woods that wants to eat the likes of you."

"I've heard talk of witches—from farmers coming to the forge," Gunder said, facing front again and forcing a smile, letting his brows unfurl. Ben reached into his pocket and passed around a biscuit for each. Neither he nor Niall had been able to eat much at supper, and the offering eased their nervous anticipation.

When the fire burned steadily, Niall pulled a sharp knife out of its sheath and held it over the dancing red flames. The chatter ceased as the serious portion of the evening loomed before them. His hand grew hot. Sure the blade was now sterile, he held it up, reflecting light in each set of eyes around the fire.

A tiny breeze fanned the flames. Smoke curled into an animal-like shape. It held still for several seconds before slowly drifting off into the night, holding its form until it was well into the tall trees.

"Did you see that?" Gunder asked, his eyes big and his mouth wide open.

"It looked like a creature—with wings," Ben said.

Niall glanced into the trees surrounding the campfire. He did not see or hear anything, but the hair on the back of his neck prickled. A chill ran up and down his spine. He turned back to the fire and took a big breath. "Here's to brotherhood. I shall never let down those who sit with me tonight. Loyalty to each other—forever—shall be our creed hence forth, whatever comes. I shall always be there for you, Gunder, and you, Ben, when you need me, and I seal my word with my blood—joined together with yours—as brothers forever."

When he was done speaking, he sliced across his palm in a single swift cut in first one palm and then the other, then handed the knife to Gunder, who did the same and passed it on to Ben. Niall glanced down at his hands where tiny beads of blood welled up along the stinging cuts. He looked over to see Ben staring blankly at the knife, and then those big blue eyes looked up into his. He gave his friend a nod and an encouraging smile. Ben drew himself up, and the knife's blade flashed again.

"No matter what comes, nothing shall come between me and my brothers," Ben pledged, swallowing hard when he was done.

"I shall never let my brothers down," Gunder added stoutly. They pressed their palms to each other's palms and held tight. A tingle of electricity crossed from hand to hand.

"Brothers," Niall began, and then all three voices finished, "Forever!"

Niall was proud of what they had done, and, despite the pain, it felt good to have done it.

They held tight for many long moments, letting their blood mix to seal their pledges. Finally, Ben straightened a little, then let go of Niall's hand to sweep the bangs out of his eyes.

Embers fell into themselves in the fire. Sparks flew up, showering the area with light for a brief moment. Some fell outside the ring. Gunder reached out and stirred the wood.

Niall sat quietly until Ben's eyes caught his attention. Leaning in, Ben whispered, "I thought I just saw something moving behind Gunder. Something very dark."

The three boys held their breath and slowly turned. Shadows danced among the trees. A cold shiver ran up Niall's spine.

Chapter Three

The days settled into gloom and cold, a long winter unappreciated by children and adults alike. Niall listened with only half an ear to the afternoon's history lesson. Everything was dull since the blood ceremony, but being inside was especially boring. He loved being outside where their lessons led them wandering about the woods. Even helping his father or practicing archery was preferable to sitting indoors.

"Proper perspective is difficult at best," the bespectacled tutor lectured. "Take, for instance, the battle between Niregon and Tyregon a few centuries ago. Both sides thought they won the ugly affair, when in fact, it was a draw," Lynmeer said, pacing back and forth and occasionally stamping his cane for emphasis. "Ironically, both sides left historical documents stating that they were the winners."

"How could both sides think they won?" Niall asked.

"Good question. I suppose because neither was wiped out, they assumed they had the better end of it. The point is, Niall, each side saw and recorded a different outcome of the same event."

"How—" Niall stopped mid-question, trying to assess the look coming over his tutor's face.

"I believe we have covered this topic quite sufficiently," Lynmeer stated, sitting down.

"But—"

"Tea! Moralia, my dear, we need tea and biscuits. I seem to have bored my young student to distraction, for he has resorted to beginning his current discourse with the word 'but,' which I cannot understand considering his elite education."

Moralia smiled. "Of course, Lynmeer, I was just thinking of that myself. I do believe we all need a break." She put her embroidery down and rose slowly, stretching before heading to stoke the fire. The tea brewed and she set out a plate of Lynmeer's favorite biscuits. Niall knew Lynmeer had been his mother's tutor in the difficult years after her parents died from the plague. Her devotion to him was more than fondness for a favorite teacher. She often spoke of how much she needed his shoulder for her tears in her loneliness after their deaths.

After tea was served, Niall settled into his chair and listened less and less. His mother and Lynmeer visited about which herbs could be used to make an exquisite brew, and which held good medicinal qualities, to be sure, but tasted simply dreadful. Their voices faded into the background as his mind wandered and softened. Thoughts floated aimlessly like the white seeds of dandelions on a breezy day.

Niall walked nonchalantly in the cool morning air. He stopped abruptly and stood stockstill under the Knurly tree canopy. Curiosity over what had lain here beneath the enormous shuttlecock ferns, tamping down the moist grass in a large oval shape held him still.

Golden brown mushrooms lay on their sides, flattened or broken off. In this spot the air was warmer, like being under thick quilts after a long night's sleep. The hair on the back of his neck tingled.

"Hello, young man," said a very dapper-looking gentleman in a long gray coat and plaid cravat. Niall jumped back, startled by the sudden appearance of a man, one who was certainly not dressed for traipsing about in the forest, walking the same path that Niall was following. Graying hair framed a kind face, and he leaned on a beautifully carved cane. Niall saw no weapon, which was unusual in these parts. His father never left the cottage without his bow. "If wild game presents itself," his father said, "you must be prepared. It could mean our survival."

Few walked in these remote woods, and no one that Niall knew of lived in the direction this man had come from. This particular path ended on the far eastern side of the kingdom near the south sea at Nanty's Bay, but here it was not much more than a deer trail used for hunting.

Niall fingered his small bow, its presence reassuring to the young lad in the unusual circumstance he now found himself in. He had never met anyone, much less a stranger, in this part of the woods so far from the village. The gentleman smiled, waiting for the boy to introduce himself, or show some reaction. Niall peered deep into the dark eyes, and was surprised to recognize himself reflected back. For some reason, the image he saw was comforting. His breathing returned to normal.

"Let's try again. Good day, Niall. I am your tutor, Lynmeer."

"You know my name?"

"Yes, of course. I have come to Knurlysham to be your teacher. Did your mother not tell you to expect me?"

"No, today is Tuesday, so we are expecting Mrs. Poshly, but no one else that I know of. My father's gone to dig peat. He would have stayed at home if we were expecting company, other than Mrs.

Poshly, that is." Niall answered honestly. The gossipy neighbor had a shrill voice and a large brood of undisciplined children.

"Well, Niall Thomas Thoralt, I am your tutor, mentor, professor and trusted advisor for the next several years," the man replied. "Previously, I was your mother's tutor, and now I am to be yours."

"I didn't know I was to have one."

Lynmeer sighed. "I have come to give you lessons once per week, for the time being. It shall be determined in the future if and when it shall be necessary for me to come more often."

"Really?"

"Yes, really. You must get out of the habit of asking silly questions. It is an absurd waste of our time when there is so much to learn."

"What must I learn?"

Lynmeer peered over his spectacles. "Leadership, for example. This kingdom's future is in peril, so leadership is one of our most obvious concerns."

"Niall. Niall! Wake up!" Moralia shook her son, whose head had steadily drifted downward and finally lay prone on the table. "You've been dozing, and your tea is cold. Lynmeer is leaving for the day. You need to see him out, please."

Centuries Earlier—Before The Great Dragon War

The Great Hall of Ayhrland was lit by hundreds of tiny flameless lights. Deep in the heart of the magnificent cave, a meeting of the Elder Council was about to begin. The hall was unusually crowded. Angry voices filled the space, heating the cool stone walls of the cave. The issue of human rights was to come before the council, and this issue had split the dragon world for some time now. Tails swished when dragons tried to convince those who disagreed to join the other side.

All seven dragon clans were represented: the Dorns to the north, the Doons from the west countries, the Meers who kept the skies, the Thanes of the lowlands, the Eahs to the east, the Gaxes from the south, and the Dores of the waters, each represented by one of the Elder Council members sitting high on the great polished stone bench at the end of the room. The land surrounding the Caves of the Council was neutral territory, a beautiful place known to the dragons as Ayhrland.

Juldorn lifted her gavel and brought it down in a thunderous boom. A lone word from a dragon near the back of the audience floated through the air as the room fell silent. All turned their eyes to the dais. As the oldest council member, Juldorn sat as Chief Elder, mitigating disagreements among these dragons for close to ten centuries. An appointment to the council lasted a life time, and as dragons could live for thousands of years, the council did not change often. She feared the issue before them today, though, was the harbinger of great change for the dragons. Be it good or bad, she could not foresee.

Dragons who had a dispute could wend their way through the system of lower councils elected in each clan. The process was long and complicated, ensuring that only issues of major import made their way to the Elder Council. They met six times each year, and their word was final.

A young dragon, Aleah of the Eah clan, had worked her way through this system, eventually gaining permission to petition the Elder Council for a decree protecting humans from cruel treatment by dragons, behavior that had begun a few decades earlier and was growing in acceptance. Juldorn motioned to the young dragon to come forward and present her argument.

Aleah stepped forward, bowing low in genuine reverence for the body of Elders before her. She was a beautiful lavender dragon, articulate and studious in pursuit of knowledge, interested in every field of science, and now deeply disturbed by the actions of some dragons toward the humans.

"Your Honors, I am petitioning this council to ban the recent interference with humans in all of our lands. Though their numbers are increasing, humans are defenseless against dragons. They possess no magic. They have no way to protect themselves from cruel treatment. They are now being used as creatures for sport, taunted and bullied, played with as if they had no feelings, all for the entertainment of heartless dragons. It is barbarous and cruel. Worst of all, it is not honorable. It is not the way of dragons; cruelty is not our history. Where is our nobility, if we condone such acts of torture and mistreatment?"

Aleah stopped to take a breath. She could hear feet shuffling behind her. Her scales tingled. She lifted her head higher. "I ask that we no longer allow such behavior and punish those who commit these atrocious acts. I ask for a decree from this Council to include a separation from the humans, two worlds if you will. When a dragon is in the presence of humans, he or she should take human shape, so as not to frighten or unduly influence the humans. And finally, there should be no magic in the presence of humans. A dragon who uses magic in their presence should suffer perhaps aging would be appropriate."

A great clamor arose among the dragons. Never had such an edict been proposed as long as any of them could remember. Again the gavel banged.

"Thank you for hearing me, your Honors," she said, stepping back. Her passionate plea had many in the hall nodding their heads, but as many murmured in opposition.

"Thank you, Aleah. You have spoken well," Juldorn said. "We shall take this petition under advisement, and a vote shall be forthcoming at our next session two moon cycles from now. There are no other issues at this time. We are adjourned!" The gavel sounded the conclusion of the meeting.

Aleah's shoulders slumped. She gathered her papers, knowing she should have expected the Council to take their time in making such a monumental decision. The humans' plight was so obvious, though, she had wanted a resounding proclamation in front of this crowd, this night.

"Very articulate, young lady. Too bad you have not chosen a topic to get involved with that you can possibly win. Perhaps you should study astronomy instead of anthropology."

Aleah's tail stiffened. She looked up into the shiny eyes of Moordoon, his sleek black skin reflecting the room's light in an ominous glow. He had stepped down from his place on the dais.

"And I hear that you are one of the worst human baiters, Moordoon, and I mean worst in every sense of the word."

"Now, now, my dear, don't be petty. You should let me show you some fun. You might change your mind and stop wasting the Council's time. How about it? A midnight ride over the beautiful countryside?"

"No. Thank you." She turned and shuffled away, muttering under her breath, "not in a million centuries."

Female dragons did not usually turn Moordoon down. The rejection prickled, but not for long. He looked around and spotted Andeah, one of his co-members on the Council. She adored him and always laughed at his jokes. He must ask how she felt about the issue. The vote was going to be close, but, cocking his head as he sauntered her way, he was a very persuasive dragon.

Eight weeks later, the Elder Council once again filed into the room and took their seats on the dais. Even more dragons were crowded into the Great Hall, bumping tails and stepping on each other as they crowded together to make room. The Elders looked much older than they had the last time they came before the dragons. Their haggard faces showed fatigue. In the last weeks, intense arguments had ensued when each one gave their respective opinion in their private chambers, followed by questions and heated debate. They had not come to a unanimous decision, so before they left the private anteroom and walked into the packed public room, Juldorn spoke to the other six elders one last time.

"As is our practice, we will vote in front of our dragons, but you must remember your oath to this sacred Council of Elders. No matter the outcome," and she looked specifically at Moordoon when she said this, for he had been the most outspoken among them, "we must uphold the decision of this vote." She looked then at each dragon, waiting for their nod of agreement. Each gave it without hesitation. She looked last at Moordoon, who squinted his hard eyes at her, hoping to break her stare. She did not blink. With half a nod, he looked away.

They filed in and sat down. The room fell into a hush, waiting to hear the Council's words. Aleah was in the front row, nervous tremors radiating from her tail to her ears. Taking a deep breath, Juldorn rose to read.

"As to the petition put before this Council when last we met, in regards to dragon behavior toward humans, the Elder Council shall vote our conscience in the presence of all dragons attending. I shall now read the petition."

She read from the scroll slowly and clearly. Every last dragon from the front to the rear of the room could hear her perfectly.

At the end, she lowered the parchment and looked out on the dragons gathered before her. "If a member is in favor of the petition for human rights as I have just read to you, then that member's vote shall be yea. If the member is not in favor, they shall vote nay. If the nay votes outnumber the yea votes, then the treatment of humans shall be left up to each dragon's own moral authority."

Someone in the crowd sucked in their breath, and a faint murmur rumbled through the crowd. Juldorn banged the gavel once again, demanding silence.

"If the vote is in favor, the precise language, timeframe, and effect of the edict will be decided by this Council and presented at the next meeting. We shall vote now, and I shall vote first. I vote **yea**." She hoped by going first, she gave courage to those wavering in their decision. A smattering of clapping broke out. Instantly, Juldorn held up her hand. "Silence! If there is one more disruption during these proceedings, the dragon responsible will be banished from Council — for life!" A gasp was heard from the back of the room, but it was quickly stifled. "Moordoon, how do you vote?"

"I vote **nay**."

"That is one yea and one nay," Juldorn counted. "Evandore, how do you vote?"

"I vote **nay**," Evandore responded.

"That is one yea and two nays. Andeah, how do you say?"

Andeah squirmed in her seat. She wanted to vote yes, and had told herself she would vote yes, but Moordoon's huge presence next to her reminded her of his recently implied threats. Her head dropped, and she whispered the word, "**nay**."

"Louder, please. We must all be able to hear you," Juldorn insisted.

"I vote **nay**," she croaked.

Moordoon settled back comfortably, an arrogant grin

across his face.

Juldorn cocked her head, entirely certain of who had gotten to Andeah. "That is one yea and three nays. Gygax, how do you vote?"

"I vote **yea**."

"That is two yeas and three nays."

"Ellthane, how do you vote?"

"I vote **yea**."

Moordoon sat up, the grin gone, his nostrils quivering.

"We are tied, three each. Lynmeer, you are the deciding vote. How do you say?"

Lynmeer, the youngest member, had sat on this Council for a mere hundred years, learning by listening to the wisdom and patience of those who had come before him, slowly discerning the issues they should do something about, and when it was best to do nothing at all, letting time sort the problem out. He looked out into the audience. The lavender dragon had her eyes squeezed shut, her front toes crossed, and the color from her top half had drained to her rump.

He was torn by this vote. He believed that dragons should not need to be governed by laws. For eons, they had enjoyed the right to do as they pleased, as long as they didn't hurt other dragons. The Elder Council mitigated all disputes between the dragons, and their word was final. But the truth was, in recent years many dragons had forgone the honorable code of the past. This new concept of humans' having rights too was growing in his heart as the right thing to do, but still, the old ways were difficult to abandon. Taking a deep breath, Lynmeer looked straight ahead and spoke in a measured tone.

"I vote **yea**."

Pandemonium broke out.

Six Years Later

Ecirp and his younger brother scurried about the Great Hall, lighting lights and making sure everything was spitspot. The Elder Council was meeting tonight. Ecirp wore a somber black vest, adhering to the ancient custom of mourning. He had served Evandore, one of those who had died following that dark night six years ago when the Council voted in favor of human rights. Sometime soon, he would find a new dragon to serve, but for now he tended to the Hall. Like his father before him, and his father before him, and back as far as was recorded, service was the call of his family and the way he happily filled his days.

A week before the meeting, Juldorn sat brooding in her chambers, looking for a solution other than the obvious one before her. She could think of nothing else. It was time. Six devastating years of war followed the last meeting of the Elder Council. Nearly all of her friends and all of her family were dead. Evandore and Andeah, two of the Council members that had voted nay, had died in the fighting, and Moordoon had been grievously wounded.

She called each of the remaining Council members to her chambers. "We go soon before our dragons, those who survived, that is. Before we do, we must make a decision for the world's future beyond the edict that winnowed our demise. I believe there is no choice now but to sunder the world between humans and dragons. The magic needed for this feat to be accomplished is more than one dragon can perform. I am asking for volunteers, but it is a task that none of the volunteers will survive. After that, there can be no magic in the human's world, and they in turn shall not pass into ours."

"How many of us will it take?" Gygax asked.

"Three," Juldorn replied.

"I shall not be a part of this," Moordoon said hotly, his scars vivid against his black skin.

"I didn't think you would," Juldorn answered dryly. "I cannot force any of you to do this, but I am asking. I know of no other way. I shall be one of the three."

Juldorn looked around the room. She could tell that her protégé, Lynmeer, was about to speak. Before he could say anything, she spoke again. "I wish for each of you to think about this carefully. Come to my chambers privately within the week with your answer or further questions."

Lynmeer's shoulders relaxed with the momentary reprieve. He followed Gygax out of the chamber, deep in thought. Outside, a voice startled him out of his reverie.

"Lynmeer!" Aleah yelled. He stopped and turned toward the lavender dragon running toward him. She was winded, and he waited while she caught her breath. "I'm so glad I caught you. I just returned from my home in the east, and with all that happened since the last . . . meeting, and so much time going by, I never got the chance to tell you how much your support meant to me."

Lynmeer looked into her kind eyes. "That vote started a war that has nearly wiped dragons from the earth, turning our world upside down, and the changes are still coming."

His tone was sad, and the word "changes" scared her. "Are you sorry you supported the humans?"

She asked the very question that had vexed him since the war began. "No, Aleah. I believe change is inevitable, and I believe the humans should not be subjected to cruelty, but it has been hard to see so many die."

"My family is lost . . . I had no idea something so awful would happen." She stared at the ground for a while. "If you had known, would you have changed your vote?"

"If I had known what was coming, I would have looked for another way to deal with the human problem, but if the vote were to be held today, I would vote the same."

Aleah had not realized she was holding her breath. She reached out and touched his arm. "Would you like to get some tea and biscuits?"

Two days later, Gygax entered Juldorn's chambers. She looked up from her writings and smiled. The mutual respect from years on the Council together had grown into friendship, and eventually into love. They had even considered having a child together, but female dragons reproduce so seldom, they had yet to have a chance.

"So, what is your plan for us, my dear?"

"Ellthane has already agreed, her magic will sunder the world into two. Our magic shall guard the entrance forever after. We shall become the gate, opening only for dragons, until there are none left."

Gygax cocked his head to the side. "The Gaxdorn Gate. I like the sound of that."

Juldorn smiled wryly. "Dorngax doesn't have quite the same ring, does it? I suppose Gaxdorn will have to do."

A day later, Lynmeer appeared at Juldorn's door. He had spent the last two days in the company of Aleah, falling madly in love with her wit and curiosity. Leaving her behind and returning to the Great Hall had not been easy.

"I have come to volunteer, Juldorn," he said, stepping forward when she motioned him to come in.

"I was sure you would, Lynmeer, and I am greatly pleased that you have done so. However, your job in the future shall be to carry forward the tradition of this Council's wisdom. You are the youngest, and should, therefore, last the longest of those of us that voted in favor of the edict. Ellthane, Gygax and I shall sunder the world into two and guard the gate. You and Moordoon will be the remaining Council members. I am counting on you, Lynmeer, to uphold our honor."

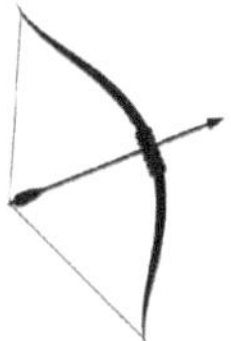

Chapter Four

The Present

As winter gradually gave way to spring, buds on the Knurly trees swelled, creeks lapped at their banks, and patience grew thin in all young things wanting to be let loose. Niall and his friends tried numerous excuses to get together for fun, rather than work, and their entreaty was finally successful one bright, sunny April morning. Together at last, freed from chores and parental supervision, they took off running, shouting and laughing for the gloriousness of being young.

The boys cavorted in the woods around the village for a couple of hours before their energy began to wane. They stood panting on the bank of Knurly Run. Ben stripped his clothes off while Gunder and Niall looked at each other, heads cocked to the side.

"Last one in is a ninny!" yelled Ben.

"All for one, I suppose," Gunder grumbled, his left eyebrow drawn up an inch higher than the right one as he surveyed the cold water.

"I suppose," Niall agreed, nodding from side to side rather

than up and down.

A minute later, loud splashes were followed by spitting, sputtering, and crude hollering.

"Mother it's cold!" Gunder scrambled up the bank five seconds after hitting the water. He shivered from head to toe. Grabbing his shirt, he used it for a towel.

The others were right behind him, pulling on their britches as fast as they could. "That cold water shriveled me up to nothing," Niall said.

"Ah, you had nothing before," Gunder responded, laughter fast on the heels of the remark. Niall was on him a second later, and they rolled this way and that way among the twigs and leaves until, as usual, Gunder sat on top, waiting for Niall to give in.

"Let's run a bit to warm up," Ben offered, still shivering even though he'd finished dressing while the other two tussled. He took off without waiting for an answer. Gunder rolled off his victim and the two of them jumped up and grabbed their remaining clothes, laughing as they tried to put them on while running. Ben led them up through the hills behind the village. Plenty warm now, he stopped to let the other two catch up, though Gunder was close behind.

"Ow," Niall grumbled, bringing up the rear.

"What's the matter?" Gunder asked, turning to look.

"Brambles. My pants are too short."

"Mine too," Ben offered. "Mother says I can stop growing any day now. I'm already as tall as my father. Anyone hungry?"

"Yes!" Gunder shouted with his usual grin. He immediately started downhill, Ben close behind. They headed straight toward the village, their hunger dictating a direct approach. A straight line would take them down a small ravine, then up a smaller hill, and down again toward the roof tops.

"Look about you, Master Niall," whispered a giant Knurly tree towering over him. Niall stood rooted to the spot, unnerved that it had spoken to him with others nearby. It was not by any means the first time a Knurly tree had spoken to him, but this was the first time with others around.

Five years earlier, traipsing through the woods, Niall had intentionally kicked a large root sticking out of the ground.

"Ouch! For goodness sake."

"Who's there?" Niall asked.

"I am."

"Show yourself . . . please," Niall added.

"I'm in plain sight, silly boy. Are you daft? Look up."

Niall slowly looked up at the great sweeping branches and glossy green leaves of a giant Knurly tree.

"I'm not daft, I'm Niall Thoralt. Who are you? Where are you?"

"I am Professor Faversham. You may address me as Professor Faversham, if you please," the giant tree responded, proudly raising its crown and shaking the uppermost leaves with a tiny flourish.

"Faversham," Niall repeated slowly.

"Professor Faversham," the tree corrected.

"How is it that you talk?" Niall asked, looking for a face on the trunk. He could not tell exactly where the voice came from.

"How do you talk?" the tree asked back.

"I don't know," Niall answered frankly. "Do all trees talk?"

"Not precisely, no."

"Why?"

A small branch fell suspiciously close to Niall's head. He scooted slightly and tried again. "Why don't all of the trees talk?"

"They wish not to, I suppose. Not to your kind, anyway."

"My kind?"

"Humans."

"Oh." Niall thought that over for a couple of moments. "Can anyone understand the trees, those trees that do choose to talk?"

A small branch in the tree next to Professor Faversham shook rather pointedly, despite a lack of breeze. "I don't know the answer to that, Niall, but few of us choose to speak because, because it isn't done among all the trees, only some of the Knurlywoods," he said softly.

"So, why did you speak to me?" Niall asked.

The small branch next over shook harder.

"Because I think you are one of us," the professor said. "However, at the moment, if you don't mind, I would like to bring up the subject of your carelessness when you traipse through our woods."

Later, at home, Niall asked his mother if she had ever heard trees talk. She looked at him pointedly and then sat down. She was silent for so long, he began to fidget.

"Please sit with me," she said, indicating there was room next to her. "When I was a child, before my parents died, I had many conversations with trees. I remember my mother telling me there was a lot to be learned from trees. After they died, I stopped going into the woods—for a long, long time. After that, I believed those conversations must have been my imagination, or maybe dreams. But now, I'm not so sure." She shrugged.

✝ ✝ ✝

"The trail," the tree indicated now as Ben and Gunder

bounded away, shaking a branch twenty feet to the right of where Niall stood. The game trail headed toward a patch of dense saplings, topping a small ridge that overlooked the quaint houses of timber and stone. In these thick woods, twenty feet of ferns and undergrowth was enough to hide an army. Niall turned in the direction indicated.

"Hold up a minute," he yelled across the flowering heather to Ben and Gunder. The two halted, turning around to see what might be the cause for delay. Niall moved away from the direction they had gone. They looked at each other. Gunder held up his hand and reversed course.

"Where'd you get to?" Gunder grunted, losing sight of Niall when he flung himself over a large tree fall blocking his way. Ben chose to go around.

"Over here," Niall said, his usually buoyant voice subdued.

They came upon him kneeling beside the body of a large deer left in the middle of the trail. The kill was at least a day old. The boys had no experience with a dead animal left to rot. Dried blood had pooled beneath the exposed shaft that pierced straight to the animal's brain. The arrow's distinct markings were unfamiliar.

Killing for sport rather than for food was unheard of in these woods. The people of Rhyaden prided themselves on living in harmony with their land, and squandering such a bounty would never have been deemed acceptable. The strangeness of this find did not end there, however. One antler was still attached to the stag's head, the other cut off, nowhere to be found in the immediate area. The one that remained had a twist at the base, one that gave it a ripple effect in a beautiful pattern of light and dark. None of the three had ever seen such a unique specimen. As he sat on his haunches, Niall's heart grew heavy at the loss of such a magnificent animal. He could not comprehend the motivation for such an act as this.

The branches above him stirred in a gentle breeze. He appreciated the gravity of the warning. Gunder came closer and silently stood near him.

Ben walked up. "Bloody awful," he said, blanching when he saw the carcass.

"A stupid waste," Gunder said, his voice hot.

Niall looked about. He was sure the tree would have warned him if danger still lurked close by. Regardless, these woods were suddenly not the playground he had always thought them to be.

He glanced at Ben, who had no desire to come any closer to the dead animal. His young friend silently stared toward the village, waiting for his companions to decide what the next move should be, his freckles enflamed from his discomfort.

Niall blinked hard.

"What do you make of it?" Gunder asked, kneeling down beside him.

He shook his head, not sure at first how to voice his thoughts without alarming the other two. "I don't know. I'll talk to my father and my tutor, see what they think."

The boys finally tore themselves away to head home. They stopped atop the last ridge to gaze down on their village. The strange arrow was tucked in Niall's quiver. He didn't know for sure, but he believed it came from the Kingdom of Baldonia.

"Do you suppose they stood up here and watched our village?" Gunder asked.

"That thought leaves a bad taste in my mouth," Ben replied, his gaze on the chimney rising above the bakeshop.

"Mine too," Niall added. "I'm not hungry anymore, Ben. I

think I'll go on home."

That evening, sitting on the front porch, both Lynmeer and Henry gazed at the arrow for a long while without speaking. Henry turned it over several times, smelling the feathers and fingering the point while Niall recounted the story of finding it. After supper, Niall saw Lynmeer off, walking with him for a ways.

"You are correct in assuming the arrow comes from Baldonia," Lynmeer said out of the blue.

Niall nodded. He looked up at his mentor. "Lynmeer, why do people go to war?"

The teacher's eyes closed. When they reopened, Niall heard sadness in his voice. "There are many reasons, Niall. Greed is high on the list, selfishness, ego, and on the other side of the coin, when people are attacked, they want to protect their country and their families."

"Does it keep happening, over and over?"

"Yes."

"Is there a way to stop it?"

"I haven't found one."

After the incident with the stag, Niall worked harder at mastering his stealth skills, and his marksmanship improved daily. Henry graduated him to a bow as long as he was tall. In this area of his education, Lynmeer seemed quite happy to step back and let Niall's father be the teacher, for Henry was skilled and patient with the bow, and with Niall.

"Father, I can hardly walk and heft this bow at the same time," Niall complained when first given his new weapon.

"You'll grow, and in the meantime, you'll get stronger,"

he said, looking into his son's eyes, his hands holding tight to his shoulders.

It had taken Henry half a year to meld the wood properly, giving it the best advantage for marksmanship and strength. He told Niall how he had come upon the Knurly branch walking home empty handed from hunting one afternoon. Sure that the branch had not been on the path that morning when he left, he bent down to throw it to the side. It was a habit of his to keep the way clear so he wouldn't stumble when he carried game home. Picking up the heavy wood, he realized there were no small twigs branching off, no knots to compromise its strength. He inspected the nearly six-foot piece further, turning it over and over.

Henry carried the prize branch home to begin the long process of making a bow. Knurlywood was too hard to cut. To make this solid piece into the right shape, he soaked the wood for over a fortnight before the first bending, and then again, and again until it achieved the proper shape of a bow, followed by daily sanding and rubbing with oil until it was smooth and perfect.

The family sat at the supper table after a tedious day working with felled trees in the long cut. Unusually quiet, Henry set his fork down and looked at his wife and son.

"If the fighting in Baldonia comes to Rhyaden, many of our young men will be lost defending our King," Henry said.

Niall's fork stopped in midair. Moralia's head lifted slowly to gaze at her husband. In the past, they had not discussed such subjects in front of their son.

"He's old enough to hear, Moralia."

"I'm not ready," she replied.

"We must be ready."

"I don't want to think that my son is old enough to be part of such a thing," she said softly. "The thought of war . . . it frightens me."

"I know, my dear, but I believe war is a reality, is it not?"

Niall kept his eyes on his plate, equally excited and scared to think he was finally old enough to hear such a conversation.

As much as the incident with the stag worried the adults, it also served to strengthen the brotherhood with his two friends. On a day not long after, the three met for a romp in the woods.

"I'm going to hide. You guys try to find me," Niall said.

"Hide? Why?" Gunder asked.

"To practice our skills. We'll all have a go. Shut your eyes and count to ten—slowly."

Gunder looked at Ben, who shrugged and closed his eyes. Gunder shook his head but shut his too and began to count.

"One," Gunder said. Niall took a step on the count and waited for the next.

"Nine. Ten." Both boys opened their eyes and looked around. They had not heard a thing beyond Gunder's voice and expected Niall to still be standing close by. They looked at each other. "How did he get away?" Gunder quizzed.

"I don't know. You stay here and watch for movement. I'll check behind these trees." It took half an hour to find Niall. He had moved three times while they searched for him.

"Your turn, Gunder," Niall said. "Become part of the ground you walk on."

"Sure," he answered.

Niall and Ben closed their eyes, and Niall began to count in a slow, steady beat. They both could tell exactly which direction Gunder trotted. When Niall reached ten, he and Ben opened their eyes and grinned. They parted slightly, each going to the opposite side of the tree they were sure Gunder was hid behind. He wasn't there, and they both stopped abruptly and looked at each other.

Laughter erupted above them.

"Ha! Not so bad, eh?"

The two on the ground admitted he had fooled them, and Gunder swung down, grinning from ear to ear. He thumped hard when he dropped and rolled into some low brambles. "Ow!"

"Now work on not giving your position away," Niall said, holding back his laughter. He turned to Ben. "Your turn."

Ben shook his head. "I'm not so clever as you two," he said, "but I'll have a go." He started away before the other two even had their eyes shut. When Niall said "ten" Gunder immediately went in the direction he saw Ben start, but Niall waited, sure he had heard something on his right side. Gunder looked around, then up into the branches.

"He can't have got much farther than this," he yelled back. Niall motioned to him and began a slow sweep to his right. Several trees were large enough to shield Ben, but one in particular had an enormous girth, drawing Niall to look there first. Ben sat behind it, a big smile on his face.

"At least you didn't find me on the first look."

"Here!" Niall yelled to Gunder. He sat down next to Ben. "I was drawn to look here because it was the biggest tree. Next time, try for one that doesn't stand out so. Good deception at the start, though."

"Thanks. I figured I had to do something for an advantage."

"Lynmeer says to become one with the tree you stand next to."

"How?"

"Hard to explain."

Gunder came and plopped down between them. As usual, the talk got around to war.

"We should have a code between us," Ben said.

"For what?" Gunder asked.

"I'm not exactly sure, but something that only the three of us will understand if we get caught by enemies," Ben replied.

"How would we use it?"

Ben pursed his lips. "I'm not sure of that either."

They got up and strolled toward the bakeshop on Ben's promise of biscuits and a cold mug of milk. Halfway there, Niall stopped. "Brothers Forever." he offered. "That's our code." They looked from one to the other and nodded.

Chapter Five

Over a decade earlier, Torgson Neuse and his young wife Isabela came to Rhyaden from the Kingdom of Niregon, across the North Sea. They had one toddler named Gunder by their side with another due soon when they stepped off the boat. Torg also brought with him a useful trade and a willingness to lend a hand to his neighbors. They bought a wagon upon arriving and headed west, looking for a village that needed his skills. Settling in Knurlysham, Torg began the arduous task of building a home and a business from the ground up.

"There is some oak here that will make good wheels," Henry said, jumping down from his wagon. He'd pulled his horse to a stop in front of the forge, situated on the edge of the village. Torg set down his hammer and walked past Henry, peering over the side. Friends for ten years now, there was much the two men had in common besides hard work. Presently they shared a mutual worry about war with the kingdom to their west.

"Looks like fine wood. You have a good eye, Henry."

"And worth a good price too," Henry added.

"Pull around back and we'll see," Torg returned.

Henry grabbed the mare's lead and clucked his tongue. She started up, and he led her around behind the barn where both men began unloading the heavy logs Henry had brought to sell. They worked side by side, hefting the larger logs together. Under the hot sun, sweat was soon dripping off both of them.

"Any news from the castle?" Henry asked.

"Nothing good," Torg replied, throwing the long, straight saplings onto separate piles for the different woods. There the wood would cure, waiting to be sawed up according to its future.

Not every tree had the disposition to be shaped into a wheel, and never Knurly trees. Oak was more inclined than other types to be melded properly, and those that were disinclined could be made into other necessities. Scraps and sawdust from the mill were used to fuel the fire in the forge, along with dead branches collected from the woods. Knurlywood burned hotter and longer than any other wood; however, it was nearly impossible to cut, wearing down the best of blades for any who had tried. The villagers in Knurlysham had learned long ago to appreciate the sturdy trees for their beauty and leave it at that.

The forge and small mill stood at the west end of town. It offered a friendly place where many a man stopped in passing to share gossip and spit without worrying about manners.

"I am hearing of strange occurrences, things that cannot be explained," Torg continued, after stopping to peer down the length of another sapling before choosing its pile.

"What kind of things?" Henry asked. Concern creased his forehead. The log he threw completely overshot the pile. Torg stopped and the two men looked at each other.

"Scary, if you ask me," Torg said, finally. He looked around before continuing. "Some say witches. I don't rightly know, and I suppose there is some exaggeration, but I don't like hearing about heads on spikes, bodies disappearing and the like."

"The Baldonians have always been cruel when it comes to their tactics. They're not above scaring people to gain the upper hand before they even get started," Henry said.

"Even my Gunder said he saw strange things in the forest when he was out with Ben and Niall."

"Now, Torg. You know those boys have mighty big imaginations."

"He swore it, Henry, and Gunder doesn't make things up."

Henry nodded agreement and drug the last, especially thick oak trunk off the wagon. "That does it. What do you think of the load?"

"The best you've brought me."

"Good. Let's have a pint and figure out the price."

"I'm thirsty for sure."

The two men started inside. "Henry, I notice I don't see your Niall so much these days. Gunder's been asking after him."

Walking beside his friend, Henry smiled. "His tutor keeps him busy when I don't."

"I see, and what would he be learning that you cannot teach him yourself, Henry? You're the smartest man in Knurlysham."

"Oh, my friend, I can assure you there is much that I do not know."

"Well, friend," Torg said, slapping Henry on the shoulder as they walked, "I think maybe I don't want to know exactly how much I don't know." Torg bellowed then, laughing in his big way, a bigness that matched his frame. When the laughter faded, he sobered again. "Tell me now, what do you think about the Baldonians? Will they cross the mountains?"

Thinking back to the many conversations between him and Moralia and Lynmeer, Henry shook his head. "I think when the real trouble comes, it will come by sea."

Chapter Six

"Niall, I can hear your every step. Have you forgotten how to move quietly?" Lynmeer asked, deep in the cool shade of the forest on a hot midsummer day. Two years had passed since the boys found the slain stag. Rhyaden was as of yet untouched by the war to the west, so fears of an impending conflict had eased throughout the land.

"Sorry, I was thinking about the fair. Father says he believes he can convince Mother to let us attend this year. It will be my first time, and I'm fourteen! All my friends have been going since they were children."

"Ah, I thought you were rather preoccupied this morning. As a matter of fact, I too think you should go this year. I will speak to your mother myself on that very subject."

"Oh, would you?" Niall exclaimed.

"Yes." Lynmeer chuckled. "As for now, though, our subject is stealth. Please, stop stepping on the leaves and sticks. Walk with them. Become a part of the ground you walk on. Melt into the tree you stand behind."

Niall sighed. The thought of his actually going to the fair made it doubly hard to concentrate on anything else.

A few weeks later, a crier came to the village. Dressed in a colorful mismatch of patched clothing, he carried a large knapsack over his back. He went first to the village square and put up a notice of the impending fair, and then he stood shouting out his news to those nearby. Others heard the shouting and gathered from curiosity. When all who heard had asked their excited questions, he went on to visit the bakeshop, the pub and the other businesses in town. Everywhere he went, he was offered a bite for bringing his news.

The road to the village made one last bend before it came out of the trees and into plain view. Horses with tall white plumes above their heads appeared pulling tall-sided red and black wagons with ornate scroll painted in gold. They marched smartly toward the village, bobbing their heads as if they waved, their coats shiny from constant grooming, silky fetlock feathers flowing behind their broad hooves.

A crowd gathered to watch the tents being set up in the open meadow southeast of town. They came in many colors, topped by white or red or yellow flags, changing the verdant green grass into a kaleidoscope of textures, heights and hues.

Excitement rose to a fevered pitch among the village's children, but they weren't the only ones to feel it. The adults enjoyed this annual break from their usual toil in the heat and humidity of summer, and they especially loved the rare chance to visit at length with friends they didn't see often. On top of the noisy bartering and commerce, contests of strength and skill added to the festivities. Each year, Niall had listened to his friends talk of the fun, and each year he had begged his parents to let him go. He could hardly believe this was the year.

Early on the first full day of the fair, Moralia insisted both her men take a good dose of the herbal concoction she had been brewing for days. Haunted by the memories of her parents' death, Moralia had told them many times how both the fair and the plague came to the village at the same time when she was ten years old.

"You know, Lynmeer first came to tutor me after my parents died. He taught me the ancient uses for the herbs and the ways of a healer. You must drink this, Niall, every single bit of it. It will keep you safe from any diseases the tinkers have brought from Cire Castle. Who knows what lies hidden in their filthy wares."

"But, Mother—"

"There is that awful word 'but' at the beginning of your sentence," Lynmeer admonished. He peered over his spectacles, looking very dapper in a long gray coat with a matching cravat and gray hat. "The beginning of anything you say is your best chance to impress your audience, and you waste that opportunity with the negative connotation of 'but.' Besides which, it sounds like you're whining."

Henry and Moralia whirled around at the sound of his voice. Lynmeer stood smiling in the doorway. His hands rested lightly on his ever-present cane. Only Niall was no longer surprised by the abrupt appearance of his tutor. To his delight, Lynmeer's arrival meant it was indeed going to be a fine day.

Grimacing at the smell wafting up in front of him, Niall put the mug to his lips and drank the brew, spitting and sputtering at the utterly awful taste.

"Mr. Lynmeer, are you ready for a fine day at the fair?" Henry asked their surprise guest. They had not expected him today.

"Please, just call me Lynmeer if you would, Henry, and yes, I shall be attending Knurlysham's annual expedition into extravagance on this glorious day. There is always something amusing to see, and I like to stay abreast of what new things are found to be entertaining or recently invented, if at all possible, and there will be good gingerbread to be had, I am sure, if I am not mistaken, which I never am."

Henry's eyebrows bunched together, and his chin jutted forward as he tried to follow the chain of words. "All right then, good," he said, shaking his head ever so slightly. He turned back to his son and added, "Off with you, Niall. Mind your manners, now. Your mother and I will be along shortly."

Niall wasn't going to leave—just yet. He waited and watched as Moralia handed her husband his own mug filled to the brim with her medicinal concoction. It not only smelled unpleasant, little bits floated in the swirling dark liquid that looked mighty suspicious. Henry sighed and donned a wry grin. He took the mug, closed his eyes and tilted it up. Gagging followed. Lynmeer and Niall looked at each other and turned away. Niall gripped the back of his chair in his effort not to laugh.

After he regained his composure, Niall got on his way, and he did not stroll. He grabbed his bow and flew into town as fast as his skinny legs would carry him, straight to the forge to look for Gunder, who was still in the midst of his morning chores.

"Come on, Gunder. We're wasting time!" he yelled, sliding to a stop just before slamming into the rock wall of the well.

"I can't help it if my father piled extra chores on me this morning. So many men have come to town because of the fair, and they all seem to have something broken they hope can be fixed before they go home. Grab that bucket and get water for the horses while I finish feeding these hungry beasts."

"Where is it?" Niall asked, twirling around. Gunder pointed to the other side of the well. "Ah, I see it," he said, setting his bow and quiver against the barn. He grabbed the bucket, attached the well rope's hook, and lowered it down.

When they were done, the two boys ran like deer before a fire, not to the meadow where all the tents were set up southeast of town, but straight into the seemingly endless woods. Their spirits soared like the wind, their shouts and laughter ringing through the trees. As eager as both were to attend the fair, Ben had to work for his family for half a day, and so they chose to wait until he could join them before they partook of the festivities.

Freedom fueled the boys as they ran, leaping over logs and splashing across quiet Knurly Run. Grunts rang out now and again when one or the other stumbled, but they only stopped to rest when they could scarcely breathe, bending over to suck in oxygen before taking off again. They planned to check out Ben's status later in the day, most likely when hunger brought them out of the woods. For now, running as fast and as far as possible was simply spectacular.

"Let's climb this tree and see what we can see," Gunder panted. Niall was worn out, and he suspected Gunder was too, but neither mentioned fatigue to the other. They were standing in front of a giant Knurly tree that had glorious knobs and branches for good hand and foot holds. A lesser tree would be worn smooth over the centuries of children and forest creatures climbing it, but the tough old Knurly's rough bark did not wear down, allowing for a good grip.

"You first," Niall said, walking up to where Gunder stood. He looked up into the ancient tree, wondering if it was a talker. Few were, and only Knurlys spoke. He wondered what many wonders this particular tree had seen. It certainly stood taller than any of its nearby neighbors.

Gunder put a hand up and grasped the first branch, hefting himself into the tree. Once he was started, the going got easier. Up and up he went.

"I can see forever from up here," Gunder cried. "It's magnificent!"

Niall stepped up and whispered softly, "Sorry if this hurts."

"Not at all, quite used to it," the tree whispered back. "Haversham's the name."

"Are you a professor?"

"Oh no, the Favershams are a different branch of the family."

"Nice to meet you. My name's Niall," he returned, hefting himself up to the bottom branch.

"What'd ya say?" Gunder yelled down. He was quite a ways above Niall. Triangular flags atop the tallest tents in the meadow were visible from where he sat.

"Nothing. Just caught my shirt is all," Niall answered, peering up through the branches to make out where his friend had gotten to. Knurly leaves, shaped like very large sycamore leaves, all but hid Gunder, though he was only thirty feet higher.

A half mile from where the two boys sat in a tree, Ben wore the bakeshop's best apron, selling warm bread, cookies and cakes to the villagers. He scanned the crowd, disappointment etched across his face. So far he had seen nary a glimpse of Niall or Gunder. He imagined they were having a grand time somewhere out there, free from the kind of responsibility that came with being a baker's son at fair time.

"Pay attention, Ben!" his mother admonished. He had not noticed her walk up to their booth, lugging a large basket full of warm bread. Her voice made him jump.

At thirteen and a year younger than his two friends, Ben had recently shot up and was now a head taller than Niall, and skinnier if that was possible. He had grown so quickly, his mother could hardly keep him in long pants to fit his slender build. He was now as tall as his father, but only half the width.

Most days he did not mind the work set before him in the bakeshop, but today, with his friends running free, it was particularly vexing to be left behind.

"Sorry, Mum."

Gwyn smiled at him, reaching up to touch his cheek. "Tsk. You look just like your father when he was younger, freckles and all."

Ben ducked his head.

"When I come back with the next batch, I'll stay here for a bit, and you can have a look at what's out there," she said, indicating the fair.

Ben's eyes lit up. "Then hurry, Mum."

Gwyn laughed as they unloaded the basket. The fine weather had brought out a large crowd.

"Hello, Mrs. Brunde," Gwyn said, waving to an acquaintance as she started back to the bakeshop. "I haven't seen you in ages. Why, your daughter is nearly as tall as you are now. How do they grow so fast?"

Ben turned to see who his mother was talking to. The loaf he held fell out of his hand and hit the ground.

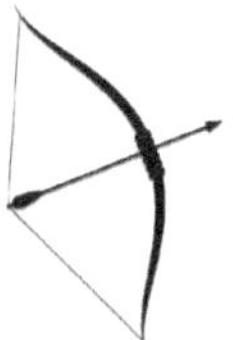

Chapter Seven

Niall waved to Ben. He and Gunder trotted across the field toward the colorful tents. Their clothes were mussed, and their hair hung limply from a quick dip to cool off in Knurly Run. They approached the Finwick tent at the same time Gwyn returned with another basket of bread and cookies. Ben's apron flew through the air as he snatched a loaf of bread and waved goodbye before his mother had a chance to utter a word.

They came together outside the ring of tents. Dropping to the grass, Ben tore the loaf he carried into three huge chunks and handed round the shares. The aroma of fresh-baked bread tantalized their senses. All three boys closed their eyes and took a bite.

"Thank you, Ben, I was plum famished," Gunder managed between mouthfuls of the soft pillowy bread. Niall laughed at his friend and offered his thanks too. He had yet to feel hungry, but as soon as he started eating the crusty warm goodness, his appetite kicked in. All three boys ate until there were only crumbs left. A loud belch interrupted the quiet. Two more followed.

"Shall we have a go at the fair?" Niall asked, mostly

recovered from the morning in the woods. They stood up and brushed themselves off.

"I saw a pretty girl," Ben said offhandedly. Both the other boys stopped in their tracks and turned to stare at him.

"A what?" Gunder asked, his eyes wide with astonishment. A bit of bread still clung to the side of his mouth. He wiped it away and shook his head, like a horse ridding itself of flies.

"A girl. She has long braids the color of honey and a wonderful laugh," Ben concluded. By the end of the brief speech, he was looking at the ground, embarrassed that he had brought up the subject. Niall saw the unfamiliar doe-eyed look in his friend's eyes before his glance fell.

"Well, then, old chap, let's go have a looksee. Gunder here doesn't even know what a girl is."

"I do so!" replied Gunder, knocking Niall in the shoulder. "I've got sisters, you daft loon."

The boys walked the noisy, crowded grounds for twenty minutes before Ben spotted the elusive girl, who stood half hidden behind her mother, watching two boys take aim at straw targets with their bows.

She was frightfully skinny in Niall's opinion, but he held his tongue. Her hair was plaited in two long braids, joined at the bottom with a strip of blue plaid tied in a bow. The same material was tied in a sash around her waist. He wondered what color her eyes were, but she was turned away from him.

Gunder watched the competition closely for a few minutes. "Let's you and I have a go," he said, poking Niall in the ribs. "We're better than those two, by a pint." Without waiting for a reply, he took off for his father's forge at a dead run. They had left their bows at the barn before their run in the woods. Niall looked over at Ben, who only shrugged. Ben was no marksman, his mind at the moment was on bows of a different sort.

No prizes were offered for the competition beyond the bragging rights for winning a round. That was obviously sufficient incentive for several of the fathers standing behind their sons. The game was organized loosely, mostly by the size of the competitor, the winner taking on all comers. If no one stepped up, that boy was declared a champion, and they started over with two fresh competitors of older age. After the small boys were done, the tenor of the banter increased. Some men began to gamble on the outcome of each round.

Gunder returned and the boys watched with heightened interest as another boy their age stepped forward and a second was pushed forward by his father. Niall looked around, wondering if his own parents or his tutor would approve of his participating, but he couldn't find them in the crowd. The first boy's arrow hit very close to center. The second boy's missed the straw entirely. The unlucky father had bet a pint of beer on his son.

"He'll be practicing a bit more before his next go!" the losing father predicted.

Laughter erupted. Niall admired him for taking it so well. Gunder grinned and elbowed Niall.

"I'll have a go," Gunder said, stepping forward.

"You will now, will you?" the first contestant's father said. "Elan here is pretty top-notch with a bow. You might not like the shame of losing."

"I can take what comes if you can," Gunder answered. The man laughed and motioned with a sweeping gesture for Gunder to go first.

Gunder was a solid lad, but his days were spent hefting and manhandling wood, not in accuracy. Because Niall took so much stock in mastering the bow, Gunder had tried his best to learn too, when he had time to practice, which wasn't often. To add his own touch and distinguish his bow from all the others, he had painted both ends blood red. At the time, Niall thought it was probably not a good choice for sneaking up on prey in the forest, but he had kept quiet.

Gunder let fly with his arrow. It landed stoutly with a solid thud. Deep into the straw, the shaft measured six inches to the left of center.

"Ach," he mumbled, stepping back.

The other boy stepped up and let fly with his arrow. It was closer to the mark, but only by an inch. The boy's father clapped him on the shoulder. "Well done, Elan! Any others brave enough to go up against my son?"

The words resonated in Niall's ears. This wasn't bravery at all, skill maybe, but there was nothing brave about shooting burlap on straw.

"I will."

Elan's father turned to look at Niall, sizing up the competition. A smile spread across his face. "Rather small for that big bow you're carrying. Did you bring your father's by mistake?"

The crowd laughed. Gunder stepped back. Elan's father again stepped away from his son, patting him on the shoulder as he did. He magnanimously motioned the new competitor forward. Niall stepped up, planting his left foot slightly forward, then drew an arrow and fitted it to the shaft. He glanced over at Elan and smiled.

Niall took one steadying breath, then drew air in slowly and held it. He let fly with the arrow. The vibration echoed through his head. In that singular crystallized moment, he no longer saw burlap and straw, but rather a beautiful stag with a twisted horn. He blinked at the strange vision. For the first time ever, he had no idea where his arrow was headed.

Thwang! Not a sound followed the arrow penetrating the target. Several seconds went by, and suddenly cheers rang out among those watching, none louder than Gunder, who clapped and hooted, jumping up and down. Several from the boisterous crowd moved forward to clap Niall on the back. The arrow stood dead center in the target.

When the clamor died down, Elan stepped up, his nerves frazzled. It wasn't easy to follow a perfect shot. The moment he let his arrow fly, his shoulders slumped. It was far to the right of center. He bit his lip.

Before the boy's stunned father could say a word, Niall graciously stepped forward and clapped him on the back. "Good job! I bet you're ready for a biscuit. Come on, I'll buy you one."

Elan smiled in surprise. He shyly looked over to his bewildered father, who didn't know what else to do, so he nodded. Two different contestants stepped forward and fitted arrows to their bows.

"That's a great bow you have," Elan said as they walked away.

"Thanks. My father made it," Niall replied.

Having previously moved to the opposite side, Ben was positioned so that when he followed the other boys, he had to pass by the girl with the long, honey-colored hair. He managed to catch her eye and smile as he went by. She blushed and looked down at her shoes. As often happens when one first falls in love, Ben promptly tripped.

Chapter Eight

In the latter half of summer, three weeks after the fair had come and gone, the weather turned dreadfully sour, at least sour was the term used by one disgruntled teacher. Dampness descended from one end of Rhyaden to the other. Everyone's mood slowly succumbed and sunk as low as the soggy heather. Gray, never-ending drizzle blanketed the land. Mist rose from the lakes as if stirred by an unseen witch. Even the streams gave off eerie vapors. The showers eventually turned to steady rain. Following days of continuous cold and wet weather, rivulets of water found their way to the small creeks. Tributaries of the Rhy River began to run stoutly, swelling until they were angry torrents, picking up debris on their wild run to the big river.

Two weeks into the miserable weather, an unexpected knock rattled the cottage door. Moralia and Niall looked at each other. They were elbow deep sorting berries for preserves.

"Who would be out in such weather?" Moralia asked, drying her hands as she crossed the room.

Lynmeer stood on the porch. He came more often now, at least three times a week except when Henry needed Niall, and even then, he often came just for tea and a visit with Moralia.

"Ker . . . chew!"

"Lynmeer, please come in. You're soaking wet.

"Thank you, my dear . . . kerchew!"

Moralia brewed him a foul-smelling concoction, adding a pinch of lavender to soften the aroma. Rummaging in her tins, she realized she was out of ginger.

"Niall, will you run to town and get us some gingerbread biscuits? They're Lynmeer's favorite, and I'm out of ginger."

"Sure!" He was off like a shot, for going meant not drinking any of her concoction poorly disguised as tea.

Lynmeer glumly sat down in front of the fire, took off his spectacles and blew his nose.

"Ghastly weather, quite."

"You poor dear. You shouldn't be out in this weather," Moralia said.

"It never rains in Ayhrland, you know," Lynmeer said, staring into a dark corner of the cottage.

"Where's that?" Moralia asked.

Lynmeer jumped slightly, suddenly aware that it was Moralia who sat beside him. "Oh nothing, my dear. You are so kind. Is the tea ready?"

Niall sloshed through the mud, jumping at times to keep on solid ground. He had gotten so bored in the horrid weather he was quite glad for the opportunity to get out. There was little to do in the cottage or the barn. His father had already sharpened every tool twice, mended all the harnesses, and rubbed every piece of leather down with oil. An hour earlier, he came to the house and told Moralia he was headed to the forge.

"May I go with you?" Niall had asked, jumping up.

"Your mother can use your help, and there's nothing for you to do at the forge in this rain," Henry replied.

His disappointment from not getting to go with his father was forgotten now that he was on his way to the bakeshop. He hoped Ben would be there. He enjoyed running, and the foul weather seemed to be breaking off. His muscles warmed up despite the damp air, losing their stiffness after days of inactivity.

"I bet the forest isn't as muddy as this track," he said out loud, turning off the wagon road and heading into the trees. He followed the same basic course as the Rindle, the small creek that ran behind their cottage and intercepted Knurly Run a mile farther west. Correct in guessing there would be less mud under the trees, he failed to take into account the rainwater dripping off the leaves above him. Before long, he was as soaked as the ground beneath him. The weather didn't cooperate one bit either. Dank clouds closed in once again, darkening the sky around him, and the mist reverted back to cold, steady rain.

An unfamiliar sound caught his attention, the din growing ominously louder the closer he got to the Run. Instead of angling toward town, he was drawn to follow the Rindle, usually a well-mannered little water course he could easily jump over. Now, swollen and dirty, it hurried to join the turbulent Knurly Run yards before the two should have met.

Niall was astounded by the change. Normally in summer, he would jump into the water to cool off on his walk to town, but the weeks of unprecedented rain had turned it into a dangerous body of swift water. He could not remember it ever being this wide or loud. Shaking his head in amazement, he turned toward town and made his way alongside the swollen river. Plodding through the tangled wet growth was slow, and he was cold. The trip to town was no longer the fun outing he had envisioned.

A blood-curdling scream pierced the heavy air, stopping Niall in his tracks. Unable to locate the source, he was sure that it came from the far side of Knurly Run. He edged closer to the water, scanning the other side through the rain. He blinked and wiped his eyes. He blinked again. There! What he first thought to be a stump must be a person, standing dangerously close to the water.

Reversing course, he moved back upstream, trying to discern what the person was holding. Another hundred feet and the desperate situation became clear. A girl held onto one end of a tree branch. In the churning water in front of her, a small boy held the other end, bobbing up and down like a cork in the roiling water.

Time slowed to a standstill. Niall contemplated how long it would take him to run to the bridge outside of town and cross, summon help from the village and get back to the girl on the other side. He weighed the options, watching the boy dip under the water in slow motion, then pop back up with a gargled yell. A second scream pierced the air.

"Go upstream before you cross. There is a log that will help you."

Niall looked up at the Knurly tree beside him. He nodded and stripped off his jacket, making his way up the Run along the water's edge. He tried to move faster, but thick undergrowth prevented sprinting and brambles clawed at his legs. Finally, he came to a log jutting out a quarter of the width of the Run. He hopped on top. Immediately a loud snap protested his weight. He ignored the warning and started across the slippery, wet log. At the end, he launched himself as far out as he could go.

The frigid water was merciless, crushing his chest, clamping his head in an icy vise. Debris picked up by the river slammed into him. He swam as hard as he could, determined not to get swept past the boy before he could reach him. His soaked clothing dragged heavily. The boy bobbing in the water was coming too fast. Niall felt hopeless, sure he could never reach the other side in time.

Fatigue set in. A soft, alluring voice told Niall to let go. "You tried, Niall. It just wasn't possible." His numb body listened, missing a stroke and letting the water propel him. It was easy now, he could relax.

Moralia looked up from her knitting by the warm fire. Her hand reached up and held onto her stone necklace. Her skin tingled. The crackling logs had burned down to a bed of glowing red coals. Lynmeer was looking out the window, a faraway look on his face. Something was not right. "Niall?" she said, coming closer and trying to see out the window too. She glanced at Lynmeer again, but his eyes were blank, as if no one was there.

A different voice welled up inside Niall, stronger and more insistent than the first had been. "You must not quit!"

He felt a presence come alongside him, breaking the force of the water. What had he been thinking? Drowning in Knurly Run? Determination flooded him. Hardened from hefting the heavy bow his father made for him, he pulled for the opposite shore.

He was almost past the boy. With a strength he did not know he possessed, Niall reached out with both hands and grabbed the flailing legs, shoving the boy up on the shore. The girl fell over backwards when he came flying out of the water. Relief flooded through Niall, but immediately he was pulled under, torn away from them by the current. He saw the girl crawl to the edge, helpless to do anything but watch him go.

"Hang on!" she mouthed as the raging water tore him away.

"William. William, are you all right? Can you hear me? Willy!" She pounded her brother's back. He gagged and coughed, forcing out words.

"Stop, Annwyn! You're killing me."

She sat back then, relieved to hear her brother speak, even if she wanted to kill him for climbing that stupid tree. What had happened to the boy in the water who saved her brother? Would he drown? Uncontrollable shivers began to wrack her body.

Downstream, a large Knurly branch that draped low over the water caught Niall. Gratefully, he grabbed ahold and made his way to the bank. Cold to the bone, he shook himself like a dog, ridding his clothes of debris and water. Shuddering, he bent over, propping his arms on his knees until he caught his breath. Straightening up a moment later, he turned upstream, walking as fast as his tired legs would go. When he got close enough to see the two children under the tree, the girl was sitting still, and the boy lay flat on the cold ground. Niall forced his legs into a run.

The girl turned at the sound of his pounding feet. Her eyes followed him but she did not move.

† † †

Moralia held the back of a chair to keep herself steady as she watched Lynmeer turn into an old man. Deep lines creased his face at the edge of his eyes. His peppered gray hair turned pearly white, and his beard lengthened to a wispy point. He moaned from great pain as if being torn apart on the inside.

"Lynmeer, what is happening? Your hair, your beard."

"Moralia," Lynmeer gasped, then drew a deep breath, "do not be afraid."

"I'm not afraid, but what has happened? Are you okay?"

"Niall needed help, and I had to use magic to help him."

"Magic?"

"Yes, and it has cost me. Now please, this is most important. I do not want you to say a word to him, or to Henry, about what you saw or what I just told you.

Moralia shook her head, trying to grasp what he was telling her.

"But Lynmeer, are you all right?"

"Yes, dear one, I will be all right. Another time, I will explain everything, but not now," he continued, breathing heavily. "I am too tired. I have to catch my breath before I can take my leave."

"Can I get you anything?"

"No, all I need is rest." His body shuddered. "On second thought, let's have another spot of tea."

Moralia hurried to brew a new pot. When she filled their

cups, Lynmeer asked for a blanket.

"Of course, I'll get one from the back room. It will only take a moment."

She left the room, and Lynmeer withdrew a tiny packet of forgetting potion from his coat pocket. Aleah had said to always carry the potion in case a human saw him in dragon form. He put a pinch in her teacup and quickly returned the packet to his pocket.

"Here you are," Moralia said, unfolding the warm knitted afghan and placing it over Lynmeer's knees.

"Thank you, my dear."

"You're welcome," she said, sitting across from him. She lifted her cup and blew to cool it, then took a sip. A quizzical look crossed her face, and she took another sip to see if she could figure out what was different.

"Your company has been delightful as always," Lynmeer said a short time later. "I'll need to be gone for a while, but Niall will have a grand story to tell you when he returns."

Unable to keep her eyes open any longer, Moralia mumbled something unintelligible as Lynmeer tucked the warm blanket over her.

The pale young boy looked much like a drowned rat. The frightened girl resembled a stone-cold statue. Niall leaned over and picked the lad up, adjusting the muddy bundle in his arms once he was upright. He looked from the girl to the village.

"Show me where your home is," Niall said. "He needs to get by a fire and get something hot in his belly." Without another word he started toward town, his tired muscles quickly protesting against the weight.

She grabbed her basket and ran to get ahead of him, stumbling once in her wet skirts but quickly picking herself back up. Niall watched her braids swing back and forth in front of him. It reminded him of something he had seen before.

The sight of a soaking wet girl and a young man carrying another equally soaked boy would have attracted attention — if anyone had been outside. Niall hoped to see someone as they neared town, for it now felt like the boy weighed two hundred pounds. Halfway down a narrow street, the girl sprinted ahead of Niall to pound on a cottage door. She nearly fell in when it was opened.

"Send someone to find my father!"

"What ever happened?" the woman cried.

"I haven't time," she yelled, already running toward the next house on the lane. The woman, still standing in the doorway, saw Niall go by carrying the sodden boy. It was enough to jolt her into action. She grabbed a heavy wrap and boots, pulled a woolen cap over her head and took off for the town square.

Niall struggled to keep following. How much farther? Carrying the boy was taking a toll. His arms felt stretched to the snapping point. He was flooded with relief when she didn't bother to knock at the next cottage, but opened the door and held it for him.

"Here!"

Niall could barely grunt in reply.

"Mother, help us. William nearly drowned!"

"Oh, mercy," the woman cried. "Hurry, get him to the fire. What happened?" She threw her mending in the basket by her chair and jumped up just as Niall came through the doorway with his muddy bundle.

It was all he could do not to drop William on the hard floor. The last six inches were excruciating. He laid the boy down and stepped back, nearly collapsing himself. The ache in his limbs changed to a prickly sensation as the blood again flowed down his arms. The children's mother knelt and began peeling wet clothes off her youngest. Soaking wet himself, Niall moved closer to the fire for the warmth it gave off.

"Get me a blanket, Annwyn."

When William was dried and tightly rewrapped in the blanket, their mother poured three mugs of hot tea and handed them around. The liquid scorched Niall's tongue, but holding the cup warmed his hands and brought a grateful smile to his face.

"Thank you so much."

"Well it's the least I could do. You two need to get into dry clothes too."

He blew on the drink, watching the hot steam swirl away. Trying again, the hot drink warmed him all the way down to his belly. Ever so slowly, his brain began to thaw and the ache in his arms faded. William's violent shivering eased up too.

"I'm Margaret Brunde. What's your name, son?"

"My name's Niall Thoralt, ma'am."

"You've saved my William's life. I'm so grateful to you."

Embarrassed by the puddle of dirty water growing at his feet, Niall rocked from foot to foot, listening to the girl give her mother details of the near calamity and rescue. Annwyn absently pulled the ribbons loose that held her braids, straightening her limp wet hair with her fingertips. Niall watched her long, thin hands play with the fine strands of hair. There was something he should be remembering. Loathe to leave the warmth, he felt increasingly awkward. He was surely staying too long. Glancing about, he wished there were a rag or something to clean the mess under his feet.

"I decided we had enough mushrooms and I wanted some tea. I turned around to find William and head back, but he wasn't beside me anymore, and then I heard him yell. He was up in a big tree, and the branch he was on broke, dropping him into the river." She stopped to take a breath.

"I held onto the branch," William said, taking up the story, "but it was so dark and cold under the water, and then something lifted me out and threw me up on the bank. Then Annwyn almost killed me pounding on my back."

"I wasn't trying to kill you," she retorted. "I was trying to get the water out of you."

"Hush there," Mrs. Brunde scolded.

"He held onto his end, and I held onto my end. We just couldn't let go. Then I saw this boy on the other side and I screamed, and he ran upstream and jumped in. He saved William, Mother. I . . . I couldn't." She sobbed, giving in to overwhelming emotion. Niall wanted to put his arms around her, to let her know she did a good job, but his feet were rooted to the floor.

Margaret put down her tea and hugged her daughter. "You did your best, Annwyn, that's what matters. Oh my," she said, backing up and brushing at her bodice, "your clothes are soaked. You need to change into something dry."

The heavy door burst open a second time. An instant later, William's father was hugging his youngest son, William. Niall recognized the boy who followed behind him. It all fell into place then. Annwyn was the girl Ben became infatuated with at the fair a few weeks back. Elan was her older brother. She must have been there with her family to watch him compete in the archery contest.

When the story was finished for a second time, William's

father grabbed Niall by the shoulders.

"Thank you, boy. I don't know how I'll ever repay you for my son's life."

"Not necessary, sir, anyone would've . . . ," Niall mumbled, his tongue suddenly tied.

"Not anyone, a HERO!" He picked Niall up and bear-hugged him until Niall thought he wasn't likely to ever breathe again.

"I'm all wet, sir, and I probably ought to go home. I was supposed to do an errand for my mum, and . . ." He trailed off, not sure how to politely leave. He was keenly aware of Annwyn standing by the table watching him as her father set him down.

"I can't think of your name, son. Who are you?"

"Niall Thoralt, sir. My father is Henry Thoralt."

"Ahh, Henry's boy, yes, yes, you're the marksman. I remember. I'm Tom Brunde." He clasped Niall's hand between both of his. "I'm so grateful to you, son."

Annwyn walked up to him then and put out a trembling hand. "Thank you, Niall, for saving my brother, and likely me too. I couldn't let go of that bloody branch, I just couldn't. The river was likely to have had us both if it hadn't been for you."

"You saved him too, just as much as me," Niall replied, suddenly feeling warm.

"My name is Annwyn." She smiled and then turned and quickly disappeared into the back of the house.

"Here, boy, have some more hot tea before you go."

The rest of the day was a blur. When he got to the bakeshop, the Finwicks listened to his brief version of the news and insisted on giving him the gingerbread free of charge.

"Oh no, really, I have the money Mother sent ," Niall replied, reaching into his pocket. The wet cloth held no coin. "Or

I did when I left home," he said.

Ben was wide-eyed in wonder when Niall told him the girl's name.

"Annwyn. What a beautiful name," Ben murmured.

"Yes, it is," Niall replied. The look in Ben's eyes was unmistakable.

When Niall got home, he had to tell the story all over again for his mother. She sat quietly by the fire with an afghan over her lap as he recounted his story. Her fingers laced together, and then apart, and then together again, again and again, but finally she relaxed a bit and even smiled at Niall's obvious discomfort when mentioning Annwyn. It was the first time she had ever heard him speak about a girl.

"I don't know why I'm sitting here," she blurted out suddenly. The two looked at each other, equally confused. Her hand clasped the stone she wore around her neck.

"I'm hungry, Mother. Could I have something to eat?"

"Of course, that's what I should be doing."

Niall watched her jump up and gather ingredients for making soup. In minutes, she put it on to boil, her motions automatic. Then she walked to the table and stopped moving as if she was mesmerized, staring down at two teacups.

"When did Lynmeer leave?" Niall asked.

"I don't know. I don't remember the afternoon at all."

"That's odd."

"Yes, it is. Change out of those clothes while dinner cooks. You need to get into something warm and dry.

Henry returned late, long after the sun went down. "Several of my friends offered pints to celebrate my son being a hero," he explained. "I was only going to stay for one, but they insisted," he added rather sheepishly. Niall could not recall his father ever coming home late, or so red in the face.

"It was a brave thing you did today, Niall. I'm mighty proud of you," Henry said.

"Thank you, Father, but I just did what anyone would have done."

"No, most would not have tried to cross that river. I don't know how you didn't drown. I've never seen the water so high."

"Father," Niall started, "it was as if . . . as if . . ."

"What, son?"

"Nothing."

"As if what, Niall?"

"It was as if someone helped me when I was in the water, but no one else was there."

Moralia's chair stopped rocking.

Henry blinked. "I can't explain that, son."

The following morning, the sun rose bright and the land glistened under drops of dew shining like diamonds on the soaked, green earth. Everyone's shoulders lightened, and the gloom of the past weeks dissipated under the warm sun. Blades of grass, matted down from weeks of rain, perked up, eagerly reaching for the sky.

Several weeks passed before Lynmeer returned to tutor his student. Niall couldn't wait to fill him in on all that happened after saving William, asking his mother daily when his tutor was to return. When at last Lynmeer appeared on the horizon, Niall flew down the road to meet him, his words tumbling out in a flurry.

"Whoa, Niall, you can tell me everything over tea."

Lynmeer smiled, listening intently as they sat at the table, occasionally grabbing another gingerbread biscuit.

At the end of his story, Niall noted Lynmeer had been unusually quiet. Then he began to notice other things. "Your hair has turned white, Lynmeer."

"Niall, don't be rude," Moralia admonished as she picked up their empty teacups.

"I have been ill, a rare affliction that causes one's hair and skin to age, I'm afraid, but I'm quite all right now. No need to worry," Lynmeer said.

"Where did you go? You were gone a long time."

"I went home to Ayhrland," came the reply.

"Ayhrland?" Niall asked.

Chapter Nine

Two Years Later

Niall pulled the harness strap through the buckle to the wear mark and looped the long end back through itself. The mare stood twitching her ears back and forth, her tail swooshing from side to side. She was going to shoulder a heavy burden the first half of this long haul. Henry had a load of fine straight oak, more than called for by local demand, so they were going all the way to Cire Castle in hopes of negotiating a greater price. When he suggested his son go along to see the sites as a way to celebrate his sixteenth birthday, Niall was quick to agree.

A week before the departure, Lynmeer approached Henry when the day's lessons were over. "I should like to tag along with you to Cire, if you don't mind, Henry. It's been a while since I was last at the castle. I'd rather like to see if the king has made any fortifications for war, you know, in the event war hasn't been averted as we have been led to believe."

"Of course you may come along. The more the merrier, I say, especially if the wagon gets stuck in the mud!"

Standing nearby, Niall heard his father's joke and laughed

delightedly. Lynmeer peered over his spectacles, one eyebrow slightly higher than the other. That particular look no longer intimidated Niall as it had a few years back.

The civil strife in Baldonia seemed to have resolved itself in the past year so traveling was no longer such a concern. Cargo ships carrying goods for trade stopped in Baldonia again, their crews reporting to Rhyaden merchants that a new regime had taken over the contentious kingdom to the west. Francis Louis DeMont had been crowned the new king. Most citizens of Rhyaden breathed much easier with the news. Lynmeer and Henry, however, believed that Rhyaden might still see trouble in the future.

The first day of their journey dawned bright and sunny. Ignoring her men's protests, Moralia dosed Niall and Henry with her most potent herbal concoction, hoping it would keep them safe for the entire journey. She knew they wouldn't take any more of it even if she sent it along.

Resigned by now to the wisdom of taking his mother's brew, Niall held his nose and took big gulps, then quickly chased it down with a glass of fresh cow's milk, the best method he'd found to cut the disagreeable taste. Henry closed his eyes and swallowed his measure, followed by coughing, sputtering and a corkscrewed expression that turned Lynmeer toward the mirror to fuss with his hair. Mother had made a particularly strong batch.

At last ready to depart, Niall hugged her goodbye.

"You have the stone?" she whispered in his ear.

"Yes, Mother, I have it."

She pulled back and smiled at him. He shouldered his quiver and bow and stepped to the horse's lead. He gently clucked his tongue, and the black mare strained to start the heavy wagon. Lynmeer and Henry reached out to give a helping push. Once it rolled, the mare settled into a steady pace.

Niall looked back to see his mother's broad smile. Henry leaned in and kissed her.

"Take care, dear. You're absolutely positive you wouldn't like to tag along?" he asked.

"And be your camp slave? No, I think not. You'll have plenty of fun without me, I imagine, and I have plans for a frolic of my own while you're gone."

Henry feigned consternation, then grinned. "All right, then. We'll be back in a couple of weeks."

Niall saluted his mother one final time, and she returned an exuberant wave. He half wished she had wanted to join them, for her campfire stories were delightful and she was the better cook of the lot, but he knew she was glad of the opportunity for peace and quiet.

Lynmeer stepped lively, his cane tapping on the hard ground, keeping time to the horse's steps. Niall began whistling, leading the entourage down the road. Bringing up the rear, Henry pulled on the ropes that secured the load as the wagon lumbered forward, ensuring it was well snugged.

They skirted Knurlysham, crossing through the meadow where the fair was held each summer instead of negotiating the cobbled streets. The meadow looked bereft without the colorful tents and the sounds of laughter.

The two older men walked side by side. Suddenly Lynmeer sneezed, surprising all three of them. At the same time, Henry was knocked to the ground from behind. When he had his feet safely under him again, he turned around to find nothing there.

Niall turned back. "You all right, Father?"

"Yes, I'm fine, just tripped is all, I guess," he said, rubbing his elbow.

Niall looked from his father to Lynmeer. "Bless you, Lynmeer."

"Thank you, dear boy. Must be the ragweed. Didn't feel that one coming at all!"

Niall looked again at his father and then turned and trotted a few steps to catch up with the mare.

"Niall, let's discuss history. Enlighten me with what you know of Cire Castle," Lynmeer queried an hour later. It was midmorning, and the initial excitement of starting such a long journey had long since worn off.

"King Stephen lives there now. His great-grandfather Richard began building Cire in the new location after the Great Fire."

"When was Cire built?"

"Ah . . . eighty years ago?" Niall knew they had covered this subject, but he had never really cared for memorizing dates. "Why did they move locations?"

Lynmeer looked down for a moment, then took a deep breath. "They chose to build the new castle closer to the middle of Rhyaden for many reasons, one of which was to centralize for trade."

"Where was the first one located?"

"Far to the east and somewhat south, near Nanty's Bay."

"What other reasons made them move?" Niall asked, his curiosity aroused.

"It has been said that magical things happened there in the past, and for the most part, people fear magic. Also, there were very bad memories from the fire."

"Magical things?"

"Yes, I said magical."

"And do you think magical things really happened there?"

"Thinking something is one thing, knowing it quite another unless a person is there to see it for themselves."

"Was the castle completely destroyed in the fire, or are there some parts still visible?"

"Quite a bit of the foundation survives, though some of the stone has fallen away over time," Lynmeer answered, falling into his lecture voice. "The new castle, Cire, has side and back wings creating an inside courtyard. Also, it has a formidable front gate and is altogether much larger and better protected than its predecessor."

"How long can they withstand being under siege?" Henry interjected, listening to the conversation.

"A superb question," replied Lynmeer. Niall perked up his ears. His father seldom joined in discussions, preferring instead to listen.

"I suppose if they took proper precautions, they could last for many months. The question then becomes whether or not King Stephen has taken any such steps of preparation."

"Isn't that what a king is supposed to do?" Niall asked.

Chapter Ten

Layla DeMont, a cousin of the newly crowned King of Baldonia, slipped quietly through the woods at the edge of Lake Arual. It was early morning, and birds should have been greeting the day with sing-song chatter, but instead there was hushed anticipation in the air. Her fellow spy, Tam, waited on the other side, hidden from sight. The girls stalked a falcon.

They were Baldonian spies, returning home from an expedition to gather information and assess the potential for invasion. King Francis DeMont wished to add more land and taxes to his kingdom. Already late, they shouldn't have been after the raptor at all, but Layla simply couldn't resist the temptation. The more difficult the prey she hunted, the more the adrenaline coursed through her body, making her oblivious to authority or consequences. She planned on leading her king's army someday, and a falcon on her shoulder would be one impressive notch on her belt.

This was her second trip to the Rhyaden countryside. She had come here with her father many years prior, too young at that time to understand his animosity toward this land. When he shot a stag outside the village of Knurlysham, she felt sorry for the beautiful creature. Crouching down, she ran her hands along the course hair, surprised at the warmth. Her father cut one side of the unique set of antlers off the head, alternately laughing and muttering to himself. Blood spurted out, splattering her with droplets.

"What? Are you afraid of a little blood? Don't be squeamish, girl," he jeered.

"May I have the other side?" Layla asked, hiding the sting of his words.

"No. I intend for it to be a warning. I want them to fear they are being watched."

He took the antler home and made a horn out of it.

Since her father's death, the horn hung on Layla's belt. In the ensuing years, she grew tall and lean, preferring one long braid for her raven hair over what the ladies of the day preferred. Joining the king's army, she used it to turn her father's animosity into her own ambition. Extremely clever, she did well.

During yesterday's climb up the mountains east of the castle, she came upon a leather canister wedged in between boulders halfway up. The contents were intriguing: a beautifully drawn map of Rhyaden.

Layla walked a hundred feet to her left from where Tam napped after the two had eaten a meal of stale bread. Not sleepy herself, she promised Tam an hour's rest and moved away so as not to disturb her. Tam had kept guard the previous night and she badly needed sleep. Moving quietly across the rocky escarpment, Layla spotted the canister and made her way over to it. She eased down, using her body to shield it from her companion's sight in the event Tam woke.

Unrolling the beautiful parchment, Layla's eyes widened

in amazement. On the map, south and east of Lake Arual, in a place referred to as Gaxdorn Gate, a shiny, coppery glow came to life before fading to a dull brown. She looked closer. Not far from the dot in faded writing, "old castle" was written near what looked like a few square blocks, as if indicating a foundation. She immediately determined she would not share this with Tam or her commanders. She would keep this a secret until the time was right for her to use it for herself. Glancing across the rocks, she sighed with relief; Tam slept soundly.

There was no way to keep the canister and hide it from Tam. Layla silently debated leaving it or coming back for it sometime, and finally folded the map flat several times despite the damage to the parchment. Lifting her shirt, she tucked it behind her back, then got up and down a few times to test the likelihood of its falling out or making too much noise.

Crossing the rocky face a half hour later, Layla yelled, "Look what I found!" She held it up for her companion to see.

"What is it?" Tam inquired, blinking the sleep out of her eyes as she sat up.

"An old leather case, lodged in those rocks," she said, pointing across to where she had been. "I wonder who lost it?" She held it out for Tam to see.

Tam took it from her and opened it. As rough and weather-worn as the outside leather was, the interior was pristine. Layla watched her oldest friend inspect the broken end of the strap, an old and ragged cut.

"Beautiful workmanship," Tam said, setting it aside. "I guess we better get going. We need to finish this area today if we are to meet our company tomorrow as planned."

✝✝✝

Early the next morning, Layla gently pulled the Rhyaden map out and quietly opened it. The same mystery happened as yesterday. The glowing coppery spot reappeared. It was as if the dot came alive for a brief moment, and then the glow slowly dissipated. She refolded the map, and gently slid it into her pack.

"Come on, Tam, wake up. I want to check out the lake."

"What?" she mumbled.

"Wake up, I said." Layla poked at her companion's rear end, and then reached down and ripped the blanket off.

"Our orders are to check out the castle and its defenses, nothing about the lake."

"We have time. Come on."

Now sitting across the lake from each other, Layla's fingers tapped a steady beat on her pant leg. They were expected at home, and these hours spent stalking a bird would garner a harsh reprimand from her commander. She knew Tam hadn't wanted to come to the lake; the girl didn't like getting in trouble. She was loyal, though, Layla thought, smiling. "Stupid, but loyal."

Layla had spotted the falcon while they ate their breakfast, and Tam had immediately reminded her that the punishment for killing a falcon was having one's eyes put out. Layla had paid no heed, dismissing the warning.

"No one will even know."

"Being left a blind beggar is worse than being put to death as a spy," Tam had argued, trying to talk her out of the hunt.

"You know I'm not changing my mind," Layla countered, smiling at Tam, "so sit and wait, or help. Which do you suppose will get us home quicker?"

The large falcon and the hunter watched each other. Despite being followed, the bird couldn't bring herself to let her nest out of sight. She had already been gone long enough to endanger the eggs while they played this cat and mouse game. Layla knew the bird's intention was to lead her away from its nest, which she could care less about. She wanted the falcon, and she used the bird's reluctance to leave the area as a means to wear her down. The chase had already lasted for hours.

The bird took a short hop to a tall spruce tree. In the moment that followed her talons' grasping the branch, she turned briefly to glance in the direction of Thorncrag where the nest was hidden. In that split second, Layla sensed her opportunity. She quickly drew an arrow as she moved behind a large tree. Shielded from her prey's sight, she set the arrow in her bow. Her patience had worn thin. After these hours spent stalking the falcon, she no longer cared about capturing it, she wanted to kill it.

Layla was sure the falcon had lost direct sight of her. A bird's instinct was always to fly, for moving made it a more difficult target. Staying still left her wide open. A crucial second ticked by; still she did not fly.

The arrow whistled keenly through the air. A human most probably would not have heard the sound, but the falcon did. At the very last moment, her muscles bunched and she arched into the air. The sharp point missed her breast, its intended mark.

Pumping her wings like she never had before, the bird made a galant attempt to survive. Her flight trajectory skewed to the left. She fought hard to right herself. Another arrow sliced through the air. She did not have to hear this one. The moment the arrow left the canopy of trees, she dipped and banked hard right, then climbed again beyond the reach of the deadly weapon.

Layla seethed. Her steel gray eyes narrowed to menacing slits. Two arrows were lost with nothing to show for it, and they were now a half day late to their rendezvous point.

"Don't say a word," Layla hissed when she rejoined Tam on the far side. Tam merely shrugged and shouldered her weapon.

Chapter Eleven

Niall watched the regal bird drift down circling the lake, his brows knitting together as he watched the unusual descent. Living and working in the woods, he didn't often see a bird of prey's sweeping flight, but it was obvious something was wrong. From this distance he could not figure out the cause, but he felt something wasn't right.

"I sometimes wonder what it would be like to fly," a nearby Knurly tree said, sighing.

Niall nodded agreement. "Me too."

Lynmeer, Henry and Niall were making their way south on a lesser used track that would take them to Lake Arual. They had left the main road that led to Cire Castle, turning south at the Jameson Bridge for an afternoon of fishing and a well-deserved rest. It had been a long journey. Unhooking the horse from her load, they hid the wagon in a dense thicket and allowed the mare to enjoy a break from her burden.

The history lectures and games of stealth had grown stale. Niall, often scouting ahead of the others, took to watching and recording the various kinds of wildlife he saw, keeping track of how many different species he could identify. He drew their likeness and described them in a small brown leather journal Lynmeer had given him, and if he didn't know the name, Lynmeer was sure to.

Lake Arual was named for a unique tortoise found in its waters and nowhere else. Averaging about a foot across, its shell was beautifully marked with striations in multiple iridescent colors. The lake had a second attribute: good fishing. Delicious anticipation spurred them down the faint trail. Niall and Henry were tired of the meals they carried with them in their sacks. Lynmeer, on the other hand, was just plain tired. The long trek had become an arduous toil for the aging man.

"I certainly am looking forward to fresh fish for dinner," Lynmeer said, stroking his white beard.

"How many will it take to fill you up?" Henry asked.

"Oh, I'd say I could easily eat three or four, if they're good sized and well cooked, of course."

Henry's head came up. Niall chuckled to himself, thinking this was when they were going to wish his mother had joined them. She had a knack with herbs that would make the fish divine. He jogged on ahead to scout the unfamiliar territory.

Lynmeer slowed to let Henry and the horse get ahead of him. He bent forward, reaching for the ground, then straightened up and arched his back for a second long stretch. A giant yawn took hold for many seconds. Looking about, he wondered if he couldn't grab a nap right here. Suddenly, he stopped and sniffed the air. Something was amiss. He looked up, spotting a pin prick of blood on a leaf, high above the ground.

"Niall, please come back and join me, if you would," Lynmeer asked.

Henry continued down the path, the horse plodding next to him. Niall heard Lynmeer call to him and turned away from watching the bird's descent. With the speed of youth, he was at his tutor's side. Curious as to what his son was up to, Henry turned around and walked back to join them.

"Do you find anything out of sorts, Niall?" Lynmeer asked, smiling at Henry. Niall scouted the area, all the while standing still, thinking and listening. His eyes hunted, sorting through the leaves and branches for something out of place.

"I saw a falcon come down near the lake ahead of us," Niall said absently as his eyes methodically searched through the trees. "She came down awkwardly. I think she is badly injured." He was at the wrong angle to see the blood drop, but he spotted something else of a far more telling nature. He quickly climbed a nearby sycamore and came back down with an arrow that had fallen into a fork in the branches.

All three gazed down upon the arrow, their hearts growing heavy. It was Henry who finally spoke.

"Exactly the same markings as the one that killed that stag the boys found a few years back."

"Yes, indeed," replied Lynmeer.

Henry looked for a good place to set up camp and tether the horse. He drew out some fishing line and headed to the lake. Lynmeer walked away, leaning heavily on his cane, seeking a tall tree to rest against.

Assuring his father he would be careful, Niall went in

search of the falcon, heading in the direction he had seen the bird descend. He had a good idea of where it must have landed, though he did not expect to find it easily. It wasn't long before he found scuff marks on the ground, one large bent feather and blood near what must have been the impact area. Other than that, there were no more clues.

The wounded bird would seek cover, Niall reasoned, so following the lake in either direction would be a waste of time. Into the woods, he thought, sweeping the ground with his eyes, watching carefully for blood spots on grass blades or more of the dark feathers.

Walking slowly, he crossed the small clearing methodically before stepping into the trees. He did not try to be quiet. Instead, he kept up a slow banter, talking softly, letting the bird know he was coming and that he was not an enemy. He finally spotted a black figure wedged between a large rock and a tree trunk, ready to fight to the death.

"It's all right, take it easy now. I'm a friend."

The falcon's wings rose menacingly. He saw that the bird stood on one leg; the other hung useless. This was not an ordinary falcon. It was so large, in fact, he questioned if it was a falcon at all. Flapping and puffing up, the bird appeared twice its actual size. The nearly six-foot wing span was nothing to sneeze at, and its efforts to intimidate him were not ineffectual. Indeed, if he hadn't known the bird was badly injured, he would have never dared approach.

The sharp talons on its good foot could tear flesh to the bone. The beak was also capable of severe damage. He also knew the bird needed help or it would eventually die. He kept his distance, talking all the while as gently as possible. How could he help?

A blanket, Niall thought. If he could throw a blanket over the head, he might be able to tend to the broken leg that hung there so pathetically. If it got loose in the blanket, though, more damage might happen. He debated leaving to go get help, but he was afraid the bird might get away and he would not be able to find it a second time.

"What should I do?" Niall asked himself.

In lecture after lecture, Lynmeer had told him to look about and think backwards if need be. Niall glanced around, keeping one eye on the bird. Nothing in the trees showed itself to be useful. The ground close by was littered with leaves and twigs, but nothing large enough or strong enough to be of help. His eyes swept closer and closer until his gaze landed on himself, and it was then he realized he wore a shirt and a tunic. He quickly removed them, knowing he was exposing bare skin to the wrath of a very large, wounded and probably very angry bird. Wrapping his left arm with the shirt, he thought out his plan. He would grab the good leg with his left hand and cover its head with his tunic. It wasn't much of a strategy, he knew, but once he had the bird caught, he would figure out the rest.

"Come now, don't be frightened. I only want to help," crooned Niall. He inched closer. The bird cocked its head, preparing to lunge despite fatigue and loss of blood.

"Listen to the boy, he means no harm," whispered a nearby tree.

Niall heard the Knurly speak. The bird hesitated.

"Extraordinary," he whispered. "I'm not going to hurt you. I'm going to help."

Backed as far into the corner as possible, the wings expanded even bigger. There was nowhere else for the bird to go, but it wasn't going to give up.

Leaves rustled in a tiny breeze off the lake. The falcon cocked its head again, this time listening to the wind. Niall saw the sliver of distraction and dove for the leg. A horrifying screech filled the air, the explosion of noise splintering his ear drums. The falcon's beak missed his ear by a hair's breadth, sinking deep into the flesh of his arm. Flapping its two powerful wings the bird lifted off the ground. Could he hang on? Ignorant of birds in general, he was keenly aware of this one's determination to escape. He tightened his grip. The bird tried harder. Keeping his head down and turned away so its beak couldn't reach his eyes, he summoned his next move.

"Now or never," he said out loud. With his left hand still gripping the good leg, he jerked the bird down and toward him, immediately pulling the tunic over its head. The bird froze in the darkness. He could feel the heart beating madly. Straddling the massive creature, he let go of the leg, quickly undid the shirt from his arm and used it to secure the tunic in place.

Then suddenly, there was no movement beneath him. He feared the worst, but didn't dare undo the binding to see if the falcon was alive, fully aware he might never get it back on. He got up slowly and carried the limp body back to camp. The dead weight hung heavy at his side. Blood was smeared down his arm from the jagged bite of the beak. He paid no mind. The wound would heal with some of his mother's balms he carried in his pack, and it might leave a great scar, the kind you could tell stories to your children about. Telling Ben and Gunder around a campfire would be outstanding.

✝ ✝ ✝

"She is female, a beautiful specimen," Lynmeer said,

examining the wound. "I must look for some fresh Toeffer plants though, for it to heal properly." He quickly walked toward a thick stand of trees.

The bird lay on her side, held securely by Henry's gentle hands. Lynmeer returned shortly with some large Toeffer leaves, his favorite medicinal plant, and the first one he had taught Niall to use. He helped clean the wound around the break and mixed a poultice in preparation for setting the leg, softly giving instructions to Niall all the while. Water lapped the shore, and a whiff of burning wood drifted by.

"Whoa, there," Henry grunted, tightening his grip. "She's coming to."

The bird struggled to wrest herself free from Henry's calloused hands, but years of wrestling logs and heavy tools gave him the advantage.

"Pull the leg firm and true, don't jerk," Lynmeer coached.

"Okay, here goes," Niall said. Sweat glistened on his forehead. He took a deep breath and pulled the leg straight.

"You did an excellent job, Niall," Lynmeer said a few moments later as he bound her leg with Toeffer.

"I wish Moralia was here," Henry murmured. "She's so good with animals. How she would love to nurse this one back to health."

Niall nodded agreement. It was obvious, however, that Lynmeer knew what he was doing when it came to avian medicine. When they were done with the leg, they righted her and held her steady until she stood on her good leg without wobbling.

Later, Henry walked down to the water's edge to clean the fish he'd caught earlier. Niall felt bad watching him go. He had seen his father's shoulders droop when Lynmeer told him he should not go near the falcon for the next few months at least.

"If she is to be Niall's bird, she must bond to him only. He must provide her food, be the smell she smells each day, the one she trusts for everything. If done correctly, they will have a life-long partnership," Lynmeer explained.

Niall sat on the ground, fashioning a hood for the big bird. He planned to put it on her head while she was still under the tunic. Blindfolding the bird would keep her quiet, and he understood her need for ample time to gain trust in him. He tried not to be too hopeful, expecting the healing to take months—if she lived. While he crafted the leather, Lynmeer leaned over and made occasional suggestions.

He had already cut leather legging straps for her good leg, tethering her to a log for the time being. In the future, he would need a leather gauntlet to work with her.

An hour later, Niall offered the bird chunks of raw fish. His soothing words did not sway her. She stood proud, her feathers ruffling at the sound of his approach. She alone would have to make the difficult choice: eat to survive or die free.

Off to the side, Lynmeer watched her refusal to take food. He pursed his lips and settled in to wait until Henry and Niall went to sleep. Deep into the night, he whispered to the beautiful black bird, "He will never harm you. Trust him, as I do. Niall is the one I have come to serve."

"Man causes all of our problems," she answered hotly.

"That is partially true, but one must not attribute those failings to all men; this boy is a good one," Lynmeer replied. "I am training him to fight for his kingdom when the time comes, and he will need a good friend then, a loyal one he can trust with his life. In the meantime, my dear friend, you need him."

Morning came and Henry was up first, building a fire to ward off the chill of the night. It wasn't long before he had his line out in the water, and again they ate fish fresh from the lake. After wolfing down a few bites for himself, Niall offered the bird chunks of raw fish that hadn't made it into the pan. This time, the falcon reached out into the hooded darkness and carefully took a piece from Niall's outstretched hand, easily guided by the smell. Several morsels went down in the same manner, until she bobbed her head and took no more.

"Nan. I shall call her Nan," Niall said, smiling from ear to ear. Later, wearing a clean shirt over his bandaged arm, he looked around the camp, feeling blessed at how things had turned out. His father sat near the fire watching him feed the bird. Lynmeer had once again wandered off. The bright early sun reflected off the lake in a magical display of twinkling diamonds.

He had long ago come to accept the fact that amazing things happen. After all, he talked with trees. Nan's initial acceptance of food was only the first step. From here forward, any future bond between them was up to him and how he treated her, and patience. Regardless of the outcome, he would be forever grateful for the opportunity.

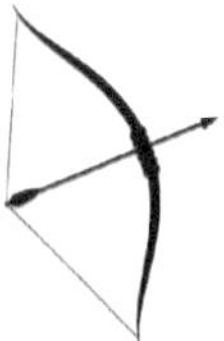

Chapter Twelve

"How did you ever catch her? She's so big!" exclaimed Ben.

The boys sat in a semicircle around a campfire, admiring the beautiful bird who sat tethered to a nearby branch. Her leg was not completely healed yet, but once she had accepted her new position in life, she had done so without reservation.

A novice at the art, Niall genuinely tried to be a good falconer. Despite his lack, each day's lessons brought the boy and the bird a tiny bit closer.

Though dutifully warned not to go close yet, to let Nan have time to get used to him, Gunder fidgeted. He finally got up and walked boldly toward the bird and was met with an ominous hissing. Wings rose, doubling the bird's size.

"Whoa!" Gunder exclaimed, freezing in his tracks.

"Easy, Nan, easy," Niall said, standing up and walking over to stand between the two. "I told you to be patient," he said, then turned back to the bird. "This is Gunder. He's my friend, girl, take it easy," he crooned. "She's touchy still. You fellows ought to wait till next time before you try to pet her, give her more time to get used to you. She'll come around, I'm sure of it."

"Whatever you say," Gunder said, backing away slowly and sitting back down next to Ben, whose eyes had enlarged considerably. When Gunder returned to his seat unscathed, Ben's face crinkled and he opened his mouth to tease him. Gunder outweighed Ben by a good forty pounds, and none of it was fat. Ben closed his mouth instead and remained silent.

"We had stopped to fish in Lake Arual when I saw her drifting down," Niall said, continuing with his story. "I knew something was wrong by the awkward way she was flying, sort of listing to the side."

"But how did you get close to her?" Gunder asked.

"She was badly hurt so I wrapped my shirt around her head, but not before she bit my arm," he said, pulling up his sleeve to show his friends the scar from her beak. It too had been wrapped in Toeffer and was healing well. "Being in the dark sort of paralyzed her, and I was able to carry her back to camp. Father held her steady, and my tutor told me what to do, how to splint her leg, how to wrap it with Toeffer and then how to bandage it. He knew what herbs to put in her water and he showed me how to make her hood and the legging. I didn't know anything, really. I'm sure she would have died had it not been for him."

"It's amazing she lived, Niall," Ben stated. "She's so beautiful. What a shame if she had died."

"I didn't know the herbs would work for birds too. Still, I'm not sure I would have even thought to use them unless my tutor had been there. Nan's lucky. Lynmeer says she'll be fine," Niall said. "The rest will be patience."

"You've done a marvelous job," Ben said. Niall smiled at the genuine compliment. Ben's admiration for what they did to save the bird was obvious.

"It's hard to believe she is sitting so quiet, this close to us," Ben added.

"And it's plenty close enough!" Gunder exclaimed, laughing away his earlier discomfort.

The discussion finally turned away from the bird and on to the rest of the adventure as they prepared their dinner. Niall said little of the boring hours of simply trudging down the road, but he made the most of the funny anecdotes he could remember. Both Lynmeer and Henry shared a similar dry sense of humor.

"Get on with it," Ben said suddenly. "Tell us about Cire Castle! Is it glorious? Did you get to see the king?"

"I didn't go to the castle," Niall replied.

"What? What do you mean you didn't go!" asked Gunder. The only thing that had made Niall's going without the two of them bearable was the fact that they knew he would come home and share every detail of the wonders he saw.

"I couldn't go with Nan still so weak. I didn't want to leave her unprotected, and she has to be fed by hand. So, I stayed at our camp near the lake while Father and my tutor went on to the castle with the lumber."

The two boys stared at Niall. The only noise to be heard was fat crackling when it dripped off a roasting lamb shank and hit the red coals beneath.

"You walked all that way and you didn't get to see the castle," Gunder repeated, almost more to himself than to the others. Then he drew a big breath. "I'm sorry you had to miss it."

"Yes, awful and yet, a worthy sacrifice for her," Ben added, turning again to look at the beautiful Nan sitting like a royal princess on her throne. "With such a powerful ally, a man could do almost anything." He turned back to the other two. "But that means, fellas," he said, sweeping his bangs out of his eyes, "we can be all together the first time we see the castle."

"I suppose you're right," Niall said, smiling as Ben's grand idea sunk in. "I hadn't thought of that, but you are totally right! We shall go together."

"I did get to see one of the Arual tortoises," Niall told the boys later as they licked their fingers. The roasted meat was gone but for a few chunks kept back for Nan. They had devoured it sizzling hot straight from the fire, dancing it on their tongues to cool it.

"I've heard about them," Ben said. "Are they as beautiful as they say?"

"Yes. The colors on its shell reflected light like jewels, and they're very fast," Niall noted, throwing more wood on the fire to ward off the evening chill. "As soon as one heard me, it dove into the water and was gone."

"You were lucky to see one at all, from what I hear," offered Gunder. "By the by, did your father say anything of the castle's preparations?"

"He had lots to say, and much of it wasn't complimentary. After selling the lumber, they went to the mews to see what they could learn to help me with Nan. The Master of the Mews, a Mr. Grote, didn't give them the time of day, but one of his apprentices, one by the name of James, sought them out afterward. He told them plenty."

"But about the castle, not just the falcon?" Gunder queried.

"Yes, Father asked him all kinds of questions about whether the castle was prepared for siege and the like," continued Niall. "James said they have no stores of food set aside. King Stephen doesn't know how to prepare for war, so he goes hunting or gives parties. His troops are in disarray, their equipment as well as the castle are in a state of neglect. It's as if he can't be bothered."

"What about the soldiers?"

"He didn't have much hope for anyone else taking charge; the king has evidently not fostered discipline, and there is a lot of squabbling from lack of leadership." Niall answered. "James told Lynmeer he should be a soldier. He doesn't have the touch to be a falconer, but no one listens. He is secretly training himself to the sword. It is a difficult task because he is given so little time off from his chores in the mews. Father liked him a lot. He said he's young and strong and has a good heart."

"Your father is a good judge of character, that's what my father says," interjected Ben. "I'm afraid it sounds like the Baldonian king might have an easy time."

"Father said those very words," Niall said glumly. "Their visit wasn't very encouraging, that aspect of it at any rate." Then he shortly brightened up and added, "But he got a good price for his lumber, and I got Nan, so overall, it was an exceptional adventure."

Niall looked over at the beautiful falcon sitting on the tree branch on the other side of their camp fire. The growing worry of Rhyaden's defenses would soon enough weigh heavy on all their minds, but for now, he had a falcon to train.

There were other perplexities for the boys to consider and discuss that night, not the least of which were their growing thoughts about the young girls of the village. The boys talked late into the night, making plans in the event of war, watching the fire burn down to glowing coals before covering up to sleep.

Chapter Thirteen

Annwyn walked differently, more deliberately than when they younger, Niall noticed, catching a glimpse of her headed in his direction. A month had gone by after returning from Cire, and Niall had not been to town until today. The first thing he noticed was the sun shining on her honey-colored hair. It was swept back atop her head now, no longer falling in braids like it had when they first met.

He didn't understand why his chest constricted when he saw her. After he had asked his father a few awkward questions about girls, Henry had stuttered through an explanation about feelings, and what those feelings might lead to. The cumbersome talk had not really helped. After that, he decided the best course of action was steering clear of females altogether. In the case of Annwyn, Ben had liked her first anyway, and that dictated Niall stay away.

He knew she had seen him when he stepped outside the bakery. Her steps hastened in his direction. He was sure she would want him to quell or confirm the rumors about his falcon, or explain his absence from town of late.

"Why, Niall, I haven't had the pleasure of seeing you in such a long time. Wherever do you keep yourself these days?"

"Good day, Winnie. What have you got yourself up to?" Niall answered. He held a rather large sack of gingerbread biscuits at his side.

"You know I prefer to be called Annwyn," she replied softly, her golden hair mirroring the sunlight. Niall found the glossiness distracting.

"Yes, I do. Are you headed to the bakery?"

"Why, yes, mother wants some cake to celebrate my father's birthday, but—"

"I'm sure you'll find something splendid in Finwick's. Have a lovely day, Winnie." Giving her a slight bow, Niall walked on.

He thought it best not to have a conversation about what he was up to because, in truth, everything he did nowadays was about falcons and preparation for war, nothing to be sharing with this disarming girl whom his best friend adored.

He heard her say "but" as he hastened away. Calling her Winnie infuriated her, he knew, but he couldn't help himself from teasing her. Rounding the corner, he glanced back. She had already stepped inside the bakeshop.

Good old Ben, Annwyn thought, pulling open the door. He was so predictable and steady, not at all elusive like Niall. Why Ben was best friends with him was beyond comprehension, regardless of Niall's past heroism. He was hardly to be seen these days anyway, and his insistence on calling her Winnie so juvenile. She stopped for a moment to collect herself and stepped through the door.

Ben could always be found right here, working dutifully in his parents' store. He had told her previously that his father would rather he was out back hefting the heavy sacks of flour, but the ladies of the village bought far more goods from him than they did from anyone else in the family. She had no doubt of that.

Tall and filling out nicely, Ben had an infectious smile and an irresistible dimple. His hair had darkened and the freckles had faded. His charm and good looks were a combination that few female customers, including herself, could resist.

"Well . . . hello . . . what brings you here this morning?" Ben asked, looking up.

"Mother would like a celebration cake," she said, walking up to the counter.

"I'm sure we can find something suitable if you need it right away, or did you want to order one for a later time?"

"For today," Annwyn said, adding another smile. She took a moment to look at what he offered.

"So, what have you fellows been up to lately?"

"Uh . . ." Ben stammered. "Nothing, really. How about you?"

"Oh, just the same old thing," she murmured, edging closer, reaching out to dust imaginary lint off his sleeve. "Come on, Ben, surely you boys have done something interesting lately. I heard Niall went to Cire Castle. Was it simply divine?"

"Uh . . . well, Niall didn't actually go to the castle, you see," Ben said, breathing in her intoxicating scent. "His father did, though. Said it was mighty interesting." He backed up and began rearranging the baskets of bread and biscuits that were on display.

Annwyn's exasperation climbed another notch. What was going on, and why weren't they telling her? She turned away and feigned interest in a basket of pumpernickel, giving the flush of her frustration time to dissipate. Drawing a deep breath, she turned to try again and at that very moment, Gwyn Finwick came bustling through the front door.

"Why, Miss Annwyn, how are you this fine morning? How is that dear mother of yours? I haven't seen her in just the longest time."

"Ah, Mother, I'm so glad you're back," Ben interjected before she could answer. "I need a bit of a break, and Father has a chore he wants me to do out back, so I'll leave Miss Annwyn in your capable hands and go get it done for him. I'm sure you two have a lot to catch up on."

Without waiting for a reply, he fled to the back room and past his aunts steeped in the pleasant aroma of flour and vanilla. Annwyn heard a distant door slam.

Her mouth dropped open. Gwyn smiled at the retreating figure of her son and shook her head. "Now what can I help you with, my dear?" she asked.

✝ ✝ ✝

Niall hurried toward the edge of town where the Neuse forge was located. Always a bustling place, farmers came there needing their wagons repaired or brought in a plowshare that had snapped off and needed replaced. Men came for gossip too, and today in particular, many were standing about talking while they waited. Torg was too busy to notice Niall siphon Gunder away for a few minutes of discussion behind the back wall of the barn.

"We need an adventure, Niall," Gunder lamented. "Father has me working nonstop while he's off scouting the countryside. Then when he's home, he's behind and we're twice as busy!"

"What's he looking for?" Niall asked.

Gunder shook his head. "He comes home exhausted and dirty, that's all I know, but I've got us some more iron," Gunder said. "A man came by and traded with father for a wheel. He said the wheel would be more useful since he was moving his family to a bigger town."

"I wonder why he's moving?" Niall asked.

"That I don't know, but Father said it looked like the man and his family hadn't eaten well in a while. I asked if I could use some of the iron to try and make something for myself, and he said I could make what I wanted, he didn't have time to mess with it."

"Good. We need a long, stout piece that will reach from the side of the stall to the trapdoor. I think I've worked out a way to open the door that will be invisible from above."

"You have?" Gunder asked.

"Well, I hope I have. We'll use a long strap underneath the floor to go from the left side of the stall to the latch. It has to be stout enough to lift the trapdoor high enough for us to grab the edge and pull it up. Once we're inside and the door is down, it can be bolted from underneath."

"Ah . . . I hadn't thought of that, and you're right, there's no need to lock it from the top. Anything else?"

"The smaller the door, the less weight to lift. I figure if you can get through the opening, then it's big enough. We can figure out the rest as we go."

"Cutting in the door and moving dirt without Ben's father noticing is going to be tricky," Gunder said.

"Ben has that figured out. We'll have to be ready when his father next goes to Milltown for flour. He's always a day there and a day back. Ben thinks there's some room beneath the entire barn to spread the dirt out."

† † †

Eighteen months later, a month before Niall's eighteenth birthday, Niall and Henry sat rocking on the porch after supper. Moralia was inside, cutting cloth scraps to make blankets.

"Let's walk. I think I ate too much stew," Henry said, patting his stomach.

"Sure," Niall answered. He stood up and leapt off the porch.

Henry used the steps, following his son toward the road. They walked in comfortable silence.

After a quarter mile, Niall reached down and picked up a rock. He flung it down the road, watching it bounce several times before disappearing into the trees. "We dug a chamber under the Finwick barn to store weapons," he said, looking over at his father.

"Did you now? That's a big undertaking," Henry said, putting his arm around Niall's shoulder. "What purpose did you have in mind for it?"

"A place to store weapons."

"Ah. The very topic I was wanting to discuss," Henry said.

"Weapons?" Niall asked.

"No," Henry chuckled. "No, not weapons, exactly. I don't want to worry your mother, though. I'd like to keep this between us, all right?"

"You and Mother always discuss everything," Niall replied.

"The thought of your going off to protect our kingdom is a difficult subject for her," Henry said, his voice low, "but the fact is, you and Ben and Gunder are old enough to fight if it becomes necessary."

Niall nodded, and then suddenly his head cocked sideways and he leaned slightly forward. "Someone's coming down the road."

Henry instinctively pulled Niall behind him as he scanned the road, his hand on the hilt of his knife nestled in its sheath on his belt.

"Oh, it's Lynmeer," Niall said, waving to his tutor.

Henry relaxed and they continued. Getting closer, they could hear the man tapping his cane in rhythm to the song he whistled.

"Hello." Lynmeer greeted the two. "Taking an evening stroll, are you? It's such a delightful evening, I couldn't help but get out myself."

"We were about to discuss what our roles should be during an invasion, Lynmeer. It would be good to have your input."

"Glad to be of service. What is the area of your concern?"

"None in our village wish to be ruled by the Baldonian king. It seems to me that many of our young men are going to want to join King Stephen's army if there is an attempted takeover, but I fear for our village. Some must stay here to protect it," Henry answered.

"That is a valid concern, Henry. It will take someone who is experienced and respected to lead the villagers if they are attacked."

"Who do you suggest? We should bring them into our discussions," Henry asked.

"You, my dear Henry. You are the one who can best protect Knurlysham."

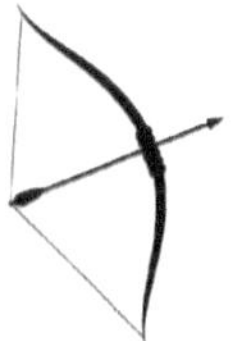

Chapter Fourteen

"Send for my cousin, the spy," King DeMont ordered. His general whispered to a guard and the man quickly left the room. The general and the king had been discussing their plans for the last hour. A map of the Rhyaden kingdom was spread out before them. "Turtle bay is too shallow for large ships, but our longboats should be fine. It is almost directly north of Cire. I think it will do nicely."

"Yes, my Lord. I agree," General Bickford said.

"All right, then. Our plans are set. I have, ah . . . family matters to discuss with my cousin. Leave me now. You may begin your preparations for the invasion," he said, brandishing a devilish smile.

General Bickford bowed and left the room. The king didn't have long to wait. A knock came fifteen minutes later.

"Ah, come in, come in, dear cousin."

Layla shut the door carefully behind her. The king had never before addressed her as such, and this summons was her first to his private chambers. The unusual request put her on alert.

"You summoned me, your Majesty?"

"I did indeed. Your work as a spy has given me invaluable information concerning the invasion we are planning," the king replied.

Layla's eyebrows shot up. Her mouth opened, but she quickly shut it without a word.

"Yes," the king said with a smile, "the invasion of Rhyaden will begin within a fortnight. General Bickford will lead the first assault. Captain Lodall will follow with a larger, second contingent as soon as they are prepared."

"And what is your wish of me, your Majesty?" Layla asked. Her eyes were lit with speculation on what her role was to be.

"You and I have one thing in common, do we not?" he asked, pouring himself a drink and indicating the same for her.

"No, thank you, my Lord," she said, shaking her head. "I'm not sure what you are referring to."

"Our family heritage. We are both DeMonts, as was Valdorn's mother. Our family should have taken the Rhyaden throne after King Charles' death!"

Layla showed her careful nature now. "Of course, your Majesty. At the time, the Walford side, the wife's side of the family, prevailed, however controversial."

"They did indeed— then! I have no intention of repeating that history."

"Pardon, sir?"

"I do not intend to lose the Rhyaden Crown this time," Francis said. He saw the flame of intrigue light in Layla's eyes before it could be masked.

"You have made mention in your reports of how poorly trained King Stephen's troops are, have you not?"

"Yes, my Lord. Poorly trained or not trained at all," Layla answered.

"Then victory should be easy."

"Their land is very different than ours, most notably the abundance of deep forests. It will be a different kind of warfare than what our troops have trained for," Layla cautioned.

"Surely my troop's discipline will handle everything that comes its way."

"Yes, my Lord." She hesitated, then asked, "Is there something in particular you wanted of me?"

"Your grandfather lost title to his lands in a gambling debt, did he not?"

Layla's back stiffened. "Yes, your Majesty."

"And your father drank himself to death, did he not?"

"He was killed in a skirmish with other soldiers," she replied, her voice flat.

"But he was drunk, if I recall. You, however, have shown great potential in my army. I think you might enjoy a chance to regain some of those lands your grandfather lost, perhaps even a title to go with them. I have such a proposition for you, if you are interested?" The king watched her reaction carefully. He saw the gleam in her eye, and he knew he had her.

"What do you need done, my Lord?"

"I wish for you to kill King Stephen. The general thinks he is to capture him for ransom, as is customary, but I do not want the nonsense of negotiation. I simply wish to add their kingdom to mine, and for that, King Stephen and any other heirs to the throne must die."

"A bold move, your Majesty."

"Can you do this task?" the king asked.

"Of course, your Majesty. It will be my honor to avenge our family—in your name, of course."

The king smiled. "You will be amply rewarded. General

Bickford knows you are to sail with him. He also knows you have a mission for me and will not be under his command. He does not like that fact so I would advise you to make as nice with him as you can."

"Yes, sir. I have a trusted second, Tam Upworth. She has proved herself very useful. Am I allowed to take her along?"

"All right. I'll let the general know. Do not tell her your mission. That must be kept between you and me only. Understood?"

"Yes, your Majesty."

"Good. You are dismissed," he said, waving his hand.

Layla bowed and left the room. She could not hide the gleam in her eyes.

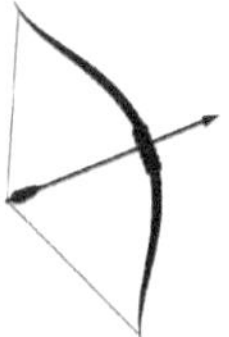

Chapter Fifteen

Water lapped the shores of Turtle Bay in the cold gray light of predawn. The cry of distant gulls broke the stillness as the birds fished for their breakfast in the cold waters of the North Sea. Longboats slipped quietly ashore, the oars stowed for silence. The warriors disembarked without a word. They already had their orders. Hand signals directed the offloading. Two men were left behind to guard the boats in the event the raid was discovered and a speedy retreat was needed.

Niall woke with a start. His vivid dream was unsettling, but worse still was the dreadful feeling something was terribly wrong. He flung himself out of bed. Pulling on his pants, he grabbed a shirt, and then his long legs thumped down the ladder steps two at a time. Grabbing a biscuit, he left the cottage and headed to Nan's protective enclosure.

"Something is wrong. I can feel it, but I don't know what," Niall said, shivering in the cold air as he fed her.

She shook slightly, stretching out her long, glossy wings.

"What should I do, Nan?"

"I would have breakfast, if I were you," Lynmeer answered, standing in the doorway.

"Oh, goodness, you startled me," Niall said.

"Why don't you give her an extra ration this morning, Niall."

Niall looked at his mentor, wondering what he knew, but he fed his falcon without asking any questions.

They returned to the cottage a short while later. His mother stood at the stove stirring porridge when the two walked in. His father stood close to the fire he had just stoked.

"What have the two of you been up to so early this morning?" Moralia asked when they came in. Her raven-colored hair was tied back, but tendrils of curls escaped to frame her face, and though her voice was even, her soft gray eyes could not hide her worry.

Niall was about to mention his dream, but Lynmeer began first. "There is news from the castle. Baldonia has invaded Rhyaden."

Moralia gasped.

"I'd love a cup of tea, if you have the kettle on," Lynmeer said, taking his coat off and hanging it on a hook near the door. "Niall, how about some breakfast?"

Eating when he truly didn't feel like eating, Niall hoped the meal wouldn't come back to haunt him later. He listened to his father and Lynmeer discuss the invasion.

"I'm going to join the fight at Cire," Niall finally blurted out.

"No, no, Niall, you mustn't go," his mother began.

"Stopping Baldonia at the castle is the best way to prevent them from coming to our village," he replied.

"Niall's right. I should go too," Henry said.

"The village would be defenseless without you, Father. We've already discussed this. You know where the weapons are stored and what should be done. Ben and Gunder will go with me, I am sure of it. You should stay here, as we planned."

When breakfast was over and the dishes cleared away, they went over the plans. Niall sat quietly, leaning back in his chair and hoping his meal would soon settle.

"Baldonia's army has landed on the north shore, close to the castle," Lynmeer concluded. "Maybe they'll never get this far west, but we can't be sure. King Stephen's army is frightfully ill-equipped and not in the least bit ready to take them on, but there is more than battle readiness for you to be prepared for," he said, looking directly at Niall. "Unless you wish to pay taxes to the Baldonian king, you will see fatherless children and starvation for those left behind afterwards."

They sat quietly, taking in the old man's words. He gently patted Niall's shoulder, looking at the quiet faces around the table.

"Fighting is not the only honorable choice a man has in order to end conflicts," Lynmeer continued. "Someday… someday I hope mankind will learn that, but that day is not yet come."

"Why Niall?" Moralia blurted out, biting her lip.

Henry gave his wife a sorrowful look, sharing her pain. The fighting would affect everyone, he knew, whether they went into battle or not.

Niall looked from his mother's frightened face deep into the eyes of his tutor. He saw his own reflection, as he had long ago, but it was not a boy standing there this time. A man looked back at him, a man with a falcon on his shoulder. He took a deep breath and squared himself.

"This choice is mine, Mother. I must go."

Niall felt no fear for himself, but rather sorrow for the pain his leaving caused his parents. A short time later, Moralia finished packing a satchel of biscuits and healing herbs for her son. While the men talked quietly at the table, she went into her room. Niall followed her and found her kneeling in front of her cedar chest. Hearing his footsteps, she looked up and smiled as she lifted the lid. On the left side, wrapped in her mother's lace shawl, lay a tiny leather pouch. She took out the pouch and turned it over, feeling the soft leather. Then she reached up and took the stone necklace from around her neck, removed its chain and put it into the pouch. The stone had been given to her by her mother, and her grandfather before that. She did not know its origin. She had given it to Niall once before when he turned sixteen and traveled to Cire Castle.

"Niall, you must take this again. Never let it out of your sight. My mother told me her father gave it to her, and it is sacred to our family. You must never lose it and must pass it on to your firstborn. I want you to have it always now. It will keep you safe," she said, pressing the leather into his hand.

Niall opened the leather drawstring and dropped the stone into his palm. The purple was so deep it was nearly black. "What is it made of?" he asked, holding it up to the light.

"I don't know."

"Thank you, Mother. I promise I will keep it with me at all times." He placed the rock back in the leather pouch and drew the string tight.

Moments later, they rejoined the others in the kitchen. Henry fell silent. Lynmeer's eyes softened as he stared at the tiny leather pouch in Niall's hand. He cleared his throat and then turned to Moralia. "My dear, you have my love and gratitude for all of your gracious hospitality," he said, taking her hand and bowing as he gently kissed her fingers.

He turned to her husband. "Henry, I hope we shall meet again. I am too old to join in so you take care of yourself. You have raised a fine son who will do Rhyaden proud. His success will be due in no small part to all he has learned from his mother and from you. Now, I bid you goodbye. It is time for us to go."

Henry stood straight as they shook hands. Lynmeer bowed again and nodded to Niall, who was fighting the large lump forming in his throat. He bit his lower lip and grasped Lynmeer's hands in his own.

"Thank you, Lynmeer, thank you for everything!"

"You are most welcome, Niall. We shall meet again." They nodded to each other.

Cane in hand, Lynmeer retrieved his coat and went out the door. He headed east following the same hunting trail into the woods where Niall and he had first met. He looked far older now.

Tears welled up in his mother's eyes. She did not speak. Silently hugging her son with an iron grip, she finally let go and handed him his pack. Henry walked his son to the front steps. Niall now stood taller than Henry, his shoulders broad and straight.

"Take care, son. Come home to us safe and sound."

"I will, Father. I love you."

Niall turned away. He put the leather pouch in his pocket, slung the pack and his quiver over his shoulder and walked to the enclosure where Nan waited, ready.

Scary times were ahead. Niall was sure Nan would go with him, but it was imperative to him that she accompany him of her own free will. If she didn't choose to follow him into battle, he wanted her to fly free once again. He quietly slipped her tethers off, removed her hood and stuffed the leather gauntlet into his pack.

Nan cocked her head and looked at Niall. She stepped gently onto his shoulder and thus their journey began. Niall could not help but wonder how long before, or if, he would ever walk this road again.

In the still, sleepy village, Niall sought out his friends. The sun was rising, and the early morning mists were floating away in whispers. Gunder was out back of the forge, washing in a pail of water next to the well, singing in his deep baritone. The sound put a smile on Niall's face.

Because Nan accompanied him, Niall hailed his good friend before getting close. She did not disappoint him, sitting calmly astride his broad shoulder.

"Niall, what in the world are you doing here so early, and with Nan? Is something wrong?"

"Baldonian troops landed and are headed toward the Castle to conquer Rhyaden."

"How do you know that?"

"My tutor brought word. I am headed to Cire Castle. My father should be here soon. He is going to organize the villagers to defend Knurlysham. He knows of our plans and where the supplies are."

"You're sure we should go to Cire," Gunder asked, "rather than stay and defend Knurlysham?"

"I am going to fight for our kingdom."

Niall stepped closer to his oldest childhood friend. Nan's grip tightened slightly on his shoulder. "Are you coming?"

"Of course!" The two looked into each other's eyes. Nan shifted position and her movement broke the spell.

"I will get Ben. Grab what you need and meet me in a half hour on the north side, near the oak grove."

"My father will hate this," Gunder said.

"Your mother too. You don't have to go, Gunder, but time is short. If you aren't there, I will understand."

"We go together." And with that said, Gunder turned and headed to the house.

Niall made his way through the cobbled streets. His nose pinched when he passed the pub, making him hurry to avoid the sharp odors. Smoke curled out of a few chimneys where the inhabitants were up and starting breakfast. The dark windows of the bakeshop affirmed his thought that it would not be open this early, but he was sure the ovens in the back would be fired and filled with loaves of bread. He navigated the long narrow alleyway between the bakeshop and Mr. Grumm's Emporium. At the back, he pounded on the bakeshop's rear door. As Niall raised his hand to knock again, Flin Finwick pulled open the heavy wood door.

"Why, Niall, whatever brings you here this early?" Flin asked. He squinted, having left his glasses on the table. When he saw Nan he backed up, astonished at the large bird sitting on Niall's shoulder.

"I need to see Ben, sir. Troops sent by Baldonia's king are attacking Cire Castle, and I am leaving to join our forces."

"What did you say? Who's doing what?"

Niall opened his mouth to answer when the door was flung back by Ben.

"I'm going with you, hold up a minute," Ben said, tucking in his shirt.

"No, you're not!" the startled Mr. Finwick bellowed at his son.

"I have to go, Father. I'm sorry, but I will come back. I promise."

Niall spoke up. "My father will be coming here shortly to help prepare the village. Will you help him, Mr. Finwick?"

Ben leaned against the wall and pulled a heavy leather boot over his foot. He looked at his father as he gave the boot a yank.

"Of course I'll help Henry, of course, but that doesn't mean you boys should go traipsing off to the castle. You'll get yourselves bloody well killed!" Mr. Finwick spluttered.

Ben hopped forward, shoving his other foot into the second boot as he went through the door. "Come with me. I'm going to show you where we've stored extra weapons. Keep what you yourself can use and share the rest with Henry. Please, Father, do whatever Henry asks you to do. I'll return as soon as I can."

"But . . . my glasses . . ."

Niall stepped aside. Ben was already out the door, headed to the barn at a brisk pace. Flin hesitated, looked at Niall and then followed. Niall came behind, knowing how difficult this must be for the baker whose only variance to each day was how the weather affected his ovens.

The poor man was in a bit of shock. A well-worn apron covered his rotund figure, and his uncombed hair stuck out in several directions. Niall could hear him muttering about bread in the ovens and a cold breakfast.

Ben rolled the barn door open, and Flin and Niall followed him inside. Ben showed his father the trapdoor, revealing the chamber underneath. His father stood dumbfounded at the preparations that had gone on right under his nose.

Ben showed him how to open the trapdoor from above and bolt it from underneath in the event the family needed to hide.

Flin stared down into the chamber, amazement written across his face. Niall glanced from the hole to Mr. Finwick's girth, hoping he would fit.

Ben climbed down into the chamber and retrieved the sword he had practiced with in his spare time. Glancing a final time at the stores as he went up the wood steps of the ladder, he couldn't help but be proud of the job the three of them had done. While his father looked on in total amazement, Ben lowered the trapdoor and covered it again with straw and dried manure.

Flin looked at his son. "You've grown so tall when I wasn't looking." His voice wavered, and he drew in a long breath. "I can't imagine how you boys did this."

"It was Niall's idea," Ben said.

"Ben and Gunder and I have all been working on it for a long time, just in case, you know, in case the Baldonian king invaded, and, well ..."

"I'll tell your mother. Best not wake her with this kind of news, or you'll never get away. Good luck to you, son, and come home as soon as you can." Trying hard to keep the emotion out of his voice, Flin grabbed his son and hugged him hard, patting him roughly on the back before letting loose. "I'm proud of you."

He looked at Niall and the great bird sitting on his shoulder. "Farewell, Niall," he said in a surprising tone of deference. "I will help your father in whatever way I can."

"Thank you, Mr. Finwick, and I'll keep an eye out for Ben."

They met up with Gunder a few minutes later near the oak grove on the edge of the village. They each carried a weapon. Nan flew overhead. No words of encouragement were needed between them, their excitement was written on their faces. They shouldered their weapons and took off at a trot, headed to Cire.

Later, when they had slowed to a walk and could carry on a conversation, Ben brought up a subject that had been worrying him for a good hour.

"I should have warned Annwyn," he said stoutly.

"I asked my father to talk to her family," Niall replied.

Ben's head jerked up. "Why?"

Niall hedged, "I knew you'd want her to know why we left."

"I don't suppose there was anymore that I could have done. I hope . . . if they know what is coming that it will help," Ben said.

Nan cawed a high screech. Under the canopy of trees that lined the road, Niall could not see her dive, but he recognized the sound of her hunting.

"Did you know I would come with you?" Ben asked.

Niall looked over at his friend and said, "Brothers Forever."

Ben smiled. "Seems strange not being in the shop today. Can't say as I mind."

"My father looked scared," Gunder said.

Chapter Sixteen

The three young warriors made record time on their journey to Cire, thanks in part to Nan. While they trekked toward their destination, she hunted rabbits and provided the meat for their meals. When they stopped at night, one started a fire and the other two dug tubers. The difference between this trip and their many boyhood overnight excursions came after the hearty meal. Now they did not laugh or scheme late into the night. As the small cook fire died after a full day of walking, the three weary travelers simply fell asleep.

After a week of travel, all three had settled into the routine. They had skirted the villages, only stopping in Glenvale when they needed a cobbler to fix the sole of Gunder's left boot.

"Traveling's not so bad," Gunder remarked, licking his fingers after wolfing down an entire rabbit by himself.

Niall chuckled as he watched his friend enjoy the meal. He wasn't hungry. They would reach the castle within two hours so, this last evening, the threesome angled to the south and then stopped early when they found a suitable small clearing in which to eat and rest. Nan was sent to scout the area so they wouldn't be caught unawares. This close to the castle made it too dangerous to follow the well-used road. The going was tougher in the dense trees and tangled vines, but darkness gave them another keen asset. Nan could see far better at night than any human.

They hadn't met anyone on the road yesterday or today. When Niall accompanied his father and Lynmeer two years earlier, the closer they got to Cire, the more tinkerers and farmers traveled the road daily, going to and from the market outside the castle. The implication of no traffic was not good.

Thinking how good it would be to have Lynmeer around to answer their questions, Niall listened to the speculation from Ben and Gunder. Together, they talked of the importance of duty and honor. Niall was careful not to whitewash war as glorious. Instead, he told them of the things Lynmeer had told him that last morning.

"He told me that sometimes fighting is necessary, but we need to understand that it is not the only honorable choice to end a conflict."

He wished he'd had more time. His tutor had come to Niall when he was eight years old; now he was eighteen. Would the image of the white-haired man limping away be the last one he had? About to engage in a battle to defend his king and castle, he turned his mind away from that which he could not control and back to the matters at hand.

He fed Nan while Ben doused the fire. Gunder wiped his hands on his pants and repacked the flint he had used to start the fire. At last, Niall turned to his friends, looking first at Ben and then to Gunder.

"This is the last chance to change our minds. There is no shame in going home to defend our village."

"What are you going to do, Niall?" Gunder asked quietly.

"My choice lies here."

"How do you know this is the right thing to do?" Ben asked. "You just told us that fighting is not the only solution."

"Baldonia has already invaded. Our king must be in a position of power to negotiate another solution. We'll have to fight now to gain that position."

"Where you go, I go," Gunder said, clapping his friend on the knee. Nan shifted her stance, her feathers ruffling slightly. Before Niall could say a word to calm her, Gunder looked the bird straight in the eye. "I had his back long before you did, Nan. We're in this together."

Nan's feathers settled down and Niall smiled. Next he looked to Ben.

"It was my idea we go to Cire together," Ben answered without being asked, "and that's what we shall do."

"All right, then," Niall began. "Here's what my father remembers about the castle."

As the evening deepened and the stars appeared, they listened to him lay out the plan he, Lynmeer and Henry had been working on since they visited the castle two years prior. "We'll come up on the south side, below the mews. There is a secret entrance known only to the falconers for getting the birds in and out. There we will look for a young apprentice by the name of James. My father said he's a good man and can help us."

Not wishing anyone to know of their approach, they silently made their way closer to the embattled castle where the forest thinned. The closer they crept, the more they smelled smoke and the acrid remains of fire.

"Can you tell what burned?" Gunder asked.

"Not from here," Niall answered. Ben only shook his head.

Hidden in the trees west of Cire Castle, far enough from the front gate to be safe from arrows, the Baldonian general studied his options. A few guards were dutifully posted around the camp, even after scouts confirmed there were no outside troops. Finding little to no resistance after the first few days, the men fell into gross neglect of duty, believing they were invincible.

Camp life was disgusting to Layla. She loathed the filth and the disgusting smells emanating from soldiers who didn't bathe. Grateful for the opportunity to be away, she and Tam scouted the surrounding territory, hunting for clues. Normally, unless the king planned a counter-attack, he would be sending emissaries to negotiate by now. Something was amiss.

The general contemplated the two obvious options. One was to wait the enemy out. That required patience, of which the general had little, but so far, he had not found a way to penetrate the castle walls.

✝ ✝ ✝

Never before had Niall been so grateful for all the hours spent practicing stealth. He knew Gunder and Ben were attempting to be quiet; still, much of the time he could hear them. It was a worry.

He moved forward. All was clear. He chirped out the sound of a cricket, and Gunder and Ben followed carefully. They had practiced a second version for danger.

High above the tree canopy, Nan finished scouting the area. Her wings stilled and she drifted down, settling into the tallest tree, watching. Niall glanced to where she sat high above them. Lifting her wings high, she slowly let them settle again. That signaled all was quiet and the bird detected no one was prowling about.

Positive he was directly across from the secret entrance he sought, Niall held up his fist when both Gunder and Ben were at his side. He unsheathed his knife and left his longbow. Ben would bring it when Niall found the door. In the meantime, Gunder fitted an arrow onto the shaft of his own bow, kneeling down to watch and give cover if Niall was spotted.

Staying in the shadows for as long as possible, Niall moved forward. To reach the actual castle walls, the only choice was to cross the open grass—one of the better defenses of the castle. He glanced up at Nan. There was a slight rustling in the Knurly tree on his right and he was sure he heard a whispered, "It's safe now." He quickly sprinted to the wall.

Covered in ivy and decades of neglect, the wall gave no indication of a door. Breathing heavy from the sprint across the open field, Niall took in a couple of long, steadying breaths, letting them out slowly to still his heart rate. He stepped carefully to his left, trying to feel the ground beneath his feet. He hoped to detect a difference, higher or lower, in front of the door, something to help mark its location in the dark. A sliver of moon glowed softly in its high perch, watching what was unfolding below, and although Niall was grateful for the help, the scant light was not enough.

Laying his hand upon the cold stone wall, he closed his eyes. A vision came to him of a falconer coming down stone stairs behind the door. On the master's gauntlet sat a huge, ebony falcon with translucent feathers, so deeply colored they were nearly blue. Niall sensed the bird was angry. The skin beneath the stone in his pocket tingled. It seemed the bird's presence was palpable, and he wondered if there was a connection to his Nan.

To his left, the tingle became stronger. He inched his way slowly, feeling for differences in the wall. Only a few feet from where he started, he detected a slight slope to the ground and had to step around a thick trunk of ivy growing up the wall, oddly giving him the impression it had been thoughtlessly allowed to grow there.

"Wait, thoughtless or deliberate?" Niall asked himself. He moved back to the right, this time squeezing in between the vines and the wall rather than going around it. His hand caught on a small metal ring in the stone. He had it.

A cricket chirped in the stillness. Gunder and Ben looked at each other. Ben had scarcely breathed since Niall's dash across the open. No one had been spotted moving about, but occasionally he heard raucous laughter coming from the Baldonian camp in the trees west of the castle's entrance.

Shouldering Niall's great bow, his sword still in its scabbard, Ben started forward on Gunder's right. Gunder was not far behind, his own red bow drawn and ready. He could not see Niall along the massive wall looming up in front of them, but they followed in the same direction he had gone. Niall suddenly appeared on their left. Without a word, he motioned for them to follow, and the three made their way to the secret entrance.

† † †

The heavy stone slid almost without sound. Niall exhaled the deep breath he had been holding in fear the door would make a dreadful racket upon opening, but the same craftsman who had cleverly hidden the heavy door had also built the mechanism that opened the door, and it would last as long as the towering walls stood guard around it.

The three young men climbed the steep stairs in pitch black, each holding the shirt of the one in front. When one of them stopped, all three stopped. At the top, Niall felt with his hand until he located the latch. He was not fearful of waking Baldonian soldiers; now he did not want to be killed because of waking a castle watchman or an apprentice of the mews.

He closed his eyes. Holding his breath, he lifted the latch up and waited for any noise the door might make. It opened soundlessly. Niall pushed the door farther and stepped into the yard of King Stephen's falcons.

Every eye was trained on the interlopers.

Chapter Seventeen

The hair on the back of Gunder's neck prickled. He wanted to bolt or at the very least draw his weapon, but Niall's hand softly patted his arm, reassuring him enough to hold his ground. After a moment to look around, they softly walked to the rampart and looked down toward the enemy camp. They could not see into the trees, but they could see the devastation rained down upon the village. A soft moan escaped Gunder before he could stop it. Ben stood nearby, shaking his head. Niall's shoulders drooped. After a moment, they moved again, following the route Niall had memorized. Lynmeer and Henry had made excellent drawings of the castle's layout.

The young apprentice rolled over and stretched. He had slept with the birds since turning twelve, the age when he was apprenticed to the mews. His eyes closed again but he lay without falling back to sleep. Something was amiss.

At night, mews might seem quiet to outsiders, but to any who lived among the birds, there was always a chorus of tiny sounds: birds shifting their stance, preening or plucking themselves in the privacy of darkness. The silence was deafening.

James raised his head. At that very moment, a hand slipped over his mouth and forced his head back down. He bucked to throw it off, but other strong hands grabbed his arms and legs. A voice whispered reassuringly in his ear.

"Shhh. It's all right. Are you the only one here?"

Unwilling to give anything away, James lay perfectly still. How in the world did they get in here?

"My name is Niall Thoralt. Are you James? You met my father Henry Thoralt and my tutor Lynmeer two years ago."

This time he nodded in the affirmative. These men were not from Baldonia.

"Are you the only one here?"

Again he nodded and this time he relaxed slightly. The hand eased back. James remembered the two men he spoke of. They had inspired him to continue practicing with the sword despite the master falconer's disdain and to stockpile arms and supplies with which to fight the Baldonian army. At first, he had told no others of his preparations, but with subtle questioning, he had found others in the castle who agreed they should be ready "just in case." His care also kept the secret door oiled and ready.

Niall signaled for the others to release James, and the young man sat up. "I have been waiting a long time," he said. "There are others too."

"Good," Niall said. He could see James's silhouette in the darkness. He grabbed the apprentice's hand and shook it firmly. "We need a dozen or so that you trust completely and hopefully who are good with weapons," he added. There was no longer any need to whisper.

"What's your plan? How many of you are there?"

"There are three of us. Gunder here, and Ben. I also have a falcon, well trained. She waits for us on the outside. We shall go to the king first. If he agrees with my plan, I shall go back outside and take out as many of the Baldonian soldiers as possible before they know what hit them. Then the king's men can attack."

"The king is gone. Two days ago, he and the master falconer and his second snuck out the way you must have gotten in."

"Where were they headed?" Niall asked.

"Their plan was to head to the dowager house, if they made it past the invaders."

Gunder sucked in air. "Bugger!"

They were silent as they digested James's words. The king's cowardice was not good news. James's head dropped for a moment, then rose again. "How did you know how to get in?" he asked. It was such a closely guarded secret. He had only been told after five years of service to the master on pain of death if he divulged it to anyone.

"My tutor worked here a long time ago," Niall replied.

"What weaponry do you have?" James asked.

"Stealth and courage," Niall answered. Gunder and Ben both smiled at the answer. James's face slowly broke into a similar look, and he nodded agreement. It would do.

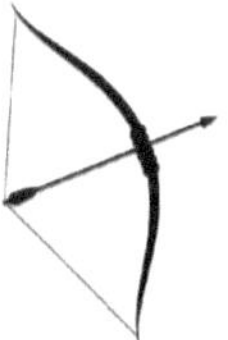

Chapter Eighteen

A Hundred Years Earlier

"Aleah, my dear," Moordoon crooned, coming up behind the lavender lady early on a splendid, warm morning. The giant black dragon had found her on the gentle, secluded slopes beneath Thorncrag, one of her favorite spots in all of Rhyaden. She sat leaning over a parchment, focused on the measurements she was plotting.

Startled by his voice, she turned around, knocking her paint jar to the ground.

"Oh drat, you buffoon! Look what you made me do. Don't call me dear, Moordoon, you have no business using that term with me."

"You are so charming when you get feisty, Aleah. Won't you come fly with me this morning? The weather is divine, and I have something beautiful to show you."

"No, I will not. Now leave at once. I wish to work in peace."

If black can get blacker, Moordoon turned the blackest black possible, except where his blood pulsed close beneath his skin and illuminated his scars. Though he quickly turned his massive head away to hide his anger, she saw the smoke hovering in his nostrils as they flared. She held her head high and stood her ground. She knew she had pricked a nerve.

"When you get tired of that little purple nit and his silly bird paintings, I will gladly show you a most extraordinary sight. You might want to include it on your map," he teased, once again in control. Perhaps he could entice her with delights other than his size and magnificent coloring.

Her eyes widened slightly. "You know, Moordoon, you should try learning how to paint. You might enjoy a little culture."

"If you feel I am neglecting my creative side, why don't you join me this morning and show me the error of my ways?"

She cocked her head to the side. "Don't be ridiculous. I have work to do, Moordoon. Good day."

He opened his mouth, contemplating a choice of retort, but closed it again and flew off.

Aleah still believed that dragons should not interfere with humans, but with all but the three of them long dead, it was a moot point. Leaving humans to their own devices was a hard sell to Lynmeer, though, who had been entrusted to look after them.

† † †

Aleah put so much time into her map and experiments, even infusing a batch of Knurly trees with magic so she could talk with them about the health of the forest, Lynmeer sought his own non-magical diversion. In manshape, he strolled into King Valdorn's castle on the east side of Rhyaden and offered his services as a tutor. Since the king's firstborn was more in need of a nanny than a teacher at the time, Lynmeer offered to teach King Valdorn how to play chess until his services as a teacher were required. A friendship blossomed and Lynmeer handcrafted a unique chess set, which he presented to the king.

In the beginning, Lynmeer easily won each match, but Valdorn was a clever student and over time he began to excel at the game. The teacher could no longer count on winning, which made no matter. He had grown to love the excellent camaraderie with the king.

As time went on, Lynmeer enjoyed his friendship and the chess games with King Valdorn more and more. Arriving unexpectedly at the castle late one evening, he was surprised to hear from castle staff that another man sat across the chess set this night. He had presented himself to Valdorn as a prince from Niregon.

"That is odd," Lynmeer said, positive the Niregon king only had young daughters.

Hearing laughter before he even passed the huge tapestries that hung in front of the doorway of the king's private game room, Lynmeer stopped and listened. He did not have to go any closer to know this was no prince from across the sea. It was Moordoon, Lynmeer's arch rival.

Beginning at their dinner, Moordoon and the king had drunk copious amounts of wine. Retiring to the game room, Valdorn explained the new game and looked forward to an easy victory. Chess was not Moordoon's objective. Losing a game was an easy price to pay to infiltrate Lynmeer's world. Moordoon had not drunk so much, however, that he couldn't sense the presence of another dragon when Lynmeer drew near. The king had just taken his rook when Moordoon's eyebrows arched and his nose quivered. Rising suddenly, he stood as Lynmeer entered the room.

"Good evening, Lynmeer," Valdorn exclaimed upon seeing the tutor. "I am teaching a new student our game! Come in and join us."

Moordoon seethed but he would not use magic and risk going against the edict of the Council. The magic Juldorn had used was too powerful, but it did not stop his anger from growing the longer he stood there.

"You should know, my Lord, that this man is an imposter. He is no prince as he has claimed," Lynmeer said.

"Whatever do you mean?" the king asked, taken back. He trusted Lynmeer, and suddenly he feared how much he had had to drink. He tried to focus on Moordoon, who did not look at him. "Guards!" Valdorn thundered.

Moordoon laughed, watching Lynmeer and ignoring the king. "As if you aren't an imposter yourself!"

The shape-shifting happened in an instant. The room was not big enough for dragons. Valdorn was knocked violently backwards, his head hitting the stone hearth before falling unconscious to the cold hard floor. His neck was broken.

At this late hour both guards were asleep at their posts, having eaten far too much at the feast earlier in the evening. When they stumbled past the tapestries, they stood frozen in shock at the sight of a huge black beast filling the room. Moordoon roared when he saw the guards, shooting flames up the walls and tapestries. Realizing he was trapped, he burst through the window, showering stone and glass on the grass below. Lynmeer shape-shifted into a dragon, roaring his own anger. He gathered himself to follow, then stopped.

Finding Moordoon could wait. He must save the king. Turning toward his fallen friend, the swish of his tail sent the two guards into the outer stone wall, knocking both out.

"Valdorn!"

As he bent over Valdorn, hungry flames licked up the walls. Lynmeer realized the danger to everyone who resided in the castle.

The room was ablaze. He must get help. He drew a long, ragged breath. Without using flame, he roared again to wake the castle's inhabitants. He then picked up Valdorn and flew through the gaping hole in the wall. His wing caught in the splintered window mullion, scraping off a handful of scales from his wing. He flew to the ground where he lay the dying king upon the wet grass. Summoning magic, he implored the king to waken, instantly groaning from the toll that using magic enacted on his own body. The paralyzed king's eyes opened. Lynmeer sighed with relief. He must get Aleah. She would know what to do next.

"I must get help. Hang in there, my friend, I will be back."

Unaware of Valdorn's broken neck, Lynmeer flew to Gaxdorn Gate, screaming for Aleah to come help. "The castle is on fire. You must help me with Valdorn. I used magic, but it is not enough. I don't know what to do next."

"You used magic in Rhyaden?" Aleah cried, knowing it could kill even the strongest of dragons.

"I had to try and save him," Lynmeer sobbed.

In those minutes while Lynmeer sought Aleah's help, oxygen streamed through the broken window, fueling the fire into a monster that buckets of water could not stop.

Valdorn's wife woke to a deafening roar and sniffed the air. Fire! Running to her child in the nursery, she pulled the sleeping boy out of his bed and thrust him into the arms of his confused nanny.

"Go, quickly, get Andrew to safety. I must find the king." With that, she was gone, running toward the room she thought her husband to be in and into the arms of the evil inferno. Giant beams fell from the ceiling already engulfed in flames, trapping her.

Lynmeer and Aleah returned quickly in human form, but they were too late to save the king. He lay dead, staring blankly beneath the stars. The queen was not to be found. A hysterical nanny sat on the grass, holding onto a sobbing child. Lynmeer and Aleah looked at each other. His gaze dropped.

"This is my fault, Aleah. I caused this. My friend is dead because of me."

"Lynmeer, you did not intend for him to die," Aleah said, squeezing his hand. "For the moment, though, we must think what to do for his son. Andrew is too young to rule this country. There is no one to protect him now. How do we help him?"

"Valdorn had cousins," Lynmeer said, trying to focus.

"There is likely to be a nasty fight over who is to rule until he is old enough, and worse yet, the winner might find a way for Andrew to fall victim to yet another 'accident,' assuring the victor stay in power," Aleah whispered.

"What are you saying?"

"I think we must take the boy away, far away for his safety, and let Rhyaden choose its next king. No one will know he didn't die in this fire."

"You were right, you know, what you've always believed. We shouldn't interfere in the humans' lives. Look what I have done. Is this plan of yours not more interference?"

"He is just a boy, Lynmeer, your very good friend's son. Don't make him suffer further for what happened here tonight."

Shortly after their conversation, Aleah offered the nanny a cup of tea. The woman was too distraught to question who gave her the welcome drink. Aleah gave a slightly different version to the boy, who took a few sips and promptly fell asleep. The nanny nodded off a few minutes later and did not waken until the following day. The boy was not seen or heard from again. Later, everyone assumed the king died jumping out the window to escape the fire, and the queen and prince were lost in the fire along with many others. The nanny had no recollection of the night's events, or how she got out of the castle.

Lynmeer later walked among the smoldering ruins. He finally found what he looked for—a small hardened stone, made from his scales that had been scraped off his wing. They had not disintegrated but rather melted together into a perfectly round marble with tiny striations of iridescent purple. He picked up the beautiful stone, turning it over to look at all sides.

In a small village on the opposite side of Rhyaden, a small, sweet boy was found a few days later sleeping in a barn with little more than a clean nightshirt on his back. The name Andrew was written on a piece of parchment and pinned to the back of his gown, and a small leather pouch hung around his neck with an unusual stone inside. The barn belonged to a childless couple who immediately took him in and fed him. The wife began sewing clothes for the little one, and her husband went to the barn where he sawed and sanded and returned with a tiny bed for the lad. Unable to have children of their own, they could not help but hope the family that had left him did not return.

The toddler could not say where he was from or if he had family. Only the two dragons knew this young lad was a Valdorn, and that fact would not be revealed for another hundred years. No one in the village had heard of a missing child, and so it was assumed a poor person passing through had left the boy in hopes of finding him a new home. In that, they were partially right. It wasn't long before news of the Great Fire at Valdorn's castle made its way to Knurlysham, and thereafter everyone's attention was diverted to speculation over who would become the next king.

Bitter fighting over who would succeed Valdorn soured the winter. Andrew's close cousins on the Valdorn side, the DeMonts, claimed a right, as did Richard Walford, a distant cousin of his father who happened to be his mother's brother. The DeMonts had larger numbers but had to cross mountains or come by sea in the frigid cold to fight. Wanting horses with them, they chose to traipse over the mountains. It turned out to be a poor choice due to the harsh winter. When they finally faced the Walford army, many had succumbed to the elements, and those that remained were weak from hunger.

Months later, the fight ended with Richard Walford crowned the new King of Rhyaden. Though bitter feelings remained between the two kingdoms, spring arrived nonetheless. The weather turned bright and warm, heralding a new beginning. The king determined his first act would be to build a new castle, far from the old one.

✝ ✝ ✝

In Ayhrland, Lynmeer worked endlessly on a miniature painting of a yellow finch, made as a special gift to Aleah for their upcoming wedding. It was almost finished.

Glancing over at the small parchment Aleah had hung close to where he worked, he smiled.

Kindness Always

Where was she now? He swished the paint brush in a cup of water and then wiped it dry, wondering as he did so where he might find her. He could not remember if she had said she was working on her map in Rhyaden today, or here in her experimental gardens.

His head lifted and he turned sideways, detecting a distant cry. The sound was not a part of the music he had been listening to. Time slowed to a stop. Dread washed over him in a nauseating wave, and his paintbrush fell to the ground. He whirled around and flew to Gaxdorn Gate. Following the source, he came through just as another far-off scream reverberated across the land. To a human, the sound was like crashing thunder. Lynmeer knew it came from another dragon, one in agony.

In her quest to make a map without magic, Aleah did not fly between landmarks, she walked in human form, measuring the distance as early cartographers would in years to come. The rudimentary method was challenging but gave Aleah a wonderful sense of satisfaction. Her goal today had been to climb Thorncrag Mountain. Reaching the high granite peak was the only remaining obstacle to completing the entire eastern side of Rhyaden on her map. Nearing the top, trees became sparse, scraggly specimens, bent low from winter winds. Loose hardscrabble lay between larger, sharp-sided rocks. She reached the top winded but thrilled with the accomplishment. The view was spectacular in every direction.

Aleah pulled a notepad out of her pack, writing down her impressions:

* hardy, tiny white flowers, very low to the ground below the tree line

* no flowers on the last 100' to the top, only gray and black granite

* the trees near the top bend in the same direction as the prevailing wind, gnarled, fascinating shapes

* very, very large bird nest below top ridge, protected by rocky overhang

Next she made sketches and wrote a description of what she could see in each direction. Then she began an estimate of distance to familiar landmarks. While her eyes swept across the landscape, she saw a large bird flying far south of the crag and wondered for a second if it belonged to the nest below. The ominous size became more distinct as it gained altitude, far too large to inhabit this nest. A twenty-foot span of iridescent black wings covered a massive body of hard muscle and strong legs ending in sharp nine-inch talons. One had to get very close to see the scars marring Moordoon's sleek skin, scars obtained in the Great War.

He did not need to get close for her to know who was flying in Rhyaden. Anger rose immediately at Moordoon for flaunting the rule of not being seen by humans in dragon form. Nor did he respect her devotion to Lynmeer.

"Drat him."

Expediency took over. She did not want to be seen. She could shape-shift, but she couldn't disappear without magic. She hoped he wasn't looking when she hid herself as best she could in a small crevice a few feet below the top.

In a vigilant canvass of the area, Moordoon spotted the human sitting on the crag top. A dragon's eyes are keen, and he spotted the human far sooner than a human could detect him. His curiosity piqued, he banked and found an updraft to take advantage of. His eyes widened to focus on the mountaintop, and then he saw the human hide. He swerved off, banking hard to the left, seething inside. It was no human. A human couldn't see this far. It was Aleah. Why was she so stubborn? What must he do to win her? He slowly descended to the gentle slopes beyond the crag and used the trees to disappear.

Waiting fifteen minutes to be sure he was gone, Aleah finally got up from where she had flattened herself. She stretched and shook her limbs before taking up her pad and trying again. It was no good. Her agitation over Moordoon's appearance in the sky spoiled the peace of the day. Why was he coming to Rhyaden as himself, not in human form as required by the edict? She packed up her bag and the canister that held her map in preparation for the descent.

She hesitated. Shape-shifting meant a quick flight home. She was sure there were no humans in sight. Staying in human form meant a long climb down the mountain, and if the black dragon returned, she would be exposed again. She straightened her shoulders, determined not to let Moordoon win the day. If nothing else, this map project had certainly taught her a newfound respect for human limitations.

Taking one final glance across the vast landscape to assure herself that Moordoon was not waiting, she started down and almost immediately slid on loose gravel.

"Gracious!" she said, catching herself.

The second time she slipped, she looked for a stick to use for balance. Finding none above tree line, she sat down and scooted down a scary chute on her bottom. This made the going down as slow as the ascent, only for different reasons.

She was now on the same level as the sturdy raptor nest. Curiosity tugged at her. She could not help but wonder if there were eggs in the nest. "How Lynmeer would love to paint the lady of this house," she thought. The nest itself would make an interesting study, one Lynmeer had yet to try on canvas. Loving to nurture his artistic side, she turned to face the rock, side-stepping for a closer look. Rocks above it protruded sharply outward, protecting the chicks underneath. If she could have seen into the nest from above, she wouldn't have had to go so close.

A scream thundered through Aleah's ears. Great flapping wings descended on her just as claws ripped at her shoulders, sending her into the solid granite overhang. Unconscious, her limp body rolled toward the edge and then free-floated for a few seconds before hitting the mountain side again.

The falcon hopped toward the edge, prepared to attack again in defense of her chicks, but there was no one there. The body was already a hundred feet below, tumbling in a sickening series of thuds down the mountain.

Sharp granite severed the tiny leather strap attached to the cylindrically shaped leather case that held the map. It floated free and then bounced twice before wedging deep in a crack between boulders.

Moments after her fall, Moordoon picked up and held Aleah's bruised body in his arms. He gently rocked her back and forth, singing softly. No magic could save her now, though he would have used it had it not been too late. He caressed her tattered wings. At the moment of her death, she had turned one final time into her beautiful lavender self.

In his grief, Moordoon was totally oblivious to Lynmeer's approach, his senses obliterated by the tears streaming down his scarred and ragged face. It was Moordoon's scream Lynmeer had heard when he emerged from Ayhrland.

Rage coursed through Lynmeer's body, turning his eyes blood red and his scales and skin morbidly black. You could not tell one from the other except their size. The two dragons became one, pitching and clawing at each other in unequaled fury, holding tight as their screams echoed across Rhyaden. Both knew they fought to the death, too close and fast for fire, or words of explanation.

Lynmeer had the advantage of rage, but Moordoon fought for his life, and eventually his larger size began to wear on the smaller dragon. Sensing the tide turn, Moordoon poured all of his remaining strength into his wings, lifting both of them off the ground. Eighty feet up he drew his muscles in tight and gave a great heave, thrusting Lynmeer toward the ground with everything he had.

Lynmeer knew he could not turn over fast enough, and dragons were incapable of upside-down flight. With his belly exposed to Moordoon's claws, he was certain to die. Thrashing in a desperate attempt to save himself, the claw on his right leg caught a ligament in Moordoon's left leg, locking the two together. The brief moment of triumph for the scarred black dragon turned to startled realization. They were both going down.

Mature spruce trees spiraled high beneath the two dragons. Unlike on the mountain's slope, with its shorter scrabbly trees, here the landscape flattened out, and the rich, black earth grew magnificent trees. One such spruce lay directly beneath the battle. Moordoon's shove had given Lynmeer's weight too much momentum for either to pull apart. The only thing preventing the dragons from hitting the ground was the spruce's thick branches.

The sudden stop shocked Lynmeer. He hung by his entangled claw, bouncing slowly up and down. Searing pain came on quickly, inching its way up his leg. Unable to bear his weight, the claw would tear itself out of his body if he hung there much longer. The giant tree shuddered and groaned under the weight of two dragons.

"Moordoon, you bastard, get yourself untangled so we can get down."

There was no response. Lynmeer raised his head and looked at his enemy. Empty black eyes stared into space. The spruce had impaled the black dragon as keenly as a spear. He heard the ugly sound of sinews in Moordoon's massive black legs begin to tear. He had only seconds to react.

Turning as far over as he could, Lynmeer hoped it was far enough. He withdrew his claws. The snagged one wouldn't let go of the muscle it had embedded itself in. The flesh of his leg began to tear as they stretched, pulling farther and farther apart. Screaming in agony, Lynmeer felt a snap. He tumbled in a flurry toward the ground, managing one flap of his wings before landing.

Lying on the cold ground, shock engulfed the purple dragon. It was some time before he came to his senses. He shook his head, gently tested each wing and then looked at his torn claw. Glancing up into the spruce, he saw the great black dragon's body. He was alive. He had won. Suddenly though, what he had lost that day seemed far worse than his own death.

"Aleah!"

Lynmeer crumpled in grief. Tears poured from the very deepest recesses of his soul, and he was powerless to stop them. He hurt to his bones, his heart broken. Hours later, he carried Aleah's body through Gaxdorn Gate and returned her to their home in Ayhrland.

Lynmeer scoured the area under Thorncrag days later. He looked first for Moordoon, for he did not want a human to stumble upon the great dragon. Moordoon's body was gone, every clue of their battle wiped clean. Lynmeer stared up into the tree. What besides magic or another dragon could have removed the huge dragon from the tree?

"I swear to you, Aleah, on my life, I will protect all you hold dear, this land and the creations you planted, and I will keep watch over Valdorn's descendants," Lynmeer sobbed. The words echoed over the countryside. The black falcon atop Thorncrag looked over the side of the nest, stilled by the dragon's words despite the clamor of her newly hatched and ever hungry chicks.

Friend or enemy, Moordoon was gone. Aleah was gone. No one to laugh with; no one to critique his paintings; no one to share his day's adventure with; no one to offer advice or encouragement; no one to correct him. He fell into a deep and dark depression in his loneliness, struggling each day between letting go and rejoining life. Weeks after the battle, he tried once again to paint, but there was no inspiration, no joy in his hand as he brushed paint onto the canvas. He desperately wanted Aleah to reappear. Paint dabbed on the end of the brush slowly dried, unused.

But life does go on. As Lynmeer's terrible ache for Aleah began to diminish, the wounds to heal and the loss to right itself, the dragon began at last to look beyond Ayhrland. He returned to travel throughout Rhyaden, visiting with the Knurly trees and watching Valdorn's son grow to manhood.

The new king, Richard Walford I, ruled Rhyaden with a careful eye on taxes, building a new castle in the middle of his kingdom. Cire was much grander and far more defensible. He was fair to his subjects and well liked, but after only ten years on the throne, he died. His son, Richard II, spoiled and lazy, had a much less successful reign. His one accomplishment was adding two more wings to the castle in order to hold far larger groups for lavish hunting parties.

† † †

"Um, excuse me, sir," a tiny creature said, his voice startling Lynmeer. The dragon stood in a small clearing in Ayhrland where he painted. It was not far from the caves wherein lay the Great Hall of the Elder Council. Now, he stared at a canvas that had been set up days ago, waiting for the first stroke.

"What? What? Who goes there? No one should go there! Who said that?"

Lynmeer swung about, looking for the owner of the voice. His tail knocked over the easel. Paint, water, brushes, all went sliding across the ground.

"Down here, sir," the voice explained.

Lynmeer looked down at the tiny green creature with large, pointed ears. He cocked his head, trying to remember where he had seen this one before. Then it came to him and his eyes widened in disbelief. It was one of the creatures who cared for the Great Hall and served Juldorn. Where he had been of late, Lynmeer had no idea, unless it was to serve Moordoon. He swelled up from his nose to his toes, about to shout the little two-foot-high creature out of his sight, and then he remembered what anger had done before, and he slowly let out the air in his lungs.

"I see, and what do you wish of me?" Lynmeer said at length.

The creature watched the dragon's rising tide of anger, and his belly tightened. Then the dragon's slow exhale gave him a glimmer of hope that he had not come in vain. His muscles relaxed. "I wondered, sir, if you have need of a servant. My name is Ecirp, as was my father's name, and his before him."

"What type of work do you do?" Lynmeer asked, raising an eyebrow.

"Whatever is required, sir, as did my father, and his father before him. I can cook and clean, and I make a delicious cup of tea. Let me show you." In a flash, the scattered paint supplies were gathered and in their place, the easel was righted and a second table had appeared with a steaming hot cup of tea and some gingerbread biscuits.

"Please, sir, I am lonely too," the little fellow said when it stood in front of Lynmeer a few seconds later. In truth, the months following his last master's death had been extremely boring, and quiet. Not at all a satisfactory way to live out one's life. Since Lynmeer was the only dragon left, Ecirp finally made up his mind to give the purple fellow a try, despite how Moordoon had described him.

"Do you have any references?" Lynmeer asked.

The little creature coughed to clear his throat. "I last worked for Moordoon, sir. It was me that brought his body home to Ayhrland." He stared at the ground, wondering if his words would raise the hackles of the purple dragon, but no hot dragon breath showered down on him as used to happen when he angered Moordoon, so he continued. "Since his demise, there have not been any other dragons to work for. I've gotten rather lonely of late." His lip trembled and his large ears turned bright pink instead of green, matching his carefully ironed pink vest. He had no long tail as a dragon does, his looked more like a rosebush thorn, and he was covered in tiny scales. Very long eye lashes framed his big black eyes.

"And why not go home to your family, if you are lonely?"

Ecirp's ears turned from pink to red at this question. "Oh my, oh my, that would be a disgrace to the family, to leave the service. Oh, no, I couldn't bring that dishonor down on my family name, even if I am the last and only Ecirp left to carry on."

Would it be disloyal to Aleah to have another fix him tea?

Lynmeer was torn by the question and spent a long time wrestling with the thought. He craved companionship for himself, but the obvious need of Ecirp to have companionship too finally tipped the balance. Lynmeer eyed the gingerbread. "I suppose it wouldn't hurt for us to give it a try."

Chapter Nineteen

The Present

A week after the three young men arrived at Cire, six men quietly followed Niall and Ben down the steps, out the falconer's secret entrance, and into the dead of night. They went the long way around the castle, headed toward the far west side of the Baldonian camp. Another six walked behind Gunder and James in the opposite direction, a shorter distance to their mutual goal. None of them wore heavy armor or weapons that could clank as they walked, only weapons of stealth—bows and arrows, knives and daggers.

They would not rescue each other if things went wrong. The mission was to quietly take out soldiers and watchmen from Baldonia to whittle down the enemy numbers. Under no circumstances were they to retreat to the secret entrance and possibly give away its location. On this they had pledged their lives. If the plan went awry, they would scatter and try to raise help from the distant villages. A prearranged signal was set for the remaining men on the inside to join the battle when it ensued.

†††

During the prior week, James had quietly talked with trusted friends in the castle. He let them know their king had fled, but good men had come from Knurlysham with a plan to help them. Few had suspected the king was gone, but even fewer were surprised to hear it. Each day their numbers grew, and finally they convened a meeting in the mews for several hours of careful strategy.

"We should begin by choosing a leader," James said during the afternoon of the first gathering. Men were sitting on bales of straw, and a few leaned against the stone walls. Gunder, Ben and Niall stood apart, their arms crossed, surveying the men who had volunteered to fight with them. Their murmuring quieted at his words.

"I vote for Niall," James said, walking over and clapping Niall on the shoulder, and then he looked over the skeptical faces in front of him. Niall, Ben and Gunder were younger than most who attended the meeting. "He came to fight for us, for Rhyaden. I don't believe there is a better man for the job."

"I'm young," Niall said, stepping forward. "I'm sure there must be valiant men among you with more experience than I."

His declaration was a surprising admission that garnered a few thoughtful nods. One gray-haired gentleman dressed in the uniform of the king's guard stepped up. His eyes were rheumy and his uniform had seen better days. Buttons appeared ready to pop in the waist area. "None of us has done any fighting in a war, Niall. I'm the oldest one here, and I should know. There hasn't been a war since three generations back. The last conflict I remember was a poor boy poaching a deer on the king's land. Turned out his father had gone blind and his family was starving. That boy was James here, and I know him as well as I know my own son. I trust his confidence in you."

"Niall, you have been training for this your whole life," Ben said.

"He's right, you are the best man to lead us," Gunder added.

Niall almost answered with "but." Then the image of his parents standing on the front porch buried the word.

A chorus of "Here! Here!" went up. The vote was unanimous. He could only hope his plan would free the castle and secure their independence. Food was running low. Word that the king had deserted the castle angered many. Niall decided to address that issue too.

"If King Stephen were here, some of you would surely have to stay behind to defend him. We would have fewer men to put against Baldonia. This way, we can all fight. His absence is in our favor."

The reasoning made sense, to Niall's credit, not the king's.

The darkness of the woods and heavy cloud cover made for slow going but obscured the men's approach. Niall held up his fist. The men stopped and scoured the area in the direction they were headed. They could hardly see yet, but their eyes were adjusting. Niall's fist still high, he looked at Ben standing next to him. Ben nodded and held up his fist, prepared to stop any man who forgot. Without sound, Niall changed his direction to a slightly wider arc than the course they had been following and melted out of sight.

Fitting an arrow into his bow, he moved toward the noise he had heard. Killing innocent animals had never been easy for

Niall. He wondered now how killing a man would feel.

He could hear the leaves whispering in the air, the bark on a nearby tree stretching as it took up more water through its roots. The smell of rotting leaves and damp moss could not mask the smell of urine and days of unwashed grime. Sweat permeated the air. The stench was disgusting.

A Baldonian soldier, having drunk too much wine, wandered away from camp to relieve himself. He never heard the arrow coming. Niall removed it and wiped the tip before replacing it in his quiver. He straightened up, and then he had to stop and breathe deeply for a few seconds, steeling himself against the unbidden reaction. This was war, he reminded himself. A minute later, he was at Ben's side. He held up one finger, and then signaled them to move forward.

The men from the castle shook their heads in disbelief. After that, they did their best, but they were hardly used to moving about in the woods at night.

"Ouch!" the tail man groaned when a small log tripped him up. Niall again held up his fist and stopped. Making his way back to the older man's side, he laid his hand upon his shoulder and gazed deep into his eyes. The man swallowed. Their lives, as well as the kingdom's future, depended on each and every one of them being absolutely quiet.

On the other side of the castle, Gunder and his men waited impatiently for ten long minutes before heading out on their own route toward the enemy camp. They waited in order to give Niall's party time to go the longer distance, but after only five minutes, Gunder sensed their restlessness. He held up his fist and the fidgeting ceased, the men unsure what his signal meant since they weren't moving. He walked from one to another, checking each man's weapon before resting his hand on their shoulder. His demeanor calmed them, and when he indicated it was time to go, he, James and the others moved forward in solidarity.

They encountered a Baldonian guard posted near the road. He was there to capture anyone who hadn't heard the news of the invasion and journeyed to the castle by chance. In the first few days, this post had caught many a Rhyaden citizen, but as of late, no one came this way, especially not in the black of night.

The dozing soldier sat with his back to a tree, facing the direction he was supposed to be guarding. Boredom served an impossibly heavy burden on his eyelids, and his chin drooped close to his chest. Gunder drew his blade and dispatched the watchman. Those close nodded approval.

Emboldened by their first success, they fanned apart and kept the same pattern. Each guard they encountered met the same fate. Circling until they were directly west of the Baldonian camp, they slowed to a crawl and finally came to a complete halt. Waiting was the hardest part of all. Gunder worried if they didn't meet up with Niall's group soon, daylight might catch them before the plan was fulfilled.

Suddenly a cricket chirped. He smiled and nodded to James. They started forward carefully, and within feet, Niall was at his side. With their fingers, they counted thirty-two Baldonian soldiers eliminated between the two groups. That was significant. Now the plan was to attack, driving the enemy toward the castle where Rhyaden soldiers waited. It was a bold move, and the element of surprise was their best weapon.

As before, they started in silence, hoping to find a few more stragglers at the edge of the enemy camp. Once the alarm was sounded, they would spread out to make as much noise as possible, yelling at the top of their lungs in hopes of sounding bigger than their numbers actually were.

Niall glanced up looking for Nan, but her dark coloring blended too well with the night.

Layla lay on her bedroll, awake in the predawn stillness. She detested the previous night's raucous behavior, never allowing herself to indulge in spirits when she was surrounded by other soldiers. Her unusual position in the army made her vulnerable to envy and resentment. She had resorted to ruthless tactics in the past, and she would use them again if necessary. The only one she trusted even slightly was Tam, asleep on the bedroll next to her.

Crickets chirped and a few birds began their morning revelry, calling for the sun to rise. The ground was hard beneath her and her bedroll did little to soften the lumps. She rolled over to get off the arm that had fallen asleep during the night. Slipping her hand down her pant leg, she scratched at numerous welts left by industrious bed bugs.

Pitching a tent in a camp such as this meant no privacy. She had not had an opportunity to bathe since they set out in the longboats. She would leave this morning and head south toward the dowager house.

Her mission, unknown to anyone in the camp, made her smile. The bonus of lands and a title made her salivate. The possibilities were endless. Since no negotiations had been offered by those inside Cire, she surmised that the king had fled. Coward.

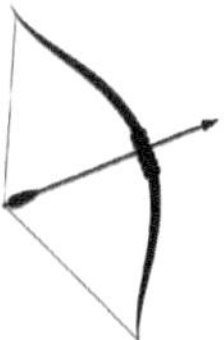

Chapter Twenty

A desperate, gargled yell rang out in camp. It quickly faltered and abruptly stopped. Stunned silence followed. Suddenly, screams and hollering erupted from both confused and frightened people trying to wake up and those trying to kill them. Men stood up, only to fall again. Nan flew overhead, adding her shrill cries to the commotion. It was an effective element, building on the confusion. Screams came from all directions now, those from above and those of the terrified prisoners within the camp who didn't know what was happening. Many of the Baldonian men had drunk far too much wine hours earlier and were still in no condition to think clearly or respond quickly. Utter chaos ensued.

Niall did not hear the noise. He moved as if he were encased in a bubble, protected from the agonizing sounds of flesh being torn open and muscles ripped apart. His arrows flew straight and true to their targets. After each, he swung to the next and drew another arrow, moving silently behind trees, never exposing himself to the enemy.

In slow motion, he watched half-dressed troops retreat in the direction of the castle, just as he'd hoped when they planned this assault. The open ground in front of Cire would give the enemy a place to regroup. The fallacy of that move was that the open ground around the castle made them vulnerable to arrows raining down by those men left inside. That was what Niall's men were counting on. Their numbers were simply too small to win in a head-to-head contest. Surprise and strategy would have to win the day.

Yelling at the top of his lungs, the Baldonian general got the attention of those nearest him, ordering them to turn and face whatever came. He roused a few to stand their ground rather than be slaughtered in front of the castle. It was a hard sell. Arrows came out of nowhere and dropped men where they stood. Many had not grabbed their shields or weapons when the initial panic erupted. There was too much confusion to mount a decent defense. Most scattered.

Niall heard the haunting blare of a horn, and his fingers held fast to the arrow fitted in his bow. Others hesitated too. The Baldonian soldier closest to him lifted his head, and Niall could see the man was heartened by the sound. The man turned and headed north, not toward the castle. Niall's arrow brought him down.

"The longboats came by sea . . . the North Sea," Niall said, repeating Lynmeer's words in his parents' cottage a few weeks ago. The sound of the horn meant retreat.

His mind raced. His eyes lifted to find Nan. She appeared to stall momentarily, then glided first one way and then the other, confirming his suspicion that the enemy was in retreat.

Yelling for his men to begin chasing their foes individually, Niall hoped to avoid giving the enemy an opportunity to regroup. He motioned to Nan. The falcon flew over the castle, cawing loudly as she swooped low and climbed high in a figure-eight pattern, the signal. Guards poured out of the castle, running toward the woods to join in the fray.

Layla sprinted from tree to tree. Tam was to her left, moving forward in the same fashion, not allowing themselves to be an easy target. These were not tactics taught for the open grasslands of Baldonia, but rather lessons learned as spies in foreign lands.

The bird. Layla had heard the raptor's screams when the enemy pounced, and now she saw the falcon flying above the castle. This was no ordinary enemy.

Niall did not allow himself to ponder the blood, the torn flesh, the empty eyes staring out of corpses. He had killed men who hours ago had been laughing and eating, men who likely also had wives, sisters and mothers waiting for their return home. No, he would not think of those things. He fought for his kingdom, for his parents, for Winnie and Gunder and Ben—people these men would kill or enslave if given the chance. Saving Rhyaden was what he had been trained for, what he had spent his entire life in preparation for. He harbored no doubts about his duty.

When the sun was straight above them, Niall ordered the men to give up the chase and reassemble in the open area outside the castle. Hours elapsed while those who were unscathed helped the wounded make their way back through the forest to the castle. Many of the women prisoners had been beaten and needed care too. Niall mixed herbs from his pack to make a soothing salve and then visited each one, administering encouragement and praise for their bravery, along with the medicine.

He bent down next to an older fellow who lay moaning on the ground holding his middle, his sallow color not a good sign. Niall saw it was the same old gentleman who had spoken in the mews. The smell emanating from the wound was putrid. Niall carefully lifted the hand that covered the deep stab wound and peeled back the torn, blood-drenched tunic. He had to shut his eyes. An enemy sword had lacerated the man's stomach and intestines, and without pressure they spilled out, mixing with his blood and clothing. Laying the man's hand back down, Niall dug in his satchel and found a leather pouch of narcissus bulbs. He looked squarely into the desperate eyes.

"Your wound is fatal, sir. You have fought bravely to defend your king and you will be remembered as a hero to the generations that follow us. That I promise."

"There isn't anything that can be done?" the blurry eyes pleaded.

"No, I'm afraid not, but I have this," he said, holding out a small bulb. "It is narcissus. It will work faster than the cruel sepsis that is soon to engulf your body from this wound."

A look of resignation came over the old man. "Thank you, sir. I'm so grateful you came to the castle, and . . . and." A spasm of coughing stopped him mid-sentence. When the coughing ceased, he wiped away the blood that dribbled out of his mouth. Looking at the dark stain, his arm reached out to Niall, who put the bulb in the man's palm and wrapped his fingers tight around it. The soldier closed his eyes and began mumbling. Niall slowly stood up and walked to the next man.

Ben came forward. He had quietly watched Niall with the dying man, unwilling to interrupt, but now he pulled Niall aside.

"I can't find Gunder. Have you seen him since we left the

castle?" he asked.

"No, I haven't. He isn't among the wounded?" Niall could see the worry in Ben's eyes.

"I checked each man. He isn't here."

Niall looked to the sky. Nan was not flying. He noticed a ruffling in a tall tree. From her high perch, she indicated a desire to come down.

"Ben, please get me some meat for Nan, and have James see to it there is food prepared for the men, yourself as well," he added. "We also need to find some willow bark to make tea. It will ease the pain for some," he said, looking past Ben to the man with the fatal stab wound.

With a sigh, he raised his hand to his shoulder and Nan lifted off, gliding down in a slow spiral until she landed softly. The men's voices quieted as those who saw her pointed out the unusually large and unfettered black falcon sitting on their leader's shoulder. Bewilderment registered on their faces.

Ben returned shortly with a small handful of meat chunks. Niall took them, thanking him, and spent a few minutes feeding his bird. During his lessons, the ritual had become an important time for Niall to think through complicated problems posed by Lynmeer. Now, he thought through the next step in the battle against Baldonia, but where was Gunder? Which came first?

A short time later, Niall walked through the woods to the spot he loosed his last arrow, scanning the ground for other arrows as he went. He was deep in thought, but he finally turned and headed toward the men, making sure that guards had been posted and the wounded had been moved inside to be cared for. Calling James to his side, they walked a short ways away from the castle for privacy.

"You're in charge while I'm gone. Post guards both close

and out a good distance. We don't want their troops amassing again just outside of sight, and, most important of all, replenish the castle supplies as quickly as possible."

"There are older soldiers here who will disagree with me as your choice."

"I'll handle them. Your preparations saved this castle, James, don't lose it now."

Some of the older men did indeed grumble when Niall first announced his decision to put James in command at the castle, despite the fact that James's preparations over the last two years had been such a big part of what saved their lives. Hearing their dissension, Niall's voice rose, and they bit their tongues, their wary eyes following every movement of the intimidating falcon.

Niall pointed to the oldest soldier among the men, motioning him forward. He had been first to open his mouth when he heard Niall's choice of leader.

"Your name, sir?"

"William. William Buckley. I, I didn't mean—"

Niall cut him off. "William, I am Niall Thoralt of Knurlysham," he said, thrusting out his hand and shaking William's as if he were greeting a proper dignitary. "Now, I wonder if you could assist me, sir?" he said, turning away and walking a short distance from the main group to talk privately under the oaks that lined the road to the castle.

"Why, certainly," William responded loudly, his demeanor once again enlarging. "Whatever you need, I'll be glad to see to it." He followed Niall, glancing behind to the men. As his head came back around, he looked straight into the glare of the falcon who sat inches away.

"Wonderful, my good man," Niall began, facing William. "You see, young James is a bit inexperienced—some might think—but you and I know he's as good a man as stands here today. I figure that with your good influence, you are the one who can lead the others into following suit with whatever James asks of them."

"Wha?" William began.

"I'll look to you to see they fall in line, right? That's why I picked you, William. I needed a good man, someone not afraid of setting the men straight," Niall finished, clapping the astounded man on the shoulder. "I'm counting on you."

Niall turned then and headed back toward the main group to give them his assessment of what they had accomplished so far. William shook his head and fell in behind, mumbling words Niall could not make out, then straightening his shoulders and marching sharply.

"Well done," the Knurly trees whispered among themselves. "Well done."

Chapter Twenty One

Niall sent Nan aloft and watched as she pumped her outstretched wings to rise through the humid forest air. Despite the circumstances, he could not help but admire her as she climbed higher and higher. Her intelligence and loyalty never ceased to amaze him. He shouldered his quiver. Ben and a handful of men had scoured the area for Gunder. They had found no trace and returned heavyhearted despite the good fortune of suffering only one death and eight wounded in this initial battle. It was their missing friend that stung so smartly, leaving heavy bands around Niall's and Ben's hearts. Niall felt Gunder was alive, but his gut told him something was terribly wrong.

Later, in the castle's great hall, Ben packed provisions into their satchels, preparing for the two of them to head out in search of Gunder. Niall came into the room and walked over to his side.

"I've thought this through, and I want you to go home to Knurlysham, Ben," Niall said.

"What?"

"Tell the villages along the way what has happened here at the castle. They need to send us anyone they can spare, especially archers, as soon as possible. This is not over by a long shot."

Ben's forehead furrowed. "He's my friend too," Ben said hotly. "It's not wise to go alone, you should know that."

"I can follow quieter and faster by myself. They have a big head start," Niall countered.

"Think about this, Niall. If you run into problems, no one will know where to look for you."

"I'll be okay. I'll have Nan with me. I'm leaving James in charge here while I'm gone. He's picked out two runners to go to the southern and eastern villages, for the same purpose I'm sending you west." Niall hesitated for a second and then added, "Check on my parents for me, will you? Tell them I'm okay."

"I should go with you, Niall," Ben said, unwilling to give in.

"We have to do what's best for Rhyaden now."

"One man against so many. It isn't safe."

"I'm not planning on going up against them. We need to know their numbers and if more are coming. Information is what I'm after, and Gunder."

Ben didn't say anything for a moment. "All right. I'll gather more help and check on our parents, but it feels wrong to leave you."

"I understand, but we really need more help here at Cire. We need . . . a lot of things." He smiled at his friend. "Please be careful going home. Baldonia may have invaded from the west by now also, as well as landed more ships."

"Do you think Gunder is dead?"

"No. He's alive, I'm sure of it, but something is wrong," Niall said.

"Take care, Niall. Promise you'll come home alive," Ben said, clasping Niall's hand.

"Brothers Forever," they said, holding tight.

The two men parted outside the castle an hour later, Ben heading west, back the way they had come just over two weeks ago. It seemed like a lifetime. Niall watched him go, his friend setting a fast pace.

Niall headed north, following a cold trail. Their enemy had left the battle scene in a hurry, leaving behind weapons and other indications of their numbers. Niall studied those clues carefully, guessing his men had killed half the enemy force that camped near the castle. What he didn't know was whether more Baldonian troops had landed and gone in different directions or waited in reserve.

An hour after parting from Ben, Niall slowed his progress. Again he sent Nan aloft for reconnaissance and stopped to pull some biscuits from his pack. There was a puzzle here, and he had yet to fit all the pieces together. Gunder was too smart not to be leaving clues unless he was dead and his body was being carried away on purpose. The retreat happened so fast, it didn't make sense that anyone carried away a heavy body.

The boys had practiced following each other's trails in the forest for years and in doing so had developed rudimentary communication by the marks they left. Twigs bent down meant they were injured. A twig broken off a bush but lying on the ground beneath it meant the enemy was close by, broken off and not there meant they were following somebody they hadn't spotted yet. He could sense there was a purpose in the lack of signs from Gunder, but he couldn't sort it out.

Nan cawed a soft warning, circling to give Niall the direction where the danger lay. He pulled an arrow out of his quiver and scanned the forest in front of him, choosing his next cover. Slipping from tree to tree, he eventually saw what Nan saw.

Two men sat near a third, who lay on the ground clutching his side. Blood dripped in a steady pulse of red, spreading slowly as it soaked the ground.

"We should go on, Gus, there isn't a thing we can do for him. They won't wait for us once they reach the boats. We'll be left behind."

"I'm not leaving my brother. I'm not gonna, and you aren't either. We're in this stupid mess together, or by golly, I'll give you the same as what Tom got," the second man threatened.

An arrow sliced cleanly through the air.

"Ahhh!" The man that had spoken first grasped at the arrow that penetrated his chest before his body slumped to the ground. The second stared in disbelief at his fallen comrade. He hesitantly raised his arms toward the sky.

Niall's voice cut the still air. "I will spare you in order for you to care for your brother, if you promise you are done fighting."

"Yes, yes, I promise," the man blubbered, looking in the direction the voice came from.

"Where is your army headed?" Niall asked.

This time, Niall's voice appeared to come from Gus's right. "North to the sea. We have longboats waiting," he said, turning the new direction.

"Do they have a prisoner with them?" came from a third location.

"I'm not su-sure," the man stuttered, totally confused now. The voice had come from behind him that time. "I remember seeing a man without a uniform, but we fell behind because of Tom's wound."

"Cover the wound with Toeffer leaves and bind it tightly to stop the bleeding. You'll find some in the trees to the west." Niall was guessing when he said this, but Toeffer was abundant and he was sure the man would find some if he kept his eyes open. "When he can travel, take him home. Don't come back. You won't be shown this mercy again."

There was nothing more to be heard, nothing but the heavy silence of deep forest. Slowly, the man brought his arms down and looked around. There was no one and no thing to indicate there had ever been anyone there. He might not have believed he had talked to a real person, except for the arrow sticking out of his dead companion's chest. His eyes traveled from the arrow up to the hollow stare of the recently departed. Rallying, he got himself up to go in search of Toeffer.

Niall heard the man tramp through the woods for over half an hour. It gave him time to retrieve his arrow and chew up a poultice to dab on Tom's wound. Looking around while his saliva mixed with the herbs, he knew these three had left the Baldonian camp without any supplies of any kind. When he finished applying the poultice, he dug into his pack and retrieved the small snare Ben had packed for him, leaving it nearby in place of the man's weapon.

† † †

Tom's brother Gus returned and looked about before dropping to his knees and applying the leaves to the wound. Finally, he went back to the dead man's body and used his knife to cut his shirt into long strips of cloth to bind the wound and staunch the flow of blood.

When Gus was finished with his administrations, he rocked back on his heels and watched his brother's shallow breathing. The pallid color above Tom's beard began to brighten, and soon his eyelids flickered and a moan escaped his parched lips. Gus procured a small flask from under his shirt and dribbled out water for his brother.

Besides the missing arrow, George's weapon was also gone. In its place was a small snare for rabbits. Gus picked it up and shook his head.

"This be dragon magic, Tom," he said.

Ben made fair time returning home, partially due to starting at the first sign of light each morning and keeping up a steady pace all day, though stopping to inform the countryside of the need for help at the castle slowed him considerably. In the beginning, he rationed the provisions he had stuffed in his bag, but he soon found it wasn't necessary. Stopping at each farm he came to, he was nearly always rewarded with a piece of mutton pie or a thick slice of bread and butter along with hearty handshakes and pats on the back. Even the poorest of peasants offered some bit of food for his journey, but those he declined.

When he rounded the last corner and Knurlysham was in sight, Ben halted and surveyed the familiar scene, grateful to be home at last. All seemed familiar, but then his eyebrows arched together.

Missing was the usual curl of smoke rising from the forge at the west end of town. There was a stillness that was not ordinary. His relief from at last seeing home faded under a deepening cloud of concern.

"State your name and business here!" a voice rang out. If he had worn the Baldonian uniform, there wouldn't have been a question. He would be dead.

Ben jerked at the words. He had been so busy surveying

the town, he had let down his guard, missing the men posted along the edge of the trees.

"I'm Ben Finwick with news of the battle at Cire Castle."

He heard scuffling to his right and boots coming from behind. Almost immediately, he found himself surrounded. He recognized the next voice and sighed with relief.

"Ben, how are you, son? How goes the war? Where are Niall and Gunder? What has happened?" Henry Thoralt blurted out. Giving Ben no time to answer, he grabbed him and hugged him tight. Henry finally pulled back and turned to one of the other men. "Geoff, go to the Finwicks' shop and tell Flin his son has returned. Be quick now." He turned again to Ben and took a breath. "Come, sit down, tell us everything you know."

Food was offered but Ben felt no hunger. Fatigue that hadn't been allowed to surface while he journeyed now left him drained. He sat down, took a long swig of water and tried to think where to begin. The task of telling all he had seen and heard was not a short one. He skipped the trip to Cire.

"The young man James was in the mews, just as you said. He was prepared for us. He's in charge of the castle now," Ben began, then his words poured out. "Niall organized everyone. We elected him leader. There was a great battle. You should have heard Nan scream."

"Whoa, son, slow down," Henry said.

Ben drew a deep breath and continued, talking slower this time. When he got to the part where Gunder went missing, though, he suddenly looked around, scanning the faces for Torg Neuse.

"Gunder's father is on patrol," Henry said, aware of whose face he searched for. "We'll send someone to relieve him."

"Niall is following Gunder's trail. If anyone can find him,

he will."

"Ben! Oh mercy, you've returned," yelled Flin, running toward them as fast as his girth allowed. He jumped up just in time to be swallowed in his father's arms.

Later, when he arrived at the bakeshop, hugs and tears, warm bread and biscuits flowed in copious amounts as his aunts and mother fussed over him. He intended to go next to Annwyn's house next, but the ladies had no intention of letting him out of their sight. After a reasonable amount of time and explanation of some of what he had done and seen, he slowly backed toward the door.

"I must run an errand. I'll be back soon." He grabbed one more cookie off the plate his aunt held.

The shop door behind him sprang open. Ben turned around just as Annwyn rushed into his arms.

"Ben! You're home."

Breathing in her clean, soapy smell, Ben buried his face in her honey-colored hair. Knowing Annwyn was safe filled him with relief. For too many miles on the trip home, he had imagined Baldonian soldiers laying waste to Knurlysham. His imagination had spared him no details.

"Where's Niall?" Annwyn asked, pulling back from the embrace.

"He's following Baldonia's army and looking for Gunder. He got lost in the battle somehow. Anyway, we could't find him."

"You left Niall by himself? Ben, how could you?"

Ben looked into Annwyn's face. The sting from her words would have hurt the boy who left home countless weeks ago, but the dying he had witnessed set in motion a subtle and growing change. He straightened his shoulders. "Niall is in charge of our army now, Annwyn. He sent me home to gather more troops and inform the villagers of what has happened up to now. I'm following his orders."

Annwyn hung her head. "I'm sorry, Ben, I didn't mean to sound like a chit. I didn't mean that at all. I, I've just been so worried. It came out wrong."

She squared her shoulders. "What do you have to do next?" she asked. "Can I help?"

"Get a bath!" Gwyn interjected loudly.

"And some clean clothes," added Wyn.

"Some proper food," said Lyn.

Ben looked into Annwyn's eyes. He kept to himself his opinion on what came next.

Niall placed the arrows in his quiver and hid the three men's bows in dense bushes before making his way north. The trail of the Baldonian retreat was easy to follow. Some of the footprints were made by bare feet of men who had left in such haste, they left behind their boots. The disarray and lack of caution from being so roundly defeated was obvious. From what the wounded man's brother had said, the routed army's goal now was to get to the longboats and go home.

Nan flew high and fast, scouting ahead of Niall. She stretched her wings and felt the delicious pull of freedom. Pumping high, then swooping for the pure joy of it, she almost missed seeing the last longboat glide onto shore. Seven other boats had already landed, the men from them having disembarked, awaiting orders.

A woman with a long, dark braid walked out from the trees to meet the commander in charge of the boats. Her stride sent a bone-chilling shiver through the falcon.

Nan dipped and turned. She did not make a sound as she flew past the rag-tag tired men from the original landing party who were hidden in the trees. Flying straight to Niall's position, she signaled the direction of the enemy.

✝ ✝ ✝

Nan's wings flared to slow her descent. She landed on Niall's shoulder, gripping tighter than usual.

"Easy, girl. What have you seen that has you so upset?"

Niall stroked the falcon's neck and chest and felt her rapid heartbeat. He wished Lynmeer were here to interpret for him. He knew he was close to the enemy, and he guessed a larger contingent of troops had joined the Baldonian forces. Beyond that, he could not guess what was bothering Nan. His eyes traveled to her leg, healed now thanks to Lynmeer's skill, but still bearing a mark where the arrow pierced her.

Her talons gripped hard as she stared off toward the sea. Niall looked into her black eyes, wondering what she saw when she was up there. Flying must be wonderful.

"Let's eat, my friend, then we have work to do."

The falcon hopped to a nearby rock. Niall pulled bread out of his pack. He ripped off pieces and handed them to Nan.

"Sorry, girl, it's all I've got to offer," he said with a grimace for her benefit.

It was sustenance, and that was important, for their next

meal could be a long time in coming. He would leave his pack hidden here in order to travel swiftly and quietly. The only thing he removed from it was the small pouch his mother had said never to let out of his sight. He took out the stone and looked at it again, always wondering what it was made of. He shook his head and put it in his pocket. Nan had calmed, and her calmness helped him organize his thoughts and prepare for what came next.

Three of Baldonia's outlying guards fell to Niall's arrows a short time later. Each of the men was posted as a lookout a ways from the main gathering camped at the edge of the trees. None of them heard a thing. There was only a soft thud as each body slid to the forest floor.

With no moon to light the landscape, he slipped undetected to the boats, and those guards also fell. He questioned the wisdom of his next move, but finally he drew his knife and slashed the mooring ropes. The boats might make noise bumping into each other, drawing men away from the main camp. That could be good or bad. He just didn't know, but he hoped somehow it would lessen his poor odds.

Niall knew he was running out of time. Sometime soon there would be a changing of the guard, or else the entire camp would be on the move come daylight. He carefully circled. Where was Gunder?

Chapter Twenty-Two

Gunder sat near several other men greedily eating their first hot meal since the surprise attack on them outside the castle. Reaching the North Sea, they had joined up with fresh reinforcements, disappointing many who hoped to get in the boats and return to their homes. Layla informed the disembarking Captain Lodall of both the battle and the loss of General Bickford. Now in command, Lodall judiciously ordered the newly landed troops to prepare a hearty meal for the battle weary men who had run in panicked disarray from the routing at the castle. The number of survivors was not good.

The only noticeable difference between the Rhyaden defector and the Baldonian soldiers was his lack of a uniform. Grime from the campaign evened everything else out. As the men's stomachs filled, they began talking and then telling stories. Gunder elicited some approval when he added outrageous exploits of his own.

"Make sure he thinks he is welcome, but don't let him out of your sight, and don't let him get ahold of a weapon," the captain told his sergeant in charge of watching the prisoner. Gunder's story for wanting to join their side was certainly plausible, but not to be swallowed whole. However, his defection afforded a great opportunity for information, and he was giving them plenty of that. It might be worth keeping him around.

"I want a bath," Layla murmured to Tam, sitting down next to her second after a long session with the prisoner, followed by a briefing with the captain.

"Me too, a long . . . hot one."

Gunder's statements reinforced Layla's assumption that King Stephen had fled. She had already surmised the king had not been the one to lead his men in the surprise attack outside the castle so she was not surprised to hear he had tucked tail and run a few weeks earlier, though Gunder could not, or would not, tell her where—yet. She assumed the king had fled to the south, most likely to the dowager house where he had banished his mother years earlier. The thought of routing His Royal Highness out, then hanging the coward in front of his own people, brought on a vindictive sneer. Most likely, though, she would slit his throat in his sleep and no one would know it was her, except King DeMont. She would take home the Rhyaden signet ring as proof.

The attack in the forest galled her. The arrows came out of nowhere, the screams were confounding and the number killed in that first skirmish was a nasty blemish. She wasn't in charge but she was there. The plan's simple effectiveness infuriated her, despite the fact that deep down she knew her own army was negligent. She wanted nothing more than to get her hands on whoever orchestrated that attack and ring his clever little neck with her own two hands.

She got up later and walked around camp, slapping a piece of rigging against her palm as she went. Its sting effectively kept her focused on the issue in front of her: whether or not this

Gunder fellow was indeed a traitor or simply a spy. Regardless of his motives, how could she best use him? Her thoughts kept shifting. Curiosity over who led Rhyaden now crept into her head. Would the prisoner's leader follow and try to save him, a weakness she would never indulge in? A smile crept over her face.

✝ ✝ ✝

Niall drew a quick breath, blinking several times. How could it be? His life-long friend sat eating and drinking among the Baldonians, the only difference being his lack of uniform. No wonder he left no trail.

The betrayal to every moment of their childhood was deep and painful for the young man hidden at the edge of the enemy camp. Bile rose in his throat and his chest constricted as he watched Gunder laugh in his big way. The sight crushed him. It took every ounce of self-control he possessed to keep quiet and not give away his position. Then a whisper floated down from the Knurly tree he hid behind.

"Be patient. All is not as it appears."

Swallowing hard, Niall blinked and looked again. Had he missed clues?

Gunder rose suddenly, and three Baldonian men rose immediately too, their hands on their hilts.

"I've got to give myself some relief." Gunder laughed, pretending he hadn't noticed where their hands went. "You all as well? Someone pick a good direction to go. I don't want to be running into any ladies now, if you get my meaning."

The men looked at each other and then chuckled as if it were sheer coincidence they had all stood at the same time.

"This way will do," the eldest of the three said, pointing east.

Gunder tipped an imaginary cap to the one who spoke, indicating he would follow, and then, in the normal course for an archer, he adjusted his quiver strap across his shoulder. The men about him took no notice of the fact that he wore no quiver.

Niall saw the movement and squinted. Looking for the tiniest of details, he held his breath as he scanned the immediate area around where the men had been sitting. If Gunder were part of this group, the bow with its distinctive red ends would not be far. He scanned the area again. It was not there.

He watched the four men walk away, one in front of Gunder and the other two following behind. The three from Baldonia were heavily armed. Gunder was the only one without a weapon. Blood flowed again to Niall's head, and for a moment he felt weak in the knees. Gunder couldn't be here of his own free will!

The difficult decision now was how to proceed. Taking on this large a number of enemy invaders by himself was foolish, and there was no time to pick them off one by one. Neither was there time to go back for reinforcements.

Nan. He could send a message with her to the castle. Would she go? He slipped quietly away and did not stop until he was back where he had left the falcon waiting, miles from the Baldonian camp.

He climbed a tree and retrieved his pack, then pulled out the gauntlet he had stuffed in the pack when he left home. Out of the soft leather he cut out one large piece. Whittling down a sharp point on a thin, stout twig, he then ignited a tiny pile of dried moss and twigs and put the sharp end to the flame until he held a blackened tip. He drew an elementary map on the leather, indicating the enemy position and numbers, then immediately smothered the tiny fire with the pack, allowing no smoke to escape. He stomped on the ashes and then buried them. Rolling the map up, he tied it with the leather string used for snugging the gauntlet around the wrist.

Dawn was minutes away. He wanted to be back at the enemy camp before they changed guards or noticed the untied boats. There was plenty of light for Nan's sharp eyes so he started the falcon on her way. He hoped she would go in the direction he pointed, not home to Knurlywood Forest. There was the possibility she would simply circle and wait for him, but he had faith she understood her mission. He needed James to get this message or his plan would fail. Reinforcements from the castle were his only hope to stop this second invasion. As the first pale streaks of gray began to illuminate the stillness, he chewed his last piece of bread, watching her fly south. She pumped her wings hard after circling once.

James lay on his bed, staring up at the ceiling. He hadn't been able to sleep much at all lately. He had worked feverishly for days, doing his best to turn the volunteers who kept showing up at the castle gate into a cohesive fighting unit. Some progress had been made, to be sure, but it seemed an uphill battle with so many untrained peasants in the mix. They were willing, but many had no skill with weapons of any kind. If many more arrived, he decided he would set some to rebuilding the burned-out cottages. The castle couldn't house many more.

Training the volunteers for battle was his highest priority once he had the castle inhabitants organized. Fresh from their recent experience, they were eager to comply with his commands. Along with his preparations for defense, he sent hunters out and ordered ovens fired up to smoke the meat they brought in. He conferred with William on what steps to take in order to better withstand another siege. Taking a cue from Niall, he put William in charge of fair distribution if such a siege occurred. The old campaigner was pleased.

All of this progress, however, did not abate his worry over Niall's and Gunder's absence. A thousand things could have gone wrong. Was he prepared to take over permanently if Niall did not return? Would the older soldiers follow him willingly?

James slept in the same cot he had used since coming to the mews. He rather liked being away from the others. His new position of command afforded him more luxury if he wanted it, but he did not. The solitary quiet and familiarity gave him the most peace for thinking through his plans. Without battle experience or schooling, he had only his instincts and common sense for strategizing the next best move. So far, those attributes had worked, but they did not diminish his anxiety.

He rolled over, listing in his head the men he would put in charge of each type of defense. He had studied them closely for days now and was gaining an appreciation for each of their strengths as a soldier. This morning he would inventory their weapons. And what came after that? There would be no going back to sleep now. The castle would be stirring soon. He might as well get up.

A long, lonely caw pierced the still air. Great wings flapped loudly, and a general uproar of unsettled birds changed the peaceful dawn into a menagerie of avian chaos. James threw off the thin summer blanket and instinctively grabbed a gauntlet before entering the mews, an old habit from his years as falconer apprentice. On second thought, he turned back and picked up a dagger too, which he slid into his belt.

There was enough daylight to distinguish each bird, and on first look, he could see nothing out of place. Then a rustling above him drew his attention up to a stone cornice high on the inside wall. There sat the beautiful, extraordinarily large black falcon that he had last seen sitting atop Niall's shoulder. His appreciation of her beauty came to him an instant before the possibilities of why she was here, alone.

Sliding the gauntlet over his hand, he took a deep breath and held out his arm.

"Come, Nan. Did Niall send you? Is he coming too?"

The bird stared at James for a long time, blinking when she heard her name. She trusted James, as far as she would trust any friend of Niall's, from a distance, preferably. However, she understood her mission to deliver the leather roll. Beyond that, she would base herself to no other man. She had been sent by Niall without a signal to return. She had no intention of becoming the property of another. Lifting her great wings, she flew straight at James.

Nan landed on his arm, much heavier than he had imagined, knocking him off balance. He stepped back to catch himself, trying to regain his composure and maintain her confidence in him.

"Good girl," he said, not attempting any other movement until he was sure she meant to stay put. It was then he noticed the thin ribbon of leather, hanging from a small leather roll that was clutched in the claw of the great falcon.

"Am I to have this?" he queried, cautiously reaching for the roll with his free hand, then sliding it out of her clutch. Nan relinquished the message without blinking. When he had it in his other hand, she lifted her wings again and hopped to a nearby stanchion.

"Thank you, Nan."

James quickly took his gauntlet off and pulled the ribbon off the roll. Unrolling it, he stared for only a half minute. The meaning was very clear. He must move quickly.

He looked up to the bird. "You have indeed done well for Rhyaden today." He saluted her and was off to gather men for the mission.

The bird looked around the mews, and then with one great surge she was airborne, leaving the other birds held captive in Cire Castle to wonder at what they had just witnessed. It would be discussed among them for countless generations to come.

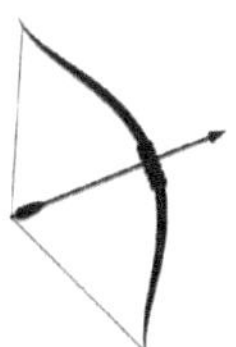

Chapter Twenty-Three

Ben poked at the wood that fueled the ovens for the bakeshop, shoving a piece to one side, then back, adding more, then spreading them out because it was too much. Some types of wood by themselves burned too hot, but others tended to burn too fast. There was a fine balance to be achieved for proper baking. Through the years, his father had shown him all the tricks to achieve uniform heat, as well as the other skills needed to be a good baker, but this morning frustration overruled skill.

"What's the matter, son?" his father asked, coming up behind Ben. He had noted the agitation that had replaced his son's even temper since his return.

"I can't seem to find the right balance of wood," Ben answered, poking sharply at the blaze inside the oven's back door.

"No, I mean, what's really wrong?" his father asked again, taking the poker out of Ben's hands and closing the iron door.

Ben turned and looked into his father's eyes. He could not help the deep sigh that escaped him. He closed his eyes momentarily to ponder exactly how to say what needed to be said.

"I have to go back to Cire, Father. It isn't right for me to stay here while Niall and Gunder fight the invasion." He looked straight into his father's eyes, expecting all kinds of argument and logic, or tears and begging. His father stood looking at him for many long moments, memorizing the width of his son's shoulders, the long legs. Finally, he reached out and put his hand on Ben.

"You have to do what is right for you, Ben. As for defending Knurlysham, Henry Thoralt and Torg have matters well in hand. Your mother and I will take care of things here in the shop, and we'll be waiting right here for you when you return. The only thing I ask, son, is that this time you say goodbye to your mother and Annwyn. It isn't right for you to go a second time without doing so."

"I will. Thank you, Father."

"Get on with you now, I've got to straighten out this fire," Flin groused, covering up his threatened composure. He reopened the oven door so he could work the wood into proper position.

Ben pondered as he walked away. He feared it would not go so easy with his mother, or Annwyn, but now that he had said it once, the worst was past. Feeling lighthearted for the first time in days, he hurried inside to put a pack together and say his goodbyes. He must find Henry too, and offer him the chance to send a message to Niall.

✝ ✝ ✝

"You've already gone once. Do you need to go again?" Annwyn asked an hour later.

"I do. I can't leave Niall and Gunder. We started this together, and I have to finish it with them."

"I understand that, but it's not fair, Ben. I want to help Rhyaden too. I just can't leave my mother and William with my father gone all the time on patrol."

"Taking care of your family is important too. Where's Elan?"

"He snuck off to join the fight. We haven't heard from him since he left. William thinks he's old enough to go too."

Annwyn sat down. Ben knelt down and pushed her tangled hair back from her face. He slowly leaned forward and startled her with a kiss on her cheek. She looked into his face, confusion lighting her eyes.

Before she could say anything, Ben said, "From the games we played as children, I know you already know how to use a knife. Come with me. There is something you need to see."

"What?"

"Come with me. I'll show you where our extra weapons are stored," he said. "It's also a secret place you can hide. I'll find you a dagger or a small knife for protection."

"How will I carry it?"

"If I know you, you'll figure that out."

Ben took Annwyn to his family's barn and showed her the secret entrance to the chamber beneath one of the stalls. There were not many weapons left in the stash. Peering down into the chamber, her eyes grew enormous.

"Your father didn't even know about this?"

"Not until we left for the castle. No one else but Henry Thoralt knows."

Ben eased down the ladder and Annwyn followed after him. They rummaged around and finally found two small knives. He made her choose one. Before they climbed out, he showed her how to close the trapdoor and bolt it from underneath. Once back on top with the door down, other than the straw being displaced, she could not tell there was a door in the floor.

"This was masterfully done," she said, admiring the clever

work.

"Thank you. It took some time working it all out," Ben said. He had noted the look of awe on her face and smiled. "You must not tell anyone, Annwyn," he instructed, kicking the straw back over the chamber entrance, "but use it if you need to." He turned and swept her into his arms before she had a chance to answer. He kissed her again, this time on the mouth.

Annwyn held herself tightly for a second, and then she let go her doubts and allowed herself to melt into Ben's arms. Her long-standing confusion over the two boys shrank in his arms. He was here, he was real.

Ben finally pulled away. "I've got to find Henry now and be off. Keep the knife with you at all times. Promise me."

Annwyn exhaled, holding her heart tightly for fear it would break. "I will, Ben, and you promise me you will come home."

"I will."

† † †

While Ben and Henry discussed the village's defenses, Moralia packed a fresh supply of healing herbs for Ben to take to her son. She looked about, frustrated. Finally, she added some gingerbread biscuits and carefully retied the leather strap. She kissed the package and held it to her heart for a brief moment. What more could be done?

Chapter Twenty-Four

Shouts echoed off the water. A guard sent to relieve the man stationed at the boats came running into camp.

"The boats are loose!"

The captain was quickly roused from his tent. "What do you mean loose?"

"The rope's been slashed. I went to relieve Jim," the guard said. "He's dead. Bled out from his chest but I didn't see no arrow."

"Can you get to the boats?"

"Five are plumb gone. I could see four out in the bay, and three are tangled close to shore."

More shouting could be heard from the water's direction. Layla slid her knife into the sheath on her belt. She fingered the antler that hung around her neck, feeling its smooth ripples.

She did not lose her cool or run to the beach in panic.

"Sergeant, bring five men to secure what boats are close. We'll use one to recover the boats out in the bay," Captain Lodall shouted. He headed toward the beach to supervise.

Layla watched her back. What surprised her was the fact that no charge came. Pacing, she tried to anticipate what would come next. Whoever was out there was extremely smart, that much was clear. She wore the same moss green tunic that provided all of them excellent cover in the forest. She would use it now to her best advantage.

"Tam! Bring the Rhyaden traitor to me."

† † †

Edging closer to where Gunder sat watching all that was going on, Niall planned to take out the three guards, arm Gunder and get back under cover before anyone had time to react. Hearing the woman's last command, he froze. He had hoped men would be sent after the drifting boats, but he had also hoped they would momentarily forget the prisoner. He pulled back behind a tree and lowered his arrow.

Someone barked out orders. The men who stood closest to Gunder grabbed him by the arms and pulled him roughly to his feet. Once they had Gunder standing, they grunted for him to move, and they followed behind him. Gunder stumbled over a vine but managed to regain his footing before going down. The closest guard prodded him to go faster.

Adrenaline coursed through Niall's veins. How many men could he take out before they stopped him? Lynmeer's voice whispered the often repeated lesson. "Never let your enemy have the advantage of your emotions, Niall."

He took a deep breath, whistled the warning chirp of the cricket and retreated into the cover of trees. Three more guards on the outskirts of the camp fell to Niall's silent arrows in the time it took to move Gunder.

The woman with the long braid down her back was carefully positioned with men all around her. Niall suspected she used them as a shield. Her uniform indicated no rank. He circled again, looking for more victims, until the crack of a whip rang out.

Gunder had many strengths and had endured many trials as a young man, but leather against his bare skin was not one of them. He was so surprised by the sharp pain, his anguished cry rang out before he knew what he did. Regret for his lapse in control fell upon him immediately. He drew a ragged breath, resolving to keep quiet no matter what. Another vicious crack sliced through the air. Blood rose, bubbling up along the edges of the welt, but he took the second lashing without a sound.

He closed his eyes and gritted his teeth, shuddering from the cruel scourge. He must not cry out, he must not, it would only bring Niall out of the trees. Straining with all of his might, the strong leather fetters held him fast until he hit the end of his endurance and collapsed.

"Oh, brave one, there is no point in wasting your strength," a woman whispered close to his ear. "You only make it harder on yourself. I can be your friend if you let me. You have a comrade out there, and I bet he would come for you if you would but call to him. Why don't you ask him to come out of the trees? That way we can put an end to this ugly pain. It isn't fair he has forced me to do this to you."

Gunder spat on the ground in front of her feet. She put her head back and laughed out loud, then stepped back. Another crack split the air. Gunder groaned and his knees buckled. The strain of his weight pulled on his arm sockets, sending a shooting pain throughout his body.

She walked forward and bent over to talk again. An

arrow whizzed by her head, so close the sharp edge sliced the outside half inch of her ear and blood spurted across her face. She screamed and dove for cover. The arrow took down a man who stood in front of her.

"Over there, over there!" she yelled, pointing in the direction the arrow had come from. Men converged almost immediately on the spot but found no sign of an archer. A breeze rose up, rippling the branches of the trees, making it impossible to listen for footsteps. Whoever had been there was gone.

Layla drew her knife and pulled his head back. "What a shame. I thought you and I could have had some fun together," she sneered.

"Never," Gunder replied. He felt calm despite the evil he saw in the steel-gray eyes. His plan to infiltrate their ranks had failed, but there must be a way to stop her.

Her sneer turned to a scowl. He could read the vicious intent unmasked in those eyes. Then his eyes fell upon the antler horn, twisted and bicolored. The stag. Gunder knew it was not probable for two different animals to have that exact abnormality. The woods outside their village came to his mind; little Ben and Niall running and laughing ahead of him under the green canopy of leaves, eating warm bread smothered with butter, and wrestling after a swim in the cold waters of Knurly Run.

There was so much he wanted to convey, to warn Niall of Baldonia's plans, their numbers and this sinister woman who thought so fast on her feet. There wasn't time.

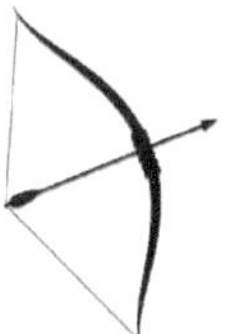

Chapter Twenty-Five

"Brothers" echoed loudly through the woods, ringing in Niall's ears, ending abruptly in a gargled bubble of blood as the woman's knife slit Gunder's throat. Niall was shielded by trees, but he saw the scowl on her face. He saw the evil in her eyes, and he knew the moment Gunder knew: she relished the kill.

Gunder slid heavily to the forest floor. Niall froze in disbelief. Never had he considered he would be unsuccessful at freeing his friend. Never had he considered Gunder would sacrifice himself to save him.

When the barrage of arrows descended on the Baldonian camp, Layla dove beneath Gunder's large frame, pulling his warm body over hers. One of his arrows sliced Tam's left arm, but by the sheer luck of turning to see where Layla had fallen, the point did not penetrate.

Others were not so lucky. Seven fell to instant death from Niall's arrows. Through the fog of his anger, he looked for the dark-haired one but could not spot her. Then a cry went up from a Baldonian archer. Niall's position had been spotted.

"Go now, Niall," the Knurly tree he stood behind

whispered.

He shook his head in defiance of the words, but the action served to clear the haze from his brain.

"You cannot save your friend, Niall, and you will not save your kingdom if you are dead. You must go now."

For the Baldonian soldier who reached the tree first, the empty space he found on the back side was astonishing. He saw movement behind another tree, but he blinked and then he wasn't sure. Years later when he recounted the tale of the great battle to his grandchildren, he described it as magic. One moment he saw a man standing there shooting arrows, the next instant the man was gone.

The shock of seeing the woman slaughter Gunder unhinged Niall. All those years of training, all that he thought he was, gone in one bloody instant. Once he was safely out of arrow range, he began to run without stealth, and he did not stop until he could no longer get air into his scorched lungs. The men who looked for him had stopped miles earlier. They were not fueled by the horror of watching their best friend endure such a vile and unjust end.

Niall's running slowed to a walk, and finally he bent over with his hands on his knees and sucked in air. Unbalanced, he had no idea where he was. Gunder's last word echoed over and over again in his head. He couldn't stop it. He understood what Gunder meant when he yelled, but now he couldn't stop the voice in his head from repeating it again and again. When he closed his eyes, the image of the whip slicing open Gunder's skin was as vivid now as it had been hours earlier.

The image of the woman's monstrous scowl brought Niall's stomach into his throat. Retching until nothing remained to come up, the dry heaves that followed caused an ache that tore at his guts. Wails of anguish spilled out. Stumbling away from his vomit, he collapsed in a sodden heap and slept.

On the following day, trees gave way occasionally to open meadows as he meandered in no certain direction. He skirted villages, not knowing if they were under siege or friendly. Saving Rhyaden no longer mattered. His father's training reminded him he should resupply himself with arrows if he was to eat, but he did not care if he ate.

Headed in a southerly direction on the third day, he heard the swift water slapping rocks before he could see it. Surprised by the size of the river, he knew it must be the Rhy.

Clothes and all, Niall waded into the cold water. Wishing to be cleansed of the nightmare, he let himself sink deeper. Another desperate swim came to mind. Funny, he thought, there was no reason to come up this time, no one to save. He slowly let the breath out of his lungs, watching the bubbles float upward. Pressure began to build in his chest. He tried to ignore it by closing his eyes, but behind his eyelids, his mother's face floated in front of him, beckoning him to rise, pulling at him until he popped above the water.

His fingers shriveled and his body numb from the cold water, he climbed up on the bank, took his clothes off and spread them out to dry. He shook his head at the foolishness of getting his boots wet, propping them upside down to drain the water. He lay naked on a patch of grass, watching the sun finish its arc for the day. As dusk began to settle in, he dressed and pulled the wet boots back on. Listening to his stomach growl, he finally went in search of something to eat, watching for wood that would make good arrows.

Tubers were plentiful in the oak and linden trees. He found a decent stick for digging and went to work. When his stomach was full, he leaned back against a tree. He felt the pouch in his pocket and pulled it out, rubbing the stone between his fingers. Comforted by the soothing action, he eventually returned it to its pouch and pulled out his knife. Rummaging in his quiver for the extra tips, He began the task of whittling new shafts. When these last tips were gone, he wouldn't be able to make more arrows without finding a village large enough to house a smithy.

He made a fire and worked a second shaft.

"What's the point?" Niall asked the dancing flames. He rolled over to his side and let sleep overtake his bitterness.

Annwyn's face smiled at him from behind the glowing embers, and her laughter rang out through the trees. Her honey-colored braids bounced up and down. Niall got up and followed her gangly gait through the trees.

She was too skinny, he thought, but he wanted to kiss her anyway. Ahead of him, she darted behind a large Knurly tree, but when he got around it, Ben was standing there, holding her hand. They both smiled, beckoning him to join them. Behind them stood a large dragon, shaking his head. Niall pulled back, frightened by the creature.

"Come with me," the dragon said.

Niall woke. Sweat glistened on his forehead. "I need to find Lynmeer," he stated to no one, staring up into the leafy trees. There was only a small rustling in the early morning breeze, no words of encouragement he secretly hoped he would hear. He assumed then that the trees had already heard of his failure to save the kingdom and wanted nothing more to do with him.

Lynmeer lived somewhere beyond the old castle. He called it Ayhrland but had said very little about it over the years, and Niall had not asked. It hadn't seemed important, but now he wished he had inquired more. He sighed and set about finishing the task of making new shafts, skillfully fitting them with his remaining tips. He looked about for feathers to use as fletching, preferring goose as his father had taught him, but he had to be satisfied with what he found for now.

Following the Rhy farther downstream, he came upon a tributary joining from the northeast. He stopped and gazed upstream along the fair-sized brook. The ground was rocky, and very possibly not the right way at all, but it headed in the general direction he thought he needed to go. If he stayed close to the brook, he had easy access to water and game. With new arrows, he was able to hunt again so he would not go hungry.

Following the water, he had a direction to go. That was something. Time passed in no connection to how far he had gone, or how far he had yet to go. The steps turned into miles as his thoughts drifted. His entire life had been for nothing. All the lessons, all the years following his tutor through the woods came to naught. He couldn't save Gunder, the finest friend anyone could ever have.

Trees at the edge of a large clearing rustled sweetly, and birds called back and forth to each other. Stone walls on a low rise in the middle of the open area indicated a foundation of magnificent proportions. His jaw dropped. It had to be the ancient castle where the famous King Valdorn lived and died. Cut stone walls still towered high in places. The scarred foundation was overgrown with moss and woody vines. He walked slowly toward the once proud home of   royalty.

One small tree grew in the middle of the largest room, perhaps the great hall, Niall thought, as he made his way past crumbling rubble to stand in the doorway. A few charred timbers butting out from the wall indicated where a staircase led to the second floor, but little else remained. Heat and flames had consumed the rest. Curiously, someone had drug a large stone from the wall and placed it under the tenacious tree, as if needing a place to sit and remember.

Back outside, Niall walked the grounds, surveying the smooth areas where barns had stood, and what must have been small homes occupied by the king's men. He made his way east toward the line of trees that lined the brook he had followed here. Thirsty, he turned toward the brook and tripped over a small boulder. Tumbling forward, he slammed into sharp rocks that cut open his chin. Blood began dripping immediately.

"Ouch!"

"What did you think was going to happen? You aren't paying a bit of attention to where you're going," the nearest Knurly tree admonished.

Anger at being mocked, followed by laughter, spilled out of Niall. "I suppose I wasn't, was I?" he replied. Picking himself up, he dusted off and gingerly touched the wound. With no pack, he had no herbs to stop the bleeding.

"I'm Niall Thoralt. Pleased to meet you. I don't suppose there's any Toeffer nearby?" he asked hopefully, looking up at the tree.

"Poeffer perhaps? I'm Laversham by the way. Nice to meet you."

"Toeffer leaves are good for healing, stopping bleeding and such," he explained, thinking perhaps the name was different on this side of the kingdom.

"There is a powerful plant called Poeffer, but I would not recommend it. Most that was started here has been pulled out." The tree shook itself a bit, and then the leaves settled down.

Niall began walking, wondering what exactly the tree meant. It would be a good thing to have some Toeffer in his quiver for just such circumstances as this. Presently, he found a small patch of a plant that looked similar to Toeffer, although the leaves were smaller.

He picked a few leaves and walked back to the tree that had spoken earlier, holding one leaf against his chin. Hoping the tree was in a good mood, he settled down to talk. The bleeding stopped straightaway, but before he could think what subject to begin their conversation with, he became lightheaded, and a minute later it felt as if he were swimming in shafts of light streaming through the trees. It was all he could do to stay upright as he leaned against the obliging tree. Although it was the middle of the morning, too early for a nap, his fingers slowly released their grip, and the leaves in his hand fluttered away in the breeze.

A century earlier, Aleah had realized the deadly potential of the new hybrid that she developed from the medicinal Toeffer parent plant. Horrified, she quickly pulled all of the Poeffer plants that she found in Rhyaden, but unbeknownst to her, a few seeds with the hallucinogenic characteristics had already fallen to the ground.

Vivid dreams visited Niall while he slept. Intense color showered down on him, and he reached out to touch the falling embers of light. One particular bright star caught his attention, dancing in front of him, enticing him to follow. He got up and tried to walk, but the ground met his foot before he set it down and he stumbled. Catching himself with his hands, he crawled instead.

The light danced ahead of him, just out of his reach.

"Where are we going?"

Laughter answered. Was that Winnie? "Ben!" he called, and then Gunder's face appeared before him. "Come on, Niall, hurry. You don't want to miss this."

"Gunder! I thought you were dead. How did you escape? Wait, you're going too fast. I'm coming. Wait!"

The face of his friend melted away, but the light still danced in the forest a little ways ahead. His hands did not feel the prickly sting of nettles or the wild rose thorns that he crawled through. Pine needles crunched beneath him as he made his way toward the pinprick of remaining light. He didn't give up until he crashed into a large boulder, teetering on the bank of the stream.

Chapter Twenty-Six

Niall woke with a horrendous headache and no idea where he was. Amazingly, his quiver was still around his shoulders and his bow lay nearby, but his hands bled from numerous scratches and his pants were badly ripped at the knees.

"That can't have been Toeffer." He groaned. He sat up and leaned against the huge boulder that had kept him from falling into the brook. When he felt able, he eased down and got a drink in the clear water.

"Please, can you tell me where I am?" he said to the nearest Knurly tree a short time later.

"You are where you are," the tree scoffed.

"But, I mean, where would that be?"

"Right here," the tree replied, clearly amused by his own cleverness.

Niall decided to take another tack. "Do you know a man named Lynmeer?"

Entertaining himself by creating riddles was the tree's favorite pastime, and it wasn't often he got the chance to show off. His friends nearby had long since tired of hearing his riddles. This last question, however, changed his demeanor. He took on a more serious tone. "Who is asking?"

"I am Niall Thoralt, of Knurlysham. I'm looking for Ayhrland. Lynmeer was my tutor and I need to find him."

The tree's branches rippled as it stretched higher. Leaves fell to the ground from the unexpected straightening, and the lower branches tried to sweep them away.

"How very good to meet you, Niall Thoralt. I am Paversham. You may call me Paversham, of course. May I call you Niall?"

"Of course, Paversham, nice to meet you. You don't happen to be related to Professor Faversham do you?"

"Distant cousin. The old coot is still well, is he? Hadn't heard news from that neck of the woods in ages."

"Yes, well, he is fine I believe. As I was saying, I've been told Ayhrland is near the old castle. Is it anywhere close to here?"

"Absolutely, yes, it most certainly is," the tree gushed, so happy to be able to oblige Niall with useful information. Lynmeer's whereabouts, and his latest student this past decade, had been well talked of.

"Well, where might it be? Can you point me in the right direction?"

"Certainly." The tree stood still, reaching as straight and tall as it could.

Niall waited.

"Where?"

"Oh, how silly of me. I'm so sorry, Niall Thoralt of Knurlysham. Here, it is right here. You are at Gaxdorn Gate, the entrance to Ayhrland."

Gaxdorn Gate? Niall had not heard that name, and he looked intently around the area surrounding the spot on which he stood. Two huge boulders were framed by towering green trees, clumps of birch filled in the middle levels and abundant berry bushes dotted the lower region. Watercress thrived in verdant clumps along the water's edge. Colorful pebbles of every hue paved the brook, sparkling in the clear water. Idyllic and peaceful to be sure, but there was nothing here out of the ordinary, nothing to indicate a gate or entrance of any kind. The proud tree stood at attention, smiling down on the young man, so pleased to be able to assist him in his quest.

Niall sighed and looked up at the tree. "I'm afraid I need a little more help. I don't see the entrance you speak of."

"Oh my . . . oh dear, I am being so very thoughtless," the tree blathered, so caught up by Niall's celebrity, he was totally oblivious to the obvious. "You must follow the water to its source and pass between the large boulders."

"Thank you, sir. You have been most helpful," Niall said graciously, glad to finally be getting somewhere. He walked out and around on the west side of the house-sized boulder that blocked the way north, only to be confronted by more immense boulders and trees on the upper side. Once there, though he couldn't find the brook. He turned south, down the other side, around similarly sized boulders until he was again at the small brook on the opposite side of where he started. He concluded the water must come from a spring between the rocks, somewhere he couldn't see from where he stood.

He took off his quiver and leaned it and the bow against a rock. He took off his boots this time, and held them under his arm, bracing himself against the cold water. "Biscuit!" he mouthed. Shivering, he wondered if the tree was playing games with him. Regardless of his dubiousness, he walked upstream in the middle of the narrow brook toward the big rocks. Sure enough, there the water bubbled up out of a hidden spring. Clear, cold water gushed toward him.

Directly behind the spring were two immense boulders, just touching each other. The closer he came, the more he felt a tingle in his pocket. The feeling excited him. This must be the right way, despite its looking too narrow to pass through.

He stepped out of the water and put his boots back on. The rock grew hot in his pocket as he got closer to the boulders, which now glowed, and there was a loud rumbling in the ground. He looked down, wishing to steady the swaying landscape. Widening his stance, he looked up to see there was now room to step between the boulders. Inside his pocket, the stone pulsed, and then he thought he heard soft music. The sound drew him forward. Once he was through the opening, the earth rumbled again behind him.

Puzzled, he turned in a complete circle. He was no longer standing in familiar surroundings. He feared he was once again under the spell of the Toeffer lookalike. For starters, water emerged from a cold spring, just as it did on the other side of the boulders, but here it appeared to go slightly uphill, merrily gurgling as it ran. He looked further, only to be more confused. Nothing made sense. He could hear music, but it wasn't singing, perhaps a harp, he thought, but he really couldn't place the origin. He asked the nearest tree where he was, but no answer was forthcoming.

"Ayhrland," he said aloud. It had to be. Lynmeer had never talked openly about his home, but enough had been said in unguarded moments for Niall to know of its existence. That much at least was comforting. He followed the brook uphill, not knowing any other way to find Lynmeer than to go looking for him.

The countryside was serene. Light reflected a rainbow of

colors in small pockets all along the pebbly path that he followed. He did not see any birds flitting past, but with that realization, a lovely harmony of bird calls began.

Niall felt peace, the first since Gunder's death. There was no sun arcing across the sky to aid in telling time, so he stopped when he wanted and kept going when he was rested. The calm was intoxicating. His heart began the arduous task of healing. When he slept no dreams disturbed him, and he was surprised each time he woke to find he wasn't hungry.

He took notice of the world he now walked in. There were no trees to be seen except Knurlywood, and all of the ground plants were unfamiliar. A few reminded him of some he knew back home, having similar leaves though smaller, but one lesson in the effects of that kind of difference had been enough. He refrained from even touching them.

The path led through an area where rows of plants stretched out parallel to each other. "It must be a farm of some sort," Niall thought, though he did not recognize anything grown there, and it appeared overgrown and untended.

Whistling a few notes of his own, he stopped at the sudden stillness that abruptly cut the air. When he stopped whistling, the music began again. That was odd. He let out a short tweet and the music stopped again.

"Lynmeer?" he called. No answer broke the stillness. "Lynmeer, it's Niall."

"He knows who you are," a small voice said.

Niall jumped. Ready to bolt in the other direction if the creature moved, he held his ground as he eyed the small thing. He was sure it had not been standing there a moment ago. Large dark eyes followed his eyes. It made no movement toward him. Niall's heartbeat slowed to normal.

Whatever it was, he decided it actually looked rather lovable, other than its scowl. Sharp teeth protruded from an overbite, or possibly they were shown on purpose. The fellow's coloring was unusual, tiny scales the color of water one second, and then celery, and then the sky, but definitely not the color of flesh. The pointed ears were enormous for its small stature, which was probably no more than three feet tall, if that. It stood on two feet and wore a blue plaid vest. Most incredible of all, of course, it talked.

"Who are you?"

"My name is Ecirp. I am Lynmeer's . . . assistant, if you will. You are not supposed to be here. He is not pleased at all."

"I'm sorry, but I need to see him."

"That is not up to you. How did you get through the gate?"

"I'm not sure. The rocks widened enough for me to pass through, but I'm not going home until I see him so I would appreciate it very much if you would be so kind as to point the way."

"Humph. No wonder you were difficult to train," the creature snuffed.

"I beg your pardon?"

"Never mind. Follow me."

Ecirp turned and walked away in a rocking shuffle. Following behind, Niall could see it had a short pointed tail that wagged from side to side. He rather enjoyed watching the odd little creature—from a safe distance. They left the path and meandered in a zigzag pattern that led him to believe he was being purposely confused. The lack of sun made it difficult to orient himself.

The creature's short legs were easy to keep up with, and before too long, they entered a quiet glen surrounded by Knurly trees. Numerous wood easels were set up with canvases in the lush grassy middle. Most were completed paintings, but a few were in the beginning stages. On one sat a portrait of a falcon. The black coloring was unmistakable. It was Nan! Niall glanced at the others. All of the pictures were of birds.

"My dear Niall. How are you?"

Chapter Twenty-Seven

Niall turned to the familiar voice and staggered back a step. At just over six feet tall, Niall was less than half the height of the dragon standing before him. An encounter with such a large beast had the distinct possibility of not turning out well. He shook his head to clear out the cobwebs. This had to be leftover effects of the Toeffer lookalike. He pinched his arm and it hurt—not reassuring in the least.

"I'm looking for Lynmeer," Niall said, swallowing to rid his throat of what had become a hard lump. "I'm Niall Thoralt of Knurlysham." He tried to stand straight and not sway in front of the dragon, whose tiny scales made a dazzling iridescent sheen across its deep purple hide.

The dragon sighed. "Hello, Niall. You've had a rough go of it, I see. Would you like to have some tea and talk about it?" The familiar voice was reassuring.

Niall blinked. He looked up into the dragon's eyes and saw himself reflected back.

"I don't understand."

"Let me help you with that," the dragon replied, shape-shifting into the white-haired Lynmeer Niall was familiar with.

"Lynmeer!"

"Yes, Niall, your tutor is actually a dragon, a very old and tired dragon."

This was not what Niall expected to hear, though he didn't really know what he expected. Perhaps he was dreaming after all.

"No, you're not dreaming, Niall. You have come to my home, Ayhrland."

Niall took that in. "Can anyone come here?"

"No, one must be a dragon to come here."

"Then how did I come here?"

"I believe you carry a stone your mother gave you, do you not? A stone that she used to wear."

"Yes," Niall replied, pulling the pouch from his pocket.

"That stone is actually a bit of me, melted by fire a long time ago. It allowed you entry."

Niall stared down at the pouch, fingering the stone inside. "Are there more dragons?" he asked, his eyes darting around the glen.

"There used to be, but I am the only one left I know of."

"I, I wanted to see you, but . . . wait, does my mother know you are a dragon?" Niall's mind was shifting rapidly.

"No, she does not."

Niall nodded. "I failed, Lynmeer. I failed Rhyaden. Gunder was killed, and I ran away. The tree said to go, so I did, but then—I didn't stop, I just kept running." The words trailed away. Gunder's face flashed before him. Niall's chest heaved, and tears spilled over.

"Let your tears out, Niall. That is how your soul cleanses itself. You won't ever forget the ugly sights you have seen, but you will heal from them in time."

Niall shuddered and wiped his face on his sleeve.

"There is no failure in learning a lesson and moving forward," Lynmeer continued, "but it does take some courage." He paused. "And so now, here you are. What do you think you ought to do next?"

"I . . . I don't know. I need your advice."

"I'm afraid there is little advice I can give you now, Niall. Your future is a decision only you can make."

"But—"

"There is that word 'but' again. You always did have trouble remembering that it is a most inappropriate way of beginning a sentence," his teacher admonished, his head tilted to the side.

The student let out his breath, and his shoulders relaxed. A small grin lit his tear-stained face.

"Uh, umm," a tiny voice interrupted.

"Oh, my, where are my manners?" Lynmeer said. "Niall, this is Ecirp, my best, and as it were, only friend in Ayhrland. Ecirp, this is Niall, my latest student."

Ecirp, now wearing a bowtie to accompany his vest, bowed and put forward a tiny hand. Niall grinned and followed suit. "So nice to make your acquaintance, Ecirp."

The little fingers felt rubbery. Niall tried to make eye contact, but Ecirp did not look up. His eyes were trained on Niall's fingernails, his aquiline nose pinched and one brow slightly higher than the other, as if he smelled something most distasteful. Niall looked at the dirt beneath his nails. There was nothing he could do about it now. He straightened back up.

"Ecirp, my dear, would you mind so very much getting us a spot of tea?" Lynmeer asked. Niall looked to see if Ecirp minded serving tea to a person with dirty nails, but the creature was gone.

He turned to Lynmeer, his puzzlement quickly turning to

amazement. Ecirp stood beside Lynmeer, laying out a tray of tea and biscuits on a nearby table.

"I brought these back from Rhyaden," Lynmeer said, "and Ecirp has copied the recipe."

"Thank you, but I'm actually not hungry," Niall said, setting himself down on a chair that had appeared at the same time as the tea.

"Of course you aren't hungry, but suit yourself," the small creature huffed, handing Niall his cup of tea.

"Ecirp, please refrain from being rude," Lynmeer admonished.

Ecirp's ears flattened, and his coloring deepened to pea green. Niall looked away and feigned interest in his ripped pant leg.

"Your paintings are wonderful," Niall said a moment later. He set his teacup down, got up and went to the closest one to truly scrutinize the work. The accuracy was astounding. Moving past each one, he recognized them, though he could not name each bird.

"Thank you, Niall. I do try to remember them as best I can."

"By the way," Niall said, suddenly remembering a question in need of an answer, "before coming through . . . what was it called, Gaxdorn Gate?"

"Yes, that is where you entered."

"I had a wound on my chin, and I put some Toeffer on it, at least I thought it was Toeffer though the leaves were smaller, but I had a most unpleasant reaction."

"That was most likely a deadly cousin of Toeffer, called Poeffer, certainly not the medicinal variety you are used to. Did you find it outside Gaxdorn Gate?" When Niall nodded affirmatively, he continued, "I feared a bit had escaped. I would stay away from it in the future were I you. I imagine you had some rather vivid dreams, did you not?"

"Quite."

"Well, ingesting it would have been quite the end of you."

"Good to know," Niall said, his eyes wide. He moved on to view another painting. When he came to the last one, he realized there had been only silence from his tutor for quite some time, not the usual lecture. He looked over to find Lynmeer snoozing.

He returned to his chair and his tea and was surprised to find it still steaming in the cup. Taking a sip, he tried to identify the flavor. There was a nuttiness to it, but he couldn't quite put his finger on it. Settling back comfortably into the seat, which rather formed itself around him, he looked about to pass the time until his friend awoke. Unaware of when it happened, he too fell asleep.

Ecirp tapped his finger as he watched the suspicious interloper sleep. In the preceding century, no student had passed through Gaxdorn Gate. What had brought him to Ayhrland? There must be something, for the boy's mother, his grandmother and his great-grandfather had also been students of Lynmeer and they had never come here. There was the possibility that Lynmeer himself had told the boy of Ayhrland, but that didn't explain this human's ability to pass through the gate.

Niall opened his eyes but dared not move. No longer sitting in the grassy glen, he was inside what looked to be a large cave smoothly polished in a glossy finish that highlighted the many colors of minerals in the rock. Numerous bird paintings adorned the walls. He raised his head and looked about. His eyes widened in bewilderment at first, and then awe. The wall opposite him was lined with shelves, top to bottom. Leather-bound journals tied with thin leather laces were stacked hither and thither on the floor, on chairs and on the shelves. Candles in brass holders gave off a warm glow, but he noticed none had flames. His eyebrows knitted together as he tried to comprehend light without a flame.

"Lynmeer has gone for an evening stroll. He shall return shortly," Ecirp chirped like proper waitstaff. He stood in the doorway.

Niall turned his head around to find the little fellow staring at him. "Is this his home?" he asked, sitting up.

"Since no other dragon lives in Ayhrland, I suppose it would be considered thus," Ecirp returned rather sarcastically, too late in remembering Lynmeer's admonishment earlier. In a more conciliatory tone he added, "We both live here, at least during inclement weather—of which there is none in Ayhrland, but, however, I suppose there is the possibility of inclement weather, so just in case, we have this abode for those times, and it comes in handy that way, or any other way, I suppose too."

Niall blinked as he tried to follow along with the little creature's words. Even though he feared his judgment might still be clouded from the Poeffer, he wasn't about to ask for further explanation. Fortunately, at that moment the purple dragon came lumbering through another entrance, a large, tunnel-like affair that seemed to open out of nowhere, or at least Niall hadn't noticed it until now.

"Oh, you're awake. Splendid then, time for tea. Of course, I think it is always time for tea, loving it as I do. Ecirp, will you do us the honor of serving us some? Yes, then, thank you so very much. I see the two of you have been getting along quite famously, and there you have it, the beauty of Ayhrland, everyone gets along wonderfully here, never any tension, although there isn't actually anyone else here to create said tension. Well, bother, and there aren't any birds either. I do love birds. Have you seen my dabbling in art, Niall?"

"I have," Niall answered, surprised at tea again already, though he supposed one as large as a dragon could have it all day long. "They are splendid. Sometimes I think they could fly right off the canvas they are so lifelike," he answered truthfully, looking at the closest canvas.

Lynmeer stretched his wings until the tips shook. Niall saw an old scar on one wing where the scales had been scraped off. Lynmeer's eyelashes uncurled to the ends and then rolled back up. He arched his neck to one side and then the other. Satisfactorily stretched, he changed into Niall's tutor in the blink of an eye and sat down in the chair opposite, hooking his cane over the arm of the comfortable deep cushion. The tea was laid out, and he motioned for Niall to join him. The ease with which he transformed was astounding. Niall was spellbound for some moments, but he eventually shook his head clear and came to the table.

"How do you do that?" Niall asked.

"Do what, my dear?"

"Change from dragon to man."

"I think it and it happens."

"Magic?"

"I suppose that is what some might want to call it; however, I am simply shifting my shape from one to another, which isn't magic, it is an ability. Now, my dear boy, what can I do for you? You have obviously come here for a reason, and you need to articulate that reason to me."

"At home, you knew what I was thinking, sometimes before I did."

"We are not in Rhyaden, are we now?" Lynmeer said, looking over his spectacles. "Why don't you simply begin."

"Why didn't you ever tell me you are a dragon?" Niall asked.

"Dragons tend to upset people. That was not my purpose as your teacher."

Ecirp quietly laid out the tea and a platter of blueberry scones. He looked up to Lynmeer, who smiled in return.

"Knowing how very much I enjoy my tea, Ecirp keeps the pantry well stocked for the occasion. So very kind, I'd say," the tutor replied, looking over at his little companion. Their obvious fondness for each other had grown through the last century together. "When I am gone to Rhyaden, he endures the time here alone, so it is very kind of him indeed to replicate some of the pleasures I enjoy while there."

"Very kind," Niall agreed. "Why don't you go with him, Ecirp?" he asked, looking over to Ecirp, "then you wouldn't have to be . . . alone."

Lynmeer's assistant was nowhere to be seen. Glancing back to Lynmeer, his tutor simply shrugged. "What else would you like to know?"

"Why did Mother and I have a dragon for a tutor?"

"I made a promise a long time ago—a promise to look after your family, and Rhyaden."

"How long have you been looking after my family?"

"For a century now, I suppose."

"Wow. Dragons live a long time then."

Lynmeer smiled. "Yes, we do."

Niall took a deep breath. "Gunder was killed by the Baldonians. It was my fault . . . and so, I don't seem to know what to do now." His head drooped, the image of Gunder's last moments resonating once again, but this time at least, tears did not spill over.

"I would like to ask you a few questions, Niall, if you don't mind."

"Of course not."

"Did you force Gunder to go with you to Cire Castle?"

"No."

"Did you make Baldonia invade Rhyaden?"

"No."

"Then how is it possibly your fault that Gunder is dead?"

"I tried to save him, but I failed. She slit his throat."

"There, you said it yourself. SHE slit his throat. You went after him, and you tried to save him, and that is the only thing that mattered to Gunder. Your friend wanted to save you, as much as you wanted to save him. Is there a reason why he shouldn't have had that opportunity?"

Niall's eyes were glued to the rock floor. "No."

"Perhaps he had a glimpse of the bigger picture, Niall. Rhyaden is still in danger."

The room was quiet.

"Think on it. Right now, though, I believe you need to get a good night's rest. We'll talk more in the morning. Good night, Niall." Lynmeer stood and took up his cane.

Ecirp returned and the tea was whisked away. He showed Niall to a small room that had a comfortable bed and iron hooks sticking out of the rock walls to hang his clothes on.

Niall woke the next day feeling wonderfully rested. He

pulled on his pants and found they were mended quite expertly, so much so, a person could not tell they had been ripped. His shirt was clean and his mud-caked boots shined like new. Sitting on the edge of the bed, he looked down at his hands. There was not a speck of dirt beneath the nails.

A new life, he thought—I shall start a new life right here with Lynmeer. Surely they could use the services of a strong young lad. There had to be plenty of tasks they could find for him to do.

Niall was still not hungry, but he ate from the platters of delicacies laid out by Ecirp, who was wearing a purple plaid vest this morning. He hoped that by eating, he would not annoy the little creature further, if that was possible.

"Lynmeer, I had a thought when I awoke this morning."

"You did? How gratifying. I rather imagine a thoughtless start to the day would be quite vexing," the dragon replied. "Any of those particular thoughts you'd care to share?"

"Well, yes, I wondered how you would feel about my staying here with you?"

"Ahh!" Lynmeer leaned back in his chair and gazed at Niall. "I do believe it is time for me to tell you a story from my past. If you are finished with your breakfast, let us go for a walk, shall we?"

They walked as they had in Niall's school days, only now they walked to music. A sweet soft melody played while they followed the stream that ran bending first one way and then another, regardless of topography. Lynmeer's cane tapped in time to the music that serenaded them as they strolled along.

"In times past, there was another dragon who looked after Rhyaden with me. Her name was Aleah. She was the most beautiful dragon, lavender in color, and sweet as honeysuckle," the dragon said, staring at the path ahead of them. "She loved Rhyaden, fiercely. Oh, she loved astrology, agronomy, art, just everything you can imagine, but Rhyaden was her joy. Her experiments are why there are Knurly trees and Toeffer in Rhyaden."

"The talking trees?" Niall asked. Lynmeer nodded.

"What happened to her?" Niall asked.

"She started a project to make a map of all of Rhyaden," Lynmeer began, looking off into the distance, "to make it as a human would, rather than a dragon."

"Why?" Niall asked.

"The challenge of it, I suppose. A dragon may use all the magic he wants in Ayhrland, but not in Rhyaden."

"Why not?"

"There was an edict for human rights, passed many centuries ago. It banned the use of magic in the humans' world. Those who disobey suffer."

"Suffer how?"

"It ages us—dramatically."

A memory prickled Niall's brain. He silently mulled over the words. A few steps further and his thoughts aligned. "Years ago, when I was swimming across Knurly Run to save young William, it was you that came up alongside me, wasn't it? After that day, your hair was white."

Lynmeer stopped beneath a Knurly tree and placed both hands on his cane. He nodded. "Yes, Niall, it was me."

"You saved my life, as well as William's. Thank you."

"You are most welcome. Now, back to my story. One day, Aleah pricked her finger, and a drop of her blood fell onto the map. It landed on Gaxdorn Gate, and as it dried, the map began to glow. She loved the effect."

"Why did it glow?"

"I suppose because it held a bit of dragon."

"That would be special!" Niall exclaimed.

"Yes, and, ironically, it was thus a magical map after all."

"What happened to it?"

"The map was lost."

"Lost?"

"There was another dragon back then. His name was Moordoon . . ."

Chapter Twenty-Eight

"So, now you know how I came to be Rhyaden's last dragon."

"I am so very sorry."

Lynmeer's head sagged. "Thank you, Niall. It was a long time ago, and yet losing Aleah is never far from my thoughts. The point I was making, however, is that if given the chance, Moordoon would have ruined Rhyaden, just as he poisoned the people of Baldonia by pitting them against each other for his own sport. I made a vow in Aleah's memory to never let that happen in Rhyaden. When I am gone, the lessons must not be lost. Someone has to be ready to lead and protect Rhyaden. Baldonia's king wishes to take Rhyaden's throne for himself." He looked closely at his student. "Surely you do not want Gunder to have died for nothing."

†††

Moralia tossed and turned, her fingers stroking her neck where the stone used to lie. Dragon essence had seeped through her skin over her lifetime of wearing the powerful stone. During the night, she dreamed of Cire Castle, though she had never been there, and a second castle that lay in ruins. She woke up sure that Niall as well as their kingdom was in trouble. She wished for a way to contact Lynmeer. His advice had always given her a sense of calm.

Gazing down at Henry in the still darkness of predawn, she traced an outline of his face in the air, stopping in particular on his lips, drawn up in a half smile, as if he were enjoying one of his dry jokes. She blew him a soft kiss and silently left the cottage, leaving behind a note to explain why she had gone.

Henry was still sleeping when Moralia tightened the saddle's cinch and then tied on a blanket for a bedroll behind the saddle. She slipped a bridle on the patient black mare and led her quietly out of the barn and down the road. Once out of sight, she mounted and began the long journey toward Cire Castle.

Riding on horseback alone was highly unusual in these troubled times, so Moralia skirted the villages and occasional cottage that cropped up along the road to Cire. She ate sparingly from her pack, adding tubers and greens from the forest to make her supplies last for the long journey.

Reaching Cire late in the afternoon a week later, Moralia dismounted and carefully hobbled the mare at the edge of a small clearing a safe distance from the castle. She was stiff and sore after a week in the saddle. Sensing turmoil around her, she circled the castle on foot, trying to ascertain its state of affairs. She saw guards atop the castle ramparts, but it did not seem to be under siege. The usual comings and goings of commerce and village life were nonexistent, however. The sight of the burned-out cottages made her shiver.

Deciding the best course was patience, Moralia hid herself in the woods where she could watch. The afternoon drifted lazily.

Squirrels and birds chattered endlessly now that the heat was retreating. Leaning against a tree, she closed her eyes to listen to the sing-song sounds of the forest at sundown. Her head jerked up, aware suddenly of voices in the distance. A tired-looking, bedraggled contingent of men trudged toward the protective spires of Cire. Rhyaden fighters were returning to regroup and resupply themselves.

Moralia looked carefully at each man in line, watching for Niall's stride. One young man at the back caught her eye. He had a limp and did not carry a bow. A shock of dark hair fell over his unshaven face.

"Ben!"

Moralia ran from her hiding place behind thick brambles and ferns toward the startled men. Several archers dropped to their knees and raised their weapons. No one loosed their arrow, too stunned at the sight of a woman encumbered by a long dress dashing across the open field. She stumbled in the long grass, caught herself, and yelled Ben's name again.

"Mrs. Thoralt?" Ben asked. His disbelief at seeing her in this place so far from Knurlysham was plastered all over his face. He stepped out of line and caught her before she bowled him over. The others looked at each other.

"Ben, is it you? Are you all right? Where's Niall?"

The men edged closer, their worn faces quizzical.

"Yes, it's me, I'm fine. A little bunged up, but I'm fine," he answered.

"Where is Niall?"

"We don't know," Ben said softly. "Ahhh!" he moaned, staggering from the pain in his leg.

"Ben! Are you all right? Let me help you," Moralia cried, grabbing his arm as he sank.

"I'll be fine, I just need a moment," he said. "Gunder was captured," he continued when the pain eased. "Niall sent a message for help, but when our men got there, he was gone . . . and Gunder was dead. No one knows where he went, or how. The fighting since has been fierce. I took an arrow in my leg so I haven't been much help. We've come back to resupply and treat the wounded."

Moralia sank to the ground next to Ben. "Gunder?"

"Yes, he . . ." Ben began. The look of anguish on her face made him stop. She didn't need to hear the gruesome details. "I'm sorry, Mrs. Thoralt."

"Oh, my dear Ben. You've been through so much." Silent tears slipped down her cheeks. She reached out and touched his face. "I can help. Do you still have the package I sent with you for Niall?"

"Yes."

"Good. I brought some also. I must go get my horse and my bag." She started to get up.

Ben reached out and grabbed her arm. "Where is Henry?" he asked. Surely she had not come alone.

"Henry is at home," she replied, matter of factly. "He is protecting the village. I came to find Niall."

"Alone? There are Baldonian soldiers everywhere."

"I am aware. I'll be back quickly." With that said, she pulled free and sprinted away.

"Wait!" he called, but she did not stop. Ben turned and looked at the other men, who looked as perplexed as he. He shrugged. "Go on to the castle. I shall wait here for her."

Two of them stayed behind with him, concerned his wounded leg made him an easy target. The rest trudged on to the castle.

"Is that really Niall Thoralt's mother? What in the world is she doing here?" asked Wallace, the older of the two who stayed behind.

"It is, and I haven't a clue how she came to be here," Ben answered.

"Maybe she knows Niall's in trouble. There was something peculiar—" he caught himself. "Maybe she has a feel for what happened."

"All mothers have special senses for their sons," Ben replied, knowing full well the man was absolutely right.

"I'm going to follow after her," Ben said, hoisting himself off the ground. "You should go on and get yourselves something to eat. I'll be along as soon as I can."

"I don't think you'll have to look too hard," Wallace said, pointing in the direction she had gone. Ben turned and saw Moralia astride the Thoralt's black mare. They watched in silence as she approached them.

"Let's go to the castle. I don't like being out here where we are subject to Baldonian arrows," Ben remarked calmly, as if her riding up to join them were an ordinary thing.

She nodded and turned the horse toward the towering walls of stone, trying to assess Ben's limp as he moved alongside the black mare. Walking was actually easier for him than standing had been so he did well at masking the true pain that aggravated his leg. Moralia offered him the ride instead of her, but he declined, and she said no more.

Once they were inside the great gate and her horse given over to a stable boy's care, Ben led Moralia to a quiet place in the courtyard outside the main hall where they could talk and not be heard. He filled her in on all he knew since returning.

"After Nan brought Niall's note, James sent troops in

the direction his map indicated. The Baldonian forces scattered quickly this time so our men were not as successful as when we caught them by surprise the first time outside of Cire."

"So, Niall went north?" Moralia asked.

"He was at the enemy camp on the North Sea when he sent word with Nan, but no one has seen him since. Our fighters have been valiant, but without Niall, they have faltered in their confidence of a victory." Ben hung his head. "And finding Gunder was . . . difficult. He'd been whipped and his throat was slit."

Moralia was mixing herbs while Ben spoke. At his description of how he'd found Gunder, she stopped. Her eyes closed. Was Niall dead too? Her hand reached up and touched the hollow where the stone had lain. Calm spread through her. No, he wasn't dead. Summoning herself to the task at hand, she took a deep breath and laid a hand on Ben.

"I'm sorry, Ben. I know how close the three of you were."

He had to look away to fight back the impending tears. Losing Gunder felt like losing his right arm. Since finding the lifeless, bloody body, anger and sadness had drained his stamina. Where was Niall? Why wasn't he here? Had he been taken prisoner? Or worse, was he dead? When a Baldonian arrow pierced his leg, he could only stare at it, sure that it was now his fate to die too.

Ben heard Moralia talking. She was explaining to him what each plant was used for and how it worked. Satisfied the mixture was ready, she ripped open the pant leg that covered his wound. The ugly abscess gave off a putrid odor.

Regaining her composure, she squared her shoulders. "Look away, Ben, and hold this stick in your mouth. Try to stay still."

"I'll be fine," he answered through gritted teeth.

"Put it in your mouth, please."

She handed him the stick. He took it reluctantly having seen her rub it with some sort of paste. She'd then added something else to her concoction for packing the wound once it was cleaned. Ben grimaced at the taste but kept it between his teeth and concentrated on the stone wall opposite where he sat. Moralia busied herself taking an inventory of the supplies between the two of them.

He gripped his pant legs and held on when the knife sliced through the putrid flesh.

The stick had done its job, though, and he did not feel any pain.

"Not too much more, Ben. The wound was going bad, but I think we've caught it in time."

Moralia patiently cleaned the foul-smelling parts of flesh away, packed the wound and put Toeffer leaves on top. The process took nearly an hour and she talked the entire time, teaching him what she was doing and why. He asked fewer and fewer questions.

Moralia looked up and saw that Ben's eyes had glazed over. Smiling, she packed up the herbs, putting only a small amount in her own satchel. She would leave the rest for him.

Using a bitter leaf to sanitize her knife before repacking

it, she heard a slow scraping sound and turned just in time to catch Ben as he slid down the wall. She managed to slow his body enough for a soft landing. When did these boys grow up, she wondered. Looking over the tattered clothing he wore, she remembered the scrawny boy of a decade ago, his face full of freckles, trying so hard to keep up with the older Niall and much bigger Gunder. Rummaging in her pack, she found her needle and some thread and went to work closing the wound. Next, she would work on the torn elbow of his shirt.

Searching the castle a while later, Moralia eventually recognized Wallace, drinking beer in the great hall with the other men who had returned to resupply. She walked over to where he sat on the long bench. The other men scooted over and made room for her to sit. They were slated to head out again in the morning and had already filled their bellies as full as they could possibly stretch them.

"Ben is sleeping on the north side of the courtyard. He needs a few days' rest. Please don't let him go with you tomorrow. Promise me," Moralia pleaded.

"You rest assured, he'll stay here. You can take care of him yourself."

"I'll be gone in the morning. I have to find Niall." She spoke softly, leaning in so only he could hear her.

"That's not right, nor proper, and I simply won't have it," he blustered, beer dribbling down his beard. "Ladies can't be running off in the woods with all these Baldonian invaders about. No sir, I mean madam."

Turning red in the face, he continued, "Your Niall is a grown man, and he can fend for himself right well, he can." Almost apoplectic, he finished his sentence by banging his pewter mug on the table. The others at the table jumped, jaws agape.

Moralia smiled at the older gentleman, searching for another tact. "Rest assured, sir, I will do nothing foolish as you say. You are so kind to think of my welfare. Thank you. I am in your debt."

Her sweetness disarmed him.

"I'll introduce you to James in the morning before we leave. He's in charge of the castle while Niall is gone, and he'll make sure Ben stays right here until his leg is mended," he assured her. "You can take care of him and the others too. There's plenty for both of you to do right here once that leg of his is healed."

The next morning, bright and early, Ben shuffled out to the bailey where James and the others congregated in preparation for their heading out to rejoin the battle. Most were newly shorn and wore fresh clothes. He, on the other hand, looked quite the mess, his hair askew and his trouser leg ripped from one end to the other.

"Whoa up there, young man. You're not going anywhere," James admonished. "Wallace here has filled me in. You're going to stay here until that leg mends. Mrs. Thoralt will look after your wound, and when she says you can travel, you can join up with the others."

Wallace stood chest out, puffed up in an old uniform newly let out with all new buttons sewed on, ready to lead his contingent of men back to the front lines.

"Mrs. Thoralt has gone after Niall," Ben informed them.

"What? What? No, no, no, she clearly understood my instructions last night for her to stay here where she would be safe. She is to look after you," Wallace blubbered.

Standing within hearing distance, a red-haired lad named Clive, who waited with the other men for their marching orders, shyly cleared his throat. "Um, beg pardon, sir."

"What?" James growled, twirling around. The young boy blanched. His arms stuck out inches past the cuffs of his shirt, and his pants fell short of his boot tops.

"S- sorry, sir, but the lady's horse wasn't in the stable this morning. I noticed it was gone first thing."

"Then why didn't you inform us first thing?" James barked.

The young man wished for a hole to open in the floor, but no such deliverance was forth-coming. The blood drained from his face under the commander's ire, his freckles popping out starkly against his pale skin.

"Oh, bother," Wallace growled from behind James, stomping in a circle, trying to think through what must be done.

"Carry on, Wallace, the men need these supplies. They are depending on you. We shall find the lady," James said.

"There is no need for anyone else to go looking for her, I can do that," Ben interjected. "My leg is on the mend, and Mrs. Thoralt left me the medicine I need to keep it healing."

Wallace's mouth opened, and then shut, his relief evident.

"All right, then," James said. "Get some food in you, Ben. Wallace, you are off. Good luck to you and your men. Save our country from the filthy mongers of Baldonia!"

Once again Wallace's chest was out, and he strutted to the head of the line.

Ben watched them go, silently wishing them good luck, and then he turned to the task of finding breakfast. He was famished.

He was certain there was no point in going after Moralia. She would find Niall, if that was possible, and bring him back, if that was possible. In the meantime, he would make himself useful today by tending the wounded as Moralia had done for him. Tomorrow he would inform James he was leaving.

Chapter Twenty-Nine

Layla made quick time heading south to the dowager house. After the prisoner died, there was no point in hanging around while their forces regrouped. Captain Lodall would take his men to capture Cire, she and Tam would find King Stephen.

Fewer trees blocked their way south of the Rhy River, so traveling was swift but less game was available for food. On the second day, they came to a large copse of trees where Layla called a halt.

"Let's hunt. I'm hungry and there ought to be deer in these trees."

"You want to hunt? Why? We have plenty of supplies."

Layla looked over at Tam. "You are welcome to eat all the dried biscuits you want. I'm eating fresh meat tonight." She pulled out an arrow and motioned for Tam to head to the east side. She would take the west.

Tam sighed and began angling away from Layla. The heather was thick, masking their footfalls. Within a few feet, Layla felt the temperature drop as she entered the trees. She stepped carefully for a hundred feet, then picked out a large tree not on any game trail in order to shield herself from sight. Tam would not be so careful. She would make enough noise to alert any deer in the copse and start them moving in the opposite direction.

It didn't take long. A twig snapped, and Layla fitted her arrow to the bow. The temptation to glance around the tree pulled on her, but she knew better. Another snap. Good the sound was not coming straight at her tree. She drew a deep breath. There.

The small campfire threw light into the surrounding trees. The girls were sated from eating a huge helping of fresh venison. Tam had fashioned a few long sticks to hold thin strips of meat above the fire while Layla had cut the backstrap. Now, they leaned back and watched the smoke curl up and around the venison, drying into something they could carry with them and eat for the next few days.

Early the next morning, they continued their journey, not stopping till midday.

"How much longer do you think?" Tam asked, chewing on a piece of dried meat.

"We never came this far south, so I really don't know. I'm hoping we're there by nightfall."

Skirting the village of Midvale in the late afternoon, they knew they were close to the big house King Stephen had sent his mother to live in when he came of age. Ample trees dotted the rolling hills surrounding the house so it was easy to avoid detection. When at last it was in their sights, Layla smiled. He must be hiding here.

When they found the best vantage point from which to watch the house, the two hunkered down and waited. Layla's concern mounted as evening drew near. Something was not right. A maid came out the back door and removed washing hung out to dry earlier in the day. Chickens ran about in their last forage for worms before roosting for the night. No horses came in from hunting. No dogs barked at the rising moon.

"I'm going to check the stable. You keep watch. Hoot like an owl if anyone approaches," Layla said. She slipped away.

Edging up to the stable was too easy. When she slipped through the door, she drew a sharp breath. No carriages awaited riders. No horses filled the stalls. No clean tack adorned the hooks on the walls. He was not here! Anger boiled over and she kicked a feed pan that went sprawling across the floor, leaving a trail of grain. She stared at the oats until their significance dawned on her. She picked up a handful and smelled them.

"Definitely not old," she said. Someone had been here. She looked around. Dung was piled high in several of the stalls. No one had mucked them of late. "Poor stewardship," she thought, pondering the scene.

Hurrying back to where Tam waited, she pointed to the front door.

"What are you going to do?" Tam asked.

"Knock."

"Knock?"

"If someone answers the door that's easier than knocking it down," Layla replied.

They sprinted across the yard. Layla stood directly in front of the heavy wood door. She lifted the brass knocker and let it fall several times.

The door opened a crack, and dark, scared eyes peeked out from behind it. Layla was ready and put her whole body into shoving it wide open. Tam bounded through the opening and caught the maid who stumbled backwards.

"Where's the lady of the house?" Layla demanded.

"No one's here. You must leave," the young girl squeaked.

Layla drew her dagger and waved it menacingly in front of the girl's face. "I'm not going to ask again."

The maid's eyes grew enormous, glued to the knife in front of her face. She slowly raised her hand, pointing up the stairs. "She's in the drawing room."

"Tie her up in the kitchen and look for any others. I'll find her royal highness," Layla said, bounding up the stairs.

"Annie, where are you? I asked for tea a half hour ago. What in heaven's name is taking so long?" The voice came from the first door on the left at the top of the stairs. Layla did not bother to knock this time.

"Your Majesty."

"Who in the devil are you?" roared the woman, rising out of her settee.

The dagger flashed in Layla's hand. "Sit back down."

The queen mother did as she was told. "Who are you?" she asked, regaining her composure.

"I am Layla DeMont, and I have come to Rhyaden to claim these lands for their rightful king— King DeMont of Baldonia."

"Why have you come here? This is my summer house. King Stephen lives in Cire Castle," the queen mother explained, as if she talked to a student.

"As did you, until your son banished you to this humble abode in the middle of nowhere. That must have stung, did it not? Being rejected by your own flesh and blood."

The queen mother opened her mouth to answer, and then sat back, looking away. Tears rimmed her eyes when at last she looked back at Layla. Something in her look pulled on Layla's heartstrings. It was a look of rejection she understood well, having experienced it throughout her childhood.

Tam came into the room. "There is a cook, an old gardener,

and the maid. That is all the servants I have found."

Layla turned back to the queen. "Not all that have been here, though, is it your Majesty? You have had company just lately, have you not?"

"No. There are just the four of us now. There were more in the beginning, but nearly everyone my son sent with me was old, except for Annie, and some have died. He does not send replacements."

"Such a thoughtful son, but you are lying to me. I saw the dung in the stables. Where did they go?" Layla said, flashing the dagger again.

The queen mother broke down in sobs. "He has abandoned me—again. I don't know where they went. He came two weeks ago. They ate and rested their horses for two days. He told me he would take me with him, and then they left. I woke up and they were gone."

"Where did he say he was going?"

"When he first came, he talked of going to Niregon to raise an army."

"What?" Tam gasped.

"As I said, he didn't tell me he was leaving, so I don't know if that was deception or his true plans," the queen mother said, her voice trailing off at the end. Suddenly, she straightened up. "King Francis is a distant relative of mine. I will write him a letter that you shall deliver, imploring him to allow me to come to his court and seek asylum."

Layla scoffed. "You have a distorted view of your — ah... cousin, King Francis."

"He understands the ethics of royal lineage. We stick together. Besides, my presence would bring legitimacy to his claim to the Rhyaden throne. I will write the letter at once. Please, instruct my cook to fix you a hearty dinner so you may strike off immediately. And send my maid. It is dreadfully past time for my tea!"

Tam stood dumbstruck. Layla loved the woman's imperviousness to the fact that she was actually a prisoner. She looked over to Tam and smiled.

"Yes, please, Tam, have the maid bring up some tea for her Highness."

"Are you—"

Layla cut her off with a wave of the dagger. "In private," she mouthed, motioning for them to leave the room.

"Let's let her believe she is in control while we search the house for clues— and booty. Besides, a well-cooked meal would be wonderful, would it not?" Layla said when they stood in the hallway. Her eyes gleamed. "In the meantime, she isn't going anywhere so let's play this game with her."

The next morning, Layla stalked the grounds outside the house. Her frustration had reached a fevered pitch after a fruitless search for jewels or money. The queen mother had insisted her son sent her here with nothing, and gave her nothing. The bills for food and supplies from the village were paid monthly, but she had nothing to do with running the household.

"Stupid! She is utterly worthless and stupid! No wonder he banished her from court," Layla ranted. She walked back to the stable, crossing the carefully brushed grounds between the house and outbuildings. "They have no horses, no help to speak of, and yet someone takes the time to sweep the road?"

Suddenly, pieces of the puzzle began to float together in her brain. She dashed into the stable and grabbed a pitchfork. She stabbed the nearest pile of dung. The tyne sank in deep and came up green.

"Fresh!"

† † †

The queen mother sat at her desk, quill in one hand, paper in the other when Layla barged through the library door.

"You lied to me! Tell me when the king left! Where is he headed?"

"What do you mean?" the queen mother asked, laying down the quill. "How dare you come in here unannounced! Get out before I call the guards and have you imprisoned!" Her eyes flashed and her cheeks enflamed as she rose from her chair.

Layla burst into laughter. "You crazy old woman, you are far more clever than I gave you credit for. Now tell me," she said, pulling her knife out of its sheath as she approached, "when did your son leave?"

The tip of the knife was now very close to the queen mother's throat. Layla watched her swallow and the color drain from her cheeks. "They left the day before you came."

"Where is he going?" Layla asked, her voice low and deadly.

"He didn't tell me, I swear. I did not lie about that. He took EVERYTHING I have." The queen's voice was begging now.

"How many men did he have with him?"

"He came with his master falconer and two others. They left with two of my servants, as well as all of my horses—something about not wanting pursuers to get fresh mounts."

"Why did you lie?" Layla asked, lowering the knife.

"He—he told me he would come back for me and let me return to court if I helped him," she answered meekly.

Layla laughed. "And you believed him," she said. The

strike was swift and unexpected. "You should not have lied to me."

The queen mother crumpled to the floor, her blood slowly spreading in a thick pool on the carpet. The letter to King Francis was still clutched in her hand. Layla bent down and jerked the queen mother's ring from her finger. It could be useful. One never knew.

Chapter Thirty

The black mare walked steadily along a road that headed east from Cire Castle. Moralia's first thought had been to go north where Niall was last spotted, but the two opposing armies were engaged there and her instincts told her that it was not only dangerous, it was not where Niall would be found.

In the early morning hours, anxious to put miles between her and the castle, she kept the mare at a fast pace. Once she was certain no one followed after her, she reined in the mare and took in the changing countryside. She had never seen this side of Rhyaden.

The rolling hills where the mare now trod were lined with elms, oaks and maples reaching high to the sky. Branches from large trees on either side met in the middle of the road, forming an airy canopy of green leaves overhead. Birds cawed out warnings when the horse ventured close to their nests. Crickets chirped as leaves fluttered in the morning breeze. Wildflowers dotted the green meadows where trees gave way to pasture. Rock fences marked one family's land from another. She marveled at the openness, while at the same time she worried it made her vulnerable.

Since the invasion, the road was no longer used for daily commerce. Vegetables lay rotting in fields without a market to sell them in. Fear kept the folk tucked in at home and out of sight. In the afternoon of the first day, a ragamuffin group from an outlying village trooped toward Cire to join the battle. Excited to join the fight, their loud talk gave her plenty of warning to hide. She went deep into the trees that lined a nearby waterway.

Late in the afternoon, Moralia was relieved when she spotted forested land once again. The open hills she'd just passed through were beautiful, but they offered very little cover and she was a bundle of nerves the entire time she and the horse were exposed. She galloped the mare to a lather in her haste to reach good cover again.

Her worry was justified. Not long after leaving the valley, the mare's ear twitched. Moralia stopped the horse to listen closely. She watched the black ears perked intently forward in front of her. Moralia trusted her horse over her own hearing and again turned the mare's head off the road.

Hesitating for a second, the mare finally took a step at Moralia's firm nudging and then moved carefully into the tangled growth. Soon Moralia heard what the horse had heard: the heavy thud of many feet. A few more steps and she slipped down off the mare. She stepped to the mare's head and led her a few more feet, then turned the mare behind the largest tree. Moralia softly rubbed her horse's muzzle.

"Hold still, girl. Don't move."

Marching past in well-ordered silence, two dozen men wearing moss green uniforms came close enough for Moralia to see sweat glistening on their brows, their unshaven faces barely masking the grime of a long march. Baldonian soldiers! Was the castle soon to come under siege again? She closed her eyes and held her breath. She did not turn her head to watch them pass lest the movement catch a marcher's eye.

The mare's leg twitched when a fat black fly landed above her hock. Moralia let her breath out and squeezed her eyes tighter. The comforting smell of her horse blanketed her. When the line of soldiers was past, she fell against the mare, grateful for her steady presence.

The thud of the soldiers' boots faded, but Moralia still did not move out of the dense copse of trees and vines. The soldiers had come so close she could smell the stench of their unwashed bodies. Her stomach rolled upward.

Some time later, Moralia cleaned herself up in a small brook. Wetting a handkerchief, she scrubbed her face and neck, rubbing hard to clean herself. Removing her shoes, she waded into the brook, hoping the shock from the cold water would help, but none of her efforts lessened the impact of the encounter. Putting her shoes back on, she took the mare's reins and walked ahead of her horse, looking for mint. She finally found the fragrant herb and picked a handful, chewing on the leaves to remove the acrid taste that lingered in her mouth.

Moralia reached to stroke the stone that hung around her neck. She had worn it since childhood, and it felt like it was there, even though it no longer was. Her heartbeat raced. "Where did I lose it?" she gasped before remembering.

Guided by something she could not name, Moralia continued the search for her son. She sensed he was alive, but in the past two days, her perception of him had clouded. The farther she traveled, the more her skin tingled. Was he hurt?

At the same time Moralia approached the old castle near Gaxdorn Gate, Lynmeer was having a rather convoluted conversation with Ecirp. The little green creature could not fathom the dragon's even entertaining the slightest wisp of an inkling that having Niall stay with them might be a thought worthy of being considered, if it were even possible.

"It is a most preposterous notion!" Ecirp exclaimed.

"And why is that, my dear friend?" Lynmeer asked, his tone gentle.

"Because . . . because humans aren't allowed in Ayhrland. You yourself voted for the edict that separated the dragon world from the human world. I was there! If he is allowed to stay, what would prevent others from following? And what about a wife for the lad? And children!" Ecirp's face turned a ghastly gray-green and his ears shook. "How could you even begin to think his living here would be acceptable?"

Lynmeer gave a slow nod of agreement. "Do not worry, Ecirp. I have made my share of mistakes when it comes to humans," Lynmeer said softly. "I wanted to hear your valued opinion, and now I have. Thank you."

Ecirp looked up into the dragon's eyes. He knew how much Niall and his mother meant to Lynmeer. A solitary tear slid down the dragon's cheek.

"I have been wondering something myself, Lynmeer. How did the boy get into Ayhrland?"

"Through Gaxdorn Gate, of course, that's the only way in," Lynmeer responded, looking at Ecirp with a quizzical expression.

"But he is not dragon," Ecirp said. "How did the gate open?"

"Ah . . . he carries a stone of my scales, melted in the Great Fire. I gave it to Valdorn's son, and each descendant after Andrew has worn or carried it since."

Ecirp paled. He reached into his vest pocket. "This one?"

Lynmeer reached out and took the round stone, nodding his head as he gazed at the purple and black bit of himself. "My scales must have enough dragon in them to allow entry, and I suppose that is what has drawn Moralia here too."

"Your essence seeped into those that wore it?"

"A small bit, I suppose. I hadn't anticipated that, I only gave it to Andrew so he would have something from someone who loved his father."

"That explains a lot," Ecirp said.

The black mare's ears perked up, then her nostrils flared. Her withers quivered, ready to take flight. Moralia listened carefully, waiting many minutes before dismounting near the small stream. Sensing no one near, she remained alert, uncertain as to why the horse was so agitated. Leaving the reins looped around the saddle horn, she bent down at the water's edge, cupping her hands and drinking deeply. She urged her horse to do the same.

Moralia had spent only a few minutes investigating the ruins. At any other time, she would have been fascinated and roamed the place for hours, but her sense of Niall's presence was heightened on the east side of the castle. She felt she would find him soon and wasted no time indulging her curiosity about history.

Moralia hobbled the mare and tied up the reins so they wouldn't break. She sank down at the water's edge and drank again from her cupped hand, then backed away from the brook on her knees and leaned up against a tree, grateful to rest. The long ride had worn her out.

Her eyelids drooped in the warmth of the afternoon. A little nap would be good, she thought, then she could find Niall. He must be close by, for she had no urge to go any further.

✝ ✝ ✝

Lynmeer and Niall walked to the small glen where the easels were set up. The dragon picked up a small palette and put it back down again.

"I have two subjects we must discuss, Niall."

Niall nodded. He'd been waiting for the dragon's decision.

"First. We've come to the conclusion that your staying in Ayhrland is not in your best long-term interests. There is no one here for you to fall in love with, or marry, or have children with if you'd like."

Niall nodded. It was the answer he'd expected, but he hadn't really thought of that reason, and it brought to mind Winnie and Ben.

"And second, your mother has come in search of you."

"How do you know?"

Lynmeer cocked his head. "I am a dragon, after all."

Niall rolled his eyes. "I wish she hadn't come," he said shortly.

"And why is that, Niall?"

"Her coming reminds me of Gunder and how he died."

"And does that remind you that Rhyaden is still in peril?"

Niall looked up into the dragon's dark pools of sight. He saw himself in the deep recesses of Lynmeer's eyes as he had each time he faced Lynmeer and his future. Nan was there, sitting on his shoulder.

Blinking, he looked away. He wasn't ready to leave the calm, soothing colors of Ayhrland, not just yet, even knowing he could not stay. He knew too, however, his mother was probably desperate to find him. "Can Mother come here?" he asked suddenly.

"This land is for dragons only, Niall."

"I know what she will wish for me to do, and I don't know if I can. I can't help but think that if I was capable of leading Rhyaden to victory, Gunder would still be alive."

"Each of us can only do our best, Niall. There are no guarantees of victory, but defeat is certain if one does not try. You must not give up!"

Niall was quiet for a long moment. He had heard those words before, under the waters of Knurly Run. The path of his future quietly opened itself before him. "All right, Lynmeer, then it is time for me to go," he said. "Thank you."

Lynmeer smiled. "You are welcome, Niall."

"Are you coming back to Rhyaden?"

"I will come shortly, but I think it will be good for you and your mother to have some time alone," Lynmeer said.

"All right, I should go." He turned around and walked toward the stream that ran uphill.

"Niall?"

The lad jumped, startled by the soft voice beside him.

"Oh, it's you, Ecirp. I'm going to find my mother. I should ask. Is there a trick to going back through?"

"Here, I believe this will help you."

The little creature held out the leather pouch that held the stone made of melted dragon scales. "It belongs to you. I took it when I mended your pants, but I realize now there was a reason for you to have it."

"What is it made of?"

"It is dragon," Ecirp said quietly, handing the pouch to Niall. "I am sorry I did not return it to you sooner."

Niall stared at the pouch. He had carried it for so long, not knowing its significance.

"You may leave here the same way you entered," Ecirp continued. "Just follow the water to the source."

"Thank you, Ecirp."

Niall put the pouch back in his pocket. He looked up to ask Ecirp if he thought they would meet again, but he was gone.

He looked back in the direction where he had last seen his tutor. He could not see anyone, but he gave a salute anyway and then turned around. Quickly walking toward the source of the brook, he heard the earth rumble as he neared the large boulders forming a solid wall behind the spring. The stone in his pocket began to tingle. Planting his feet wide to steady himself against the swaying landscape, he waited a few moments until the rumble ceased and there near the gurgling brook was a narrow gap in the rock, just enough to slide through.

Lynmeer sighed as he watched him walk away, the boy who had turned into a man, broad of shoulder, intelligent, possessing a good and kind heart, but still so young. His time tutoring Niall had gone so quickly.

"Mother. Mother, wake up."

Moralia rolled her head from side to side, the voice in her dream getting louder. Her son was climbing a tree, and she watched, afraid he would falter and fall from the great branch. Henry stood nearby, urging her to let the boy be, climbing trees was part of childhood.

"Mother, it's me. Wake up."

Chapter Thirty-One

Dawn seeped through the treetops. The black night slowly blushed with deep purple and then brightened to crimson moments before the big gold orb peeked over the horizon. Henry wondered if a storm was coming, the ache in his bones especially sharp this morning. He was on his way to relieve the third guard posting, the one closest to the road that led to Cire. Sure that this was the route the Baldonians would come, if they came, he had chosen this posting for himself when he handed out assignments.

At the end of a line of soldiers marching west, a youngster named Hobbs carried an earthenware pot swinging in a rope cradle. Inside, carefully wrapped in moss and then again in leather, were slow-burning embers with which to start the dinner fire. In another pack slung over the lad's back was dried moss, perfect for coaxing flames out of the embers with a little breath of air. Flint was not to be found in Baldonia, so soldiers and travelers alike used this method for fire. The forest provided everything else they needed. The cooks who came with Baldonia's third wave of fighters used conscripted young boys like mules for all the chores of gathering wood and carrying supplies from camp to camp. The job of carrying fire fell to the littlest fellow.

Wrenched from his younger siblings and sold into the army at the age of ten, Hobbs quickly adapted to his new life. He kept watch for his master's foul temper, kept his mouth shut and stayed out of the cook's way, or suffered a cuff to the side of his head.

Holes appeared in his thin shoes on the long march through the forest. The cook only laughed when the boy showed him. After that, each night he carefully lined his shoes with a new layer of moss. One thing was certain, this strange land full of enormous trees had plenty of moss.

Suddenly Hobbs heard the blare of a horn off to his right. His head turned in the direction of the horn, and he smacked into the boy stopped ahead of him. Six inches taller than Hobbs, the gangly youth swung around and pasted him in the chin.

"Watch where you're going, you stupid oaf!" he admonished.

The horn blared again, one long forlorn keening, followed by two short notes. The men in front began running. Hobbs didn't have a clue what he should do, and the cook, who had not been hired to fight, was busy finding himself a place to hide. Hobbs followed those in front for a few yards, and then he stopped. No one seemed to notice.

Looking left and then right, Hobbs dashed into the trees and kept going until he tripped over a vine and found himself face first in a thick clump of chest-high ferns. He stayed put, listening for footsteps. The only sounds he heard were distant cries of anguish when an arrow pierced a body, or rocks knocked men off their feet.

✝ ✝ ✝

The Baldonians had no time to form up. They had taken off at a fast pace, following the commander's lead when they heard the horn. After the road took its last turn, it left the trees and spewed the men into the open meadow like sheep to slaughter. They were easy targets for the practiced arrows of the villagers who had come on the run at the sound of the horn.

Thwack! Henry's arrow narrowly missed the commanding officer, hitting the man standing next to him. Henry took down five others in the first wave. Panic surged through the Baldonian soldiers as they realized the hopeless situation they had been led into.

† † †

Torg had been posted on the far side of the village, but his long legs brought him swiftly around to where Henry's horn blared the warning. Unlike most of the villagers who threw rocks or shot arrows from behind trees, Torg charged directly into the battle, his great sword clashing and slicing its way through flesh. Enemy blood rained over him in waves of crimson.

Suddenly, another horn sounded, this one a Baldonian trumpet. It called its men to muster around it, and the twenty-plus men still alive began to fight their way across the open field, hoping to get out of range of the sharp-edged rocks and deadly arrows.

Torg spotted Henry coming toward him at a fast clip. He raised his sword in salute.

"Torg, drop down!"

Torg heeded his friend's voice. An arrow whistled above him, slicing cleanly into a Baldonian's throat. The body stayed upright for a few seconds before crumpling at Torg's feet.

"By all that is holy, that was a shot, Henry!"

Henry came running up and helped him stand. "Are you all right?"

"Yes, and you?"

"I'm good. Stay here and check for any wounded among our men. Get them back to the village, and make sure that if any of the Baldonians are yet alive, they have no weapons to fight with."

"Where are you going?" Torg asked.

"I can pick off stragglers before they get too far into the trees," Henry yelled back, dashing in the direction the main group of Baldonians had fled.

Torg briefly watched him go, then turned toward the trees. "John!"

"Yes, Father?" John came out of the trees, running toward his father, careful not to look down at the ghastly figures lying on the ground.

"Check each man lying here and retrieve all the weapons you find, especially the arrows, even if the shafts are broken. Yell for help if you find anyone alive."

"Where are you going?" John asked. His eyes enormous at the thought of touching the dead bodies.

"I'm going to scout the woods," he answered. "You did good today, son," Torg said, laying his hand on the boy's shoulder. "This is nasty business, and I'm proud of you for standing so strong."

John turned red from the praise. "I'll take care of this, Father, don't you worry."

Torg turned and yelled toward the others coming out of the trees on the village side. "Flin!" he yelled. The two men exchanged information and then Torg was gone, into the trees in the same direction Henry had gone.

An hour later, the two men found a boy propped up against a giant Knurly tree, fast asleep. He did not wear a moss green uniform. In fact, he hardly had any clothes at all that weren't ragged remnants passed down too many times. Shoes with holes in both soles stuck out of short pants. "Poor little beggar," Torg thought, shaking his head. The boy did not belong to their village. They assumed he was a servant, left behind in the melee.

Startled eyes popped wide open when Torg lay his hands upon the boy's shoulder.

"Don't worry, lad, we won't hurt you. Is your father part of the army from Baldonia?"

Big eyes slowly shook from side to side. "Father sold me to the cook. He's mean. Please don't give me back. I'll work for you. I'm a good worker."

"I'm sure you are. Are you hungry?"

"Yes!" The eager nodding and gaunt little arms told Torg all he needed to know.

"Come on then. My missus will fix us all something to eat."

The boy got to his feet and walked between the two men. Halfway back to the village, Henry turned to his friend.

"I think you can handle the defenses here, Torg, I'm going to Cire."

✝ ✝ ✝

"I do believe we have matters well in hand," Captain Lodall said, after hearing the reports from couriers. They had come to his tent over the past few days and presented their divisions' progress in the campaign. Since the disappearance of the one called Niall, they had made steady progress.

"We must find King Stephen. I am certain the castle will fall upon hearing the news of his capture."

"What if he has fled his kingdom?" one man asked.

"Nonsense. How could he have gotten away without our detecting it? And why would those in the castle not surrender if they have no leader? Surely it makes no difference who they pay their taxes to. It's better than being dead," the captain responded.

There was only a small band of twenty Baldonian soldiers left outside of Knurlysham. They had misjudged the villagers, assuming the sleepy backwoods hamlet was unprepared for any kind of invasion. They were wrong, and worse, now they were starving.

The Baldonian captain who led the initial raid took one man with him and fled east, ostensibly to make his report to the commander-in-charge. He told his men to regroup and harry the villagers until he could return with more troops. The normal course of action would have been for the captain to send a messenger. Few of his men expected him to return.

Hunger drove the remaining Baldonian soldiers to form a plan. Two men would start the outermost cottage on fire, and while the villagers rushed to put it out, the others, already stationed around the outskirts, would slip in and find food, dispatching any villagers who weren't at the fire to their death. No prisoners. They would attempt to hold off any organized resistance until nightfall. After that, the men were on their own. Most figured to head west, over the mountains. No one mentioned returning east to rejoin the fight to capture the castle.

Chapter Thirty-Two

Niall sat beside his mother on the grassy bank of the gentle brook outside of Gaxdorn Gate. After their emotional reunion, they had much to tell each other. While Moralia talked, Niall rubbed his feet to dry them before pulling his boots back on. Once he began his story, she asked a few questions, but for the most part remained silent as he relayed the story of his journey to Cire with Ben and Gunder, the battle, and running away following Gunder's death.

She reached over and laid her hand on his. "Ben told me of Gunder's death. I'm so sorry you had to see it."

"I still see it, Mother, every day. I couldn't save him."

"War is ugly, Niall, but it has always been this way. Some speak of valor and glory, but all I see is heartache and scars that never heal. I wish it weren't so."

"You are so brave, Mother, coming all this way alone," Niall said. Suddenly his eyes lit up. "You should come with me to Ayhrland, Mother. Everything is calm and restful, beautiful really. There is no war. Baldonia's army will not invade there."

"What about your father? Maybe we could all come back

and see it together, after the war."

"After the war. What if Rhyaden falls? What if DeMont is our new king?"

Moralia gazed upon his face. "It is a huge responsibility for one so young as you, but Ben told me how it was at Cire Castle. He told me how the soldiers followed you, how brave they were under your command and how they need you now. Since you left, the men have all but given up. They are scared. It was your leadership that made the difference."

"Ben's there?" he asked.

"He returned to the castle after bringing word to our village. There was fierce fighting north of Cire, and he took an arrow in his leg. When I was there I treated the wound, and I'm sure he will recover, but he had a frightful infection. I fear Baldonia's fighters might be using some kind of poison on the tips of their arrows."

Niall stared into the trees. The grief from Gunder's death had changed him, there was no doubt.

"Watching him die was the worst thing I've ever seen."

"I understand, Niall. I watched my parents die from the plague. I sat on my mother's bed and wished I could die instead of her, but nothing I did made any difference, or changed the outcome. They died, and I didn't."

"They wouldn't have wanted you to die, Mother, you must know that," Niall said.

"With time I understood that. Time and having you helped me realize what they must have felt and wanted for me. But we don't have that kind of time now, Niall. Our kingdom will fall to Baldonia's king if you don't return soon to lead our army."

"I'm afraid."

"I am too. I know how difficult this is, but you must put

your grief aside for now. You only fail if you don't try again. You must come back."

He looked up into her face.

"You can do this, son."

"We have a king. He should be doing this."

"You're right about that, he should, but he isn't," Lynmeer said.

Niall and Moralia jumped at the voice, unaware Lynmeer had passed through Gaxdorn Gate and stood close by. "There is one piece of your ancestry I have not told you, or your mother, Niall."

"Our ancestry?"

Lynmeer sat down on a large flat rock nearby. "You are Stephen's distant cousin, the great-great-grandson of King Valdorn," he said solemnly, stopping to let the two take in his words. "That is why I came to be your tutor." Shock registered on both faces.

Finally Moralia spoke up. "Valdorn and his wife and their only son were killed in the Great Fire."

"Valdorn's son, Andrew, escaped the fire," Lynmeer said softly. "For his own safety, he was secreted away and taken to a small village far to the west where his identity was not known."

"Knurlysham?" Niall asked.

"My grandfather was Valdorn's son?" Moralia asked.

"Yes, to both questions. There was bloody fighting over who should succeed Valdorn. The winner chose to forget they had never found the boy's body. As for your royal cousin Stephen, he ran away before this fight ever began. Surely you, with all of your training, your skills and your good heart, surely you are not going to do the same."

Lynmeer's revelation was met with silence. Niall slowly

turned to his mother, who was shaking her head, trying to absorb the news.

"My grandfather was King Valdorn's son," Moralia said, but this time it was not a question.

"Yes."

"So, that's why you came to Mother, and me, and now Niall," Moralia said, recognizing the significance.

"I promised someone a long time ago, someone I cherished deeply, that I would look after Rhyaden for her. Looking after your family was an effort to accomplish that."

Niall sat without moving. His world had suddenly grown so much bigger than his mother and father, Gunder, Ben and Winnie.

"There is one more thing you ought to know. The female spy who killed Gunder seeks to kill the king of Rhyaden. Baldonia's king wishes to rule both countries as one."

The color drained from Niall's face.

"She chooses not to run away," Lynmeer stated flatly.

Memories flashed in front of Niall: Gunder, Ben and him finding the stag killed in the hills above the village. His father helping him hold the new bow when he shot the first arrow. Finding Lynmeer in the forest. Trees talking to him. "Mother is our queen," Niall declared suddenly.

"The throne must be fought for, Niall. No one will have it now without winning it, and wanting it. That might not be your mother's choice. However, the question you must ask yourself is what kind of Rhyaden do you want for your children? Before you ever knew who you were descended from, you proved yourself capable of leading Rhyaden's men. They will follow you now, if you will lead."

"Then I must get started!" Niall exclaimed.

Moralia let out a long breath.

"Mother, are you up for another journey?" Niall asked.

"Leave your mother here, Niall. You take the mare, and I shall bring her to the castle soon."

"Go, son. I'll be fine."

Niall hugged her and then pulled back, looking deep into her eyes. Would she want the throne? He could not see the answer to his question.

The old gentleman wiped his spectacles. He laid his hand on Niall's shoulder and smiled. "Keep your wits about you, Niall. Remember, don't ever let anger cloud your judgment."

"I promise. Thank you."

Niall grabbed his bow. He raced to the mare, jumped on her back and turned west. The horse was eager to run and bounded forward the moment his boots touched her sides. As the miles clipped along, Niall formed his plan, heading first to the castle to find Ben. He would rid Rhyaden of the invaders once and for all. Gritting his teeth, he tried not to be angry at himself for wasting so much time. The king had failed, but he would not.

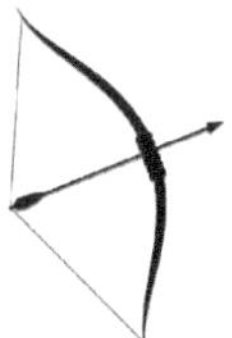

Chapter Thirty-Three

Moralia sat in the cool shade of a sycamore tree near Gaxdorn Gate while Lynmeer went to inform Ecirp of his plans. He returned bearing a blanket for a picnic, tiny sandwiches, gingerbread biscuits and a jug of steaming hot tea.

"How delightful, Lynmeer. Thank you."

"I thought you might find yourself famished after your long journey, and a little sustenance will brace you for the trip back."

"Tell me about your home," Moralia said after her first bite.

"Ah . . . Ayhrland. I feel a great sense of calm there. The colors help to create its restorative nature, and then there's the music. Such music. Inspirational music when I paint, quiet songs when I am in want of a nap, whatever I need at any given time."

"Are there others there?"

"A long time ago there were. Now, I have only one companion."

"Can anyone enter?"

"No, one must have magic to enter."

"Magic?" she scoffed. "Then how did Niall enter?"

"He carries the stone your grandfather gave to your mother, and she to you, does he not?"

"Yes, I gave it to him before he left home. I . . . I hoped it would bring him luck."

"It has magic and allowed him entry, as long as I am alive."

Moralia shook her head. "I don't understand what you mean by magic, but I'm glad he came to you, Lynmeer. He was badly shaken after Gunder's death."

"In the end, I believe he would have returned to the battle on his own. What he saw was a horrible thing for anyone to see, especially one so young, but Niall has great strength of heart. In time, he can be a great leader, if he so chooses."

Moralia smiled, then her eyebrows knitted together. There were many more questions to ask.

"There is more I need to tell you, Moralia," Lynmeer said, interrupting her thoughts. "For one, I want to apologize for something that happened a long time ago when Niall saved the boy from drowning in Knurly Run, do you remember that day?"

"Yes. Sort of. That day was always fuzzy for some reason."

"I am the reason. You watched me perform the magic, so I gave you a potion to wipe your memory. I realize now that in trying to protect you, I wasn't trusting your strength. My wife would have been disappointed in me."

Moralia's eyebrows shot up. "I didn't know you had a wife!"

"She's been gone a long time," Lynmeer said.

"I'm so sorry. Losing someone we love is so… difficult."

"And there is one other thing, one big thing that you need to know," Lynmeer said.

"Only one?" She laughed, reaching for another sandwich.

"This day has certainly been full of new things."

"Moralia, my dear, I am a dragon, the last dragon I believe, but a dragon, nonetheless."

Moralia's mouth was open, poised for the next bite. Her hand stopped in midair, frozen by the words of her white-haired tutor. She became aware of a bird singing, and then a soft breeze blowing through the leaves in the branches above her head.

"A what?"

"I know that comes as a bit of a shock, but there you have it. I am a dragon," Lynmeer stated once again.

"What?"

Lynmeer chuckled. "I'm afraid there are not sufficient words to convey my meaning, at least not in a timely manner, so I will have to show you. I'm going to back up so I don't knock you over." He backed up twenty feet. "All right, dear, are you ready?"

"What are you going to do?" she asked, afraid he had lost his mind. All this talk of magic was one thing, but this?

"I'm going to shape-shift into a dragon." And in the blink of an eye, the white-haired gentleman she had known almost her entire life became a magnificent purple dragon, three times her size.

Moralia screamed. Her hands flew up, covering her face. Seeing her reaction, Lynmeer returned to his human form.

"It's all right, my dear, please, I won't hurt you, ever."

She peeked out from behind her hands. "That thing was huge! Wait—that was you?"

Lynmeer chuckled. "Yes, my dear, dragons are very large in comparison to humans; however, in all actuality, I am considered quite small for a dragon."

Moralia's breathing slowed and her eyes softened as she collected her wits. "That scared me nearly senseless," she said.

"I'm so sorry, my dear, but I was afraid there was no better way to get through to you quickly. We have quite a trip ahead of us and it is nearing dusk. I thought we should fly at night so that I don't scare anyone else. I will set down about an hour from the castle and we'll walk from there in the morning."

"Fly?"

"Yes, my dear, you are about to have an extraordinary experience, one fit for a queen, I would say."

"How exactly? What . . . what do you mean, fly?"

"You are going to ride on my back. I shall shape-shift to dragon form, and you shall climb aboard and hold on tight, I dare say. It might be cold, so bring along the blanket.

Moralia's eyes were once again as big as saucers. Lynmeer smiled at her and gave her a peck on the cheek. "Don't be afraid, my dear, I won't let you fall. You're going to love this, I promise, and won't that son of yours be jealous when he finds out his mother got to ride on the back of a great dragon!"

A smile spread across her face. It would be a magnificent experience! Once again, Lynmeer backed up and shape-shifted into a purple dragon. She caught her breath but did not scream this time. Walking closer, she noticed the scar on his wing and his deformed foot. She knelt down and reached out to the mangled tendons, touching it softly. "Is this why the cane?"

"Yes, an old battle scar. Pull the blanket over your head. There is a slit in the middle. I'll help you up. You can sit behind my ears like you are riding a great horse. It will be windy, though, so hold on tight to my skin. It won't hurt me a bit."

"Are you sure?"

"Well, now that you ask, no, I am not. I've never had a rider before, so this is new to both of us; however, I do have very thick skin."

Moralia pulled the blanket over her head and looked up at him with a smile. Lynmeer lifted her up with his wing and she slid to the middle, grabbing ahold of the folds of skin on the back of his neck to keep from sliding right on over the other side.

"Okay, I'm . . . I'm ready."

"Hold on. Here we go."

The great purple wings lifted on either side of Moralia, enveloping her for just a few seconds before they whooshed downward. The last rays of sunlight glistened on the tiny scales, the iridescent sheen indescribably beautiful. Moralia gasped. In a lurching motion, he was up and the wings beat in deafening wumps on both sides of her head. Then suddenly, they caught air and the noise settled down as the earth dropped away.

"Are you okay, my dear?" Lynmeer asked after a few minutes, craning his head to get a glimpse of his first rider. He had carried her grandfather in a protective bundle in front of him, but never had someone ridden on his back. He could see the exhilaration on her face. Dipping his wings, he rocked a little from side to side, careful not to go too far but enough to make the ride thrilling.

"It's so wonderful, Lynmeer. The world is huge, but everything is so small from up here."   "It is a vast and lovely land, deserving of our care."

He did not go directly to Cire Castle but instead flew the length and breadth of Rhyaden, showing Moralia the entire kingdom. At the west end, he flew low over her cottage, which was strangely dark. He avoided going close to the village. Finally, he returned to the middle of the country and, circling ever higher, he crested Thorncrag Mountain. The air was sharp and cold this high, but Moralia was snug beneath the poncho. Her face was flushed and tears glistened on her cheeks from the wind in her face. Then suddenly, there before them lay the ocean lit by the moon which sat just above the horizon.

"Oh, Lynmeer. It is the most beautiful sight I have ever seen!"

He grinned from the pleasure of sharing all of this with Moralia. It had been so long since he had shared a sunrise flight with someone. His thoughts kept him silent, slowly drifting on currents, pleased to be able to show her a sight that no other human had ever seen. With the coming dawn, he angled away and circled the mountains, drawing closer to Cire. He wanted to land far from the inhabitants so they wouldn't be seen, but with this first passenger, he wanted some open ground too. He feared a sharp descent might dislodge Moralia. When she was safely on the ground, Lynmeer shape-shifted immediately, and the two walked into the woods for cover.

"We have about a half hour's walk from here," Lynmeer said.

Moralia's eyes were dancing, and a smile lit her flushed face from the wondrous flight. Lynmeer smiled at the sight. They began their walk to the castle.

Twenty minutes later, Lynmeer laid his hand on Moralia's arm. "Wait here. I want to be positive of who is in control before we waltz up to the gate."

"All right. Don't be long," she replied.

✝ ✝ ✝

"Look what we have here." A gruff voice chortled. His dirty uniform was torn, and his mouth hung open with stank breath.

Moralia turned around. A Baldonian soldier stood in front

of her. Where was Lynmeer? The dense thicket behind her gave her nowhere to run.

"Are you lost?"

Laughter rang out among the trees. "A sassy one, eh? I know exactly where I am, madam. The question is, what are you doing here?"

She thought desperately and uttered the first thing that came to mind. "I am a healer. I am headed to help those in need."

"A healer, you say," he growled, stepping closer. His rough beard and hot breath were vile. The hair rose on Moralia's neck.

"Don't you touch me!" Moralia warned, pressing against the tree behind her. Fear gripped her.

Again laughter erupted from the big man, then abruptly stopped. "Where is your mealy-mouthed king? Is he hiding in the castle?"

"King Stephen?" she asked, stalling for time.

"Do you have more than one king? Of course King Stephen! Don't play dumb with me." He moved closer to where she stood, holding his arm up in a threatening gesture.

"I have no idea where he is. I heard he ran away after the invasion. No one has seen him."

The soldier growled and backhanded Moralia. "Don't lie to me!" he shouted.

Pain rocked across her eyes. She reeled backwards, her hand coming up to protect her face. It took a moment before the haze lifted. She had never before been hit, and the shock of it was worse than the pain. Moralia locked onto the eyes of the Baldonian before her, sensing his hate. Determination replaced the fear. She would die if she did nothing.

She lunged forward and grabbed the hilt of the soldier's knife, belted at his waist. Surprise registered in the man's face at the unexpected attack. Pulling the blade out of its sheath, she prayed it was sharp.

"Arghhh," she screamed, plunging forward with all her might.

His eyes went wide as the blade pierced his skin. The tip glanced off his lower rib. She twisted the knife. Blood began burbling out of his side, soaking his uniform. He roared from the pain, and this time his blow knocked Moralia to the ground. Pulling the knife out of his side, he glared down at her in fury. Suddenly, his eyes registered surprise. He crumpled forward and landed heavily on top of her, the blade between them driven deep into her chest.

The air stank of singeing hair as it curled and shrank from the dragon's breath. Lynmeer tossed the soldier to the side. Spotting the blade, he shape-shifted and ran forward, bending down to gently pick up Moralia, cradling her in his arms. "My dear, I was gone too long, I am so sorry," he cried. Her startled eyes softened at the familiar voice.

"Where's Henry?" Moralia asked.

"He is waiting for you." Tears streamed down Lynmeer's mottled face. "You must listen carefully now, Moralia. Do you understand me?"

She nodded yes.

"I am going to heal you, but you must be prepared for what might happen to me when I do. It is a sacrifice I gladly make, Moralia. Aleah would want me to."

"Aleah?" Moralia asked. The word made her cough, and she clutched her side as a wave of pain traveled across her midsection.

"Aleah. The most beautiful dragon ever to fly over Rhyaden."

"Why didn't you tell me sooner?"

"Dragons tend to upset people, dear one. My purpose in your life was to protect you."

"What will happen?"

"It's possible I will die. I don't know for certain, but I am very old."

There was silence. Then Moralia's eyelids fluttered. She looked into the sad eyes of her oldest friend. "I wish for you to live, Lynmeer, for you to be here to protect Niall." She smiled and squeezed the hand that held hers, then her eyes drifted shut.

Moralia found herself in a misty place, following her mother across mossy rocks. Her mother was no longer distorted by the ravages of the plague, but smiling, beckoning her daughter to follow. They had not had a visit in such a long time. Moralia started forward, then she felt the hard ground beneath her and moaned.

Lynmeer set Moralia down. Hearing her soft moan, he gently kissed her. She reminded him so much of Aleah. "You are the strong one," he whispered in her ear. "You shall guide Niall." He backed away.

She felt the gentle kiss and looked away from her mother. Perhaps Henry had come? Mother could wait, she must not miss Henry. She wanted to tell him how incredibly beautiful their world is when you see it from atop a dragon.

Ecirp's grief poured out like a keen wind on the moors, and when his voice was spent, woeful sobs followed. Through blurry eyes, he tended to Moralia, mixing a potion that would make her sleep for several days, then hiding her deep in the woods under a cloak the color of the ferns. Finally, he blew his nose, straightened his vest and went to his fallen friend. The Knurly trees howled mournfully, shaking in grief and disbelief at this final sundering.

Chapter Thirty-Four

Niall drew back on the reins, stopping the mare when he first spotted the castle spires in the early morning mist. He turned around in the saddle, listening as his horse's ears perked and she danced to the side. An eerie sound came from the east. Close by, trees began swaying, and then howling. A mighty wind rocketed through the woods, throwing debris and bending branches to the ground. The ground shuddered beneath him as if a heavy door was slammed shut, and then all became quiet again.

In his pocket, a sudden, swift shock burned Niall's leg, the heat searing for a moment, and then gone. He felt for the pouch, and the hard rock was still inside. The pouch was yet warm to his touch, but it dissipated quickly. The trees around him straightened themselves.

"Something has happened, girl," he said, stroking the mare's neck in an effort to calm her. She stood twitching, her feet planted wide and ready to bolt.

After a few minutes, when nothing else happened, getting inside the castle undetected again took his attention. Deciding he was stealthier without the horse, he slipped down quietly, stroked her soft muzzle in gratitude and hid her in a small copse surrounded by dense thicket.

Niall scouted the area. Baldonian soldiers were posted here and there all the way around the castle. Rather than engage and sound an alarm, he decided to wait for night. He needed arrows so he spent the long day whittling a new supply of shanks and hunting feathers. When full darkness descended and a few stars began to light the sky, he made his way to the falconer's entrance and gained access unseen by anyone. The secret door at the top squeaked a greeting. No one had oiled the hinges of late. He flattened against the wall, fearing someone sleeping inside the mews would hear the noise. This time, however, James was not in his cot. No one was.

Niall walked down the rows, noting leaves and straw strewn about. There were none of the noises of a mews, no rustling of feathers, no shifting about and preening. In fact, he found no birds at all.

He made his way down the stone stairs from the castle mews, remembering the many turns and hallways that eventually led him to the broad chamber. There he saw men huddled on pallets, talking quietly or snoring. Turning to the closest two who sat drinking from pewter mugs at the long wooden table, Niall strode up to them without trying to be quiet, giving them a chance to see him coming first and not be frightened by his sudden appearance.

"Excuse me, do you know the whereabouts of Ben Finwick? I was told he is here at the castle."

"Why, Niall. You've come back! Everyone!" the man shouted at large, "Niall's back!"

"Please," Niall said, holding up his hand to dampen down the outburst. "Do you know where Ben is?"

"Over there," the man pointed.

Niall walked slowly past tables full of men eating and drinking to the corner where a man lay covered in blankets. The room was not cold but the man lay shivering, his disheveled hair much the same dirty color as the floor. Niall glanced about, but no one else was near. He turned back to the table where the two sat watching him, when a moan escaped from the man on the pallet.

"Niall," the voice said.

Niall whirled around. "Ben!" he exclaimed, rushing to his friend's side. "I didn't recognize you. Ben, what has happened?"

"The arrow . . . I think it was poisoned . . . your mother . . . I got better at first . . . but I ran out of what she left me . . . there were others that needed it." His words were punctuated with short, labored breaths.

Niall rummaged in the bottom of his quiver. He finally found what he sought—a packet that had a small amount of dried leaves inside. He jumped up and ran to the table.

"Bring me some water!" he commanded. One man jumped up and scurried away. Grabbing a mug, Niall emptied its contents on the floor and poured the contents of the packet into it. The man came running back with a jug of water, and Niall filled the mug.

He moved quickly back to Ben's side and propped his friend up. "Here, Ben. It's likely to taste awful, but it can't be helped. I have nothing to mask the bitterness. You must drink it all. I need to go outside and find some Toeffer to dress your wound with. I'll be back as quickly as I can."

Ben grabbed Niall's shirt. "Be careful out there. Baldonian soldiers . . . everywhere."

He held Ben's head while he took a few sips of the liquid. Ben sputtered at first from the taste but managed to get some down before he closed his eyes. "I'll try again in a minute," he said, exhausted by the effort.

"All right, then, I'll be off. Hold on, Ben. You must keep drinking this. I know it's awful, but I promise you, it will help." He got up and went back to the table where others had joined the first two looking on.

"I've got to get some medicine for his leg. Quick, tell me who is in charge and what has been happening."

"James was, till three days past," a man began. "I'm Haftley, sir. James left the castle to get supplies to the men in the north and was taken by ambush. We have most of the wounded here. We don't go outside, and the Baldonians don't come in." The man cocked his head to the side, looking at Niall rather oddly. "How did you get in?"

Niall ignored the man's question. "How many wounded are here, and how many others?"

"Probably twenty-five wounded. Some of us are ready to go back and fight, but we don't rightly know where to go. I'd say another seventy-five including women and children are holed up in the castle."

"Gather together all the men who are ready to fight. Have them pack provisions for moving fast in the forest, just in case. I'll be back as soon as I get the medicine I need."

"What about Ben there?" he said, pointing to Niall's friend on the floor.

"If I can find the right medicine, he'll recover, but I've got to hurry," Niall answered, and he turned and left the room as quickly as he had come.

Slipping out the falconer's gate fifteen minutes later, Niall froze, flattening himself behind the vine that shielded the entrance. Someone was near. Fear kept him waiting for many long seconds, too many to count, ears strained, his eyes adjusting to the dark aided only by the stars. He finally allowed himself a long shallow breath.

A minuscule rustle tickled his left ear, perhaps a mouse, so tiny was the sound. He rotated his head slightly and stared eye to eye with Nan.

"Oh grief, Nan, what a fright you gave me."

The bird blinked and stepped onto his shoulder. He could have sworn there was a smile on her face. He waited until his breathing returned to normal before finally scurrying across the open yard and into the woods. Nan flew a few feet above, settling back down when he stopped.

"I've got to find some Toeffer, Nan, and there are a few more things that sure would help. It's so bloody dark out here, but if I'm not mistaken, there is some growing where I left the mare." He cautiously moved forward, trying to be quiet and not to trip. He tamped the forest floor with his toes before setting his heels down. Still, he smacked a stump with his knee when he was looking up, and a branch caught his quiver when he was looking down. "What would Lynmeer say of my stealth now?" he thought. Eventually, though, his eyes adjusted and he remembered the lessons. "Be the ground you walk on. Be the tree you stand behind." The going got easier, but a second later Nan squeezed her talons into his shoulder. He halted immediately and the bird hopped onto a close branch, turning away from him.

Sensing the same presence that Nan did, he slowly drew two arrows and fitted one into his bow, then stepped behind the large tree on his right. He feared his abilities had dulled while he was in Ayhrland, but as the seconds ticked by, he was reassured that was not the case. Two men tramped down a game trail, their bows bumping into trees and each other. The back one held the lead rope, and Niall's mare followed behind.

"Watch where you're going, Harry. You hit me one more time with that thing and I'm going to knock yer block off!"

"Ah, shut up. You lead for a while. Why we are scouting at this time of night is beyond me because I can't see a bloody thing."

"We found the horse, didn't we?"

"Yea, and we should be riding her instead of walking."

"And get knocked off by a tree branch? You daft loon!"

The one called Harry stopped to let his fellow scout pass him by. Their uniforms were ragged and filthy. Niall could smell them before he could see them properly.

A moment later, Harry slumped to the ground. "Arghh."

"Wha'd you hit now, you clumsy oaf?" The man in front laughed, and then he too hit the ground.

Niall checked the men's pockets and found a small pouch inside Harry's shirt. Inside was a coated paper packet, and he opened it carefully. Taking a small sniff, he shook his head in anger. His mother was right. The Baldonian archers were dipping their arrows in a poison scraped off deadly frogs. His blood began to boil, but Lynmeer's last words to him came to mind immediately, cooling him off. Patting down each man, he retrieved three knives and a full complement of arrows. He sniffed each arrow and was satisfied none of them had already been laced with the poison.

"I've wasted enough time here, Nan. I've got to find the Toeffer for Ben."

Dragging the bodies off the immediate path, he hoped they wouldn't be seen come daylight. Turning to leave, he tripped over a large Knurly root and landed headfirst in a large clump of Toeffer.

"Well, Lynmeer, thank you," he said, bringing himself to his knees.

The tree coughed. "You are most welcome, sir; however, my name is Taversham."

"Oh, beg your pardon," Niall said, reaching out to break off a Toeffer leaf. "I'm Niall Thoralt of Knurlysham. I don't suppose you're any relation of Professor Haversham?"

"I rather imagine we're all related, if one were to look back far enough. Professor Haversham is most likely a distant cousin, though I've not met him."

"Well, at any rate, this saves me a lot of time," Niall said, picking himself and a good supply of the leaves up off the ground before giving the tree a respectful bow. "Do you know what happened earlier, when the wind howled so, and the ground shook?"

His question was met with silence. He could sense the tree's sorrow, but time was running out and so he continued without waiting for an answer, "I am in dire need of medicinal help for an injured man. The Baldonians have used poison on their arrows. Toeffer will be a good start," he said. "Is there anything else of good use nearby?"

The tree shook itself and then straightened up. "You might be interested in the medicinal properties of the mushrooms growing on my north side. I know it's hard for you to see in the dark. I'll shake my low branches nearest them. There is also a willow growing off to my left. You should take a few branches for pain relief, if that is needed too."

It wasn't long before Niall had all he could easily carry of the Toeffer, the mushrooms and the willow. "Thank you again."

"Absolutely, Niall, we have missed you. I hope you are able to rid us of the Baldonian trash. They have everything and everyone completely out of kilter."

"Right. Well, I shall do my best. Thank you again,

Taversham." Niall said, looking around before he started off. Clouds had now obscured even the starlight that had helped him when he first left the castle. The tree coughed discreetly.

"Cire is this way, sir." He shook his lower branches on Niall's right side.

"Right."

He started and then stopped. Getting the mare into the castle was impractical this time of night. Finally, he hobbled her again, but removed the saddle and pack. He could find them later. He buried his head in the mare's mane.

"Thank you, girl. You have served my family well. Eat and rest—and don't get caught again. I'll come for you as soon as I can."

He also left Nan outside the castle. He climbed the stairs and opened the door into the mews without fear of detection. When he entered the broad hall, Ben sat propped against a wall, a long shock of dirty hair plastered flat against his head.

Ben grinned as he watched Niall take command of the room, getting someone to boil water for making tea with the willow bark, someone else to bring a mortar and pestle to the table where he laid out his supplies. Grabbing some Toeffer leaves, he went to where Ben sat and hunkered down next to his friend.

"How are you feeling, Ben?"

"Surprisingly better after drinking that delightful concoction you left me. Do you have something equally wonderful this time?" He grimaced as Niall pulled back the blankets to get a look at the wound. The coloring was not as awful as one might have expected, but there was a ways to go.

"The Baldonians are tipping their arrows in poison," Niall explained as he wrapped the wound in fresh Toeffer. Your fever and chills are a result of the poison getting into your bloodstream, not infection from the wound. Mother did a good job here."

"Where is she?" Ben asked, lying back and gripping the edge of the blanket against the pain. "I want her to teach me more."

"She's . . . nearby," Niall answered. "I ran into a couple Baldonian archers while I was outside just now. They carry the poison in a packet. Those two won't be shooting anyone anymore, but we have to prepare as if they all have it. Wait now. I'll be right back."

Niall returned to the table, cut some willow bark to steep in the boiling water and looked carefully at the mushrooms. He wasn't sure how to use them. They looked common, but flatter with a more fluted underside than what he was familiar with. After his experience with the Toeffer-like Poeffer plant he had found near Gaxdorn Gate, he was hesitant, though he had no reason not to trust Taversham's judgment.

Wishing he had thought to ask the tree how best to administer the mushrooms, and in what quantity, he finally broke off one small piece and added it to the mug of willow tea.

"Here, Ben. This should help with the pain. There's one bit for which I'm not positive of the effects, but I'm sure it will help."

Ben drank a good deal of the tea, surprised that it didn't taste as nasty as the last concoction. Had it been bad, it wouldn't have mattered. He would have drunk it anyway. The last batch had made him feel so much better in such a short time.

"There are no birds in the mews. What happened to them?" Niall asked, as he checked the wound again.

"James let them go before he left. He didn't have time to train someone to care for them. He wanted them to be free rather than starve from neglect."

"Good thinking."

Ben nodded. He opened his mouth to praise James's bravery but hiccuped instead. A confused look came over his face. Niall had no difficulty imagining Ben had much to talk about, but it would have to wait. The mushroom must be taking affect.

Ben plopped the mug down on the floor beside him. He rolled his head from side to side. "Nooo pain," was all he managed to say. He tilted his head and closed his eyes, popping them open again. "Whoa . . ."

Niall reached out and caught Ben as he went over. Before covering him with a blanket, he checked his pulse and was relieved to find it strong and steady. He asked about and found a woman who had served as a housekeeper in the castle, or at least she had before they went to war.

"Of course I will help, sir. Ben here treated the others that are wounded and did a right fine job, up until these last few days. I'll be glad to look after him for you."

He showed her how to dress the wound with Toeffer and how to make the pain-relieving tea. He did not include anymore mushrooms in the recipe.

All the while he worked, he wished he had brought his mother with him. Someone with her knowledge needed to be at the castle, helping to tend to these wounded men. The poison that Baldonia was using added a sinister dimension that he was not sure how to treat properly. Thinking of his mother only added to his worry. Was she with Lynmeer? In his mind she was now Rhyaden's queen, and he would die if that was what it took to put her on the throne. Their last embrace lingered in his thoughts.

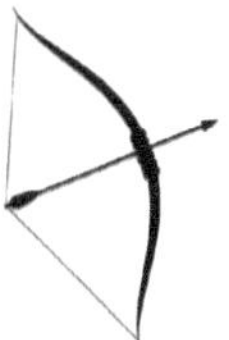

Chapter Thirty-Five

Niall opened his eyes to see streaks of colored light filtering through high stained-glass windows. He heard someone stirring the fire. Groans came from around the room where men rustled on pallets, attempting to wake up. He looked to his side where Ben lay smiling up at him.

"I'm so glad you are alive and looking better," Niall said. He stretched.

"Me as well," Ben replied. "When you were gone, I thought maybe you were dead."

Niall sat up. "I'll tell you what happened later; there isn't time now. When you are able, I need for you to go to Knurlysham. Annwyn … the village is in trouble."

"How do you know that? We've had no word from there."

"I . . . just feel it. Trust me, Ben."

"And what are you going to do?" Ben asked.

"End the war. I have to end this war."

"How?"

"I'll send Nan to search for the spy who killed Gunder. Once I know where she is, I'll figure the rest out."

"I need one more day to recover, but I'm not going back to Knurlysham, Niall. I'm staying with you. We came together, and we will end this together."

"But," Niall began, and then he shook his head. "I learned some things while I was gone."

Ben waited. There was so much Niall wanted to talk over with his best friend. "What things, Niall?" Ben finally asked.

Niall hesitated, then looked at his friend. "With King Stephen gone, someone must lead our army. So, I guess it's you and me," he replied. "Brothers Forever!"

Ben sat still, looking at Niall. His eyes reflected the dancing flames from the fire. Ben nodded his head. "Rhyaden will need a good leader after the war too."

† † †

A gentle rain had washed the air in the night, leaving a fresh scent in camp for a change. Layla knew it wouldn't last long. The warmth of the day would bring back the odor of people trapped in one place too long.

She intercepted a soldier on his way to the captain's tent. She and Tam had returned from the southern coastline an hour earlier. The man who stood before her hesitated a second too long before he spoke, and then she noted his eyelids quivering ever so slightly when he looked at her. His report of their ransacking a village far to the west seemed genuine on the face of it, but his numbers were elusive, again with those eyelashes.

"I have no news of King Stephen," the man added. He turned and walked away to give his report.

"That much I knew," she said to herself. It was obvious

not an ounce of progress had been made in breaching the castle walls. She fingered the ring in her pocket.

On the outside of the castle, soldiers were in constant frustrating skirmishes with Rhyaden fighters, whose tactic was strike and disappear. Those on the inside of the stone walls seemed to have an inexhaustible supply of food and water, arrows and boiling hot liquid to pour down on soldiers attempting to breach those walls. It was infuriating. Captain Lodall proved unable to come up with a new plan. Layla was positive he was incompetent.

Tam came running up. "It's him! He's back." Her face was flushed.

"Who?" Layla asked.

"The one they call Niall."

A smile spread across Layla's face.

"How interesting. The worthy opponent returns." She held a measure of respect for the one whose strategy had kept them from easy victory. "Perhaps if we behead him, it will be enough to demoralize those holed up inside the castle."

Tam nodded and turned to leave.

"How do you know it was him?" Layla asked, her mind still trying to decide what kind of opportunity this was before she made any kind of suggestion to the captain.

"His falcon was spotted above the castle," Tam replied.

A cold chill encased Layla. She nodded, trying to shake it off. Squaring her shoulders, she strode purposefully to the captain's tent.

"Glad you are back. Good progress has been made to the west," he said when she entered. "What have you found on your scouting trip?"

Ignoring his words, Layla started in. "The Rhyaden leader

has returned to the castle. I don't know how he got in. There has to be another entrance."

The captain stood dumbfounded. "Our scouts are on constant watch. Where did you get this news?"

"From my second; she is trustworthy."

"I can't see as it will change anything. We will stick with our plan. Eventually, they will starve. When we take the castle, the kingdom is ours, I mean to say— our king's," Lodall corrected.

"I don't believe they will wait until they starve," Layla countered.

"What do you mean? If they come out the gate without surrendering, they will be slaughtered."

"Their leader is far too clever for that. If he got in, he can get out," Layla said.

"There's no other way in," Lodall restated, his voice rising with his exasperation.

"Possibly not," she agreed, nodding her head, "but I fear we should tighten security. The men have gotten slack in their vigilance."

"Enough! I don't need your criticism of my command. You are dismissed!" Lodall was yelling now. Layla knew arguing was useless. She didn't bother to tell him of the queen mother.

"As you wish, captain."

Stepping out of the tent, Layla looked around. "I'm going to find Niall myself," she thought. "No one else will get this job done."

Inside her tent, Layla looked over to the pack she had carried everywhere she went for the past year. She picked it up off her bedroll and removed the map of Rhyaden. Curious as always about its glow, she sat down and unfolded it. No luminesce appeared. She rolled the parchment back up and walked over to the tent flap for better light. Unrolling it, disappointment sent another chill down her spine. It did not glow.

She returned the map to the leather binding and placed it in her pack. Lifting up the tent flap once again, her gaze surveyed the camp.

Far across the open area, a woman stood at a cook fire, wiping the sweat off her brow, wisps of stringy hair falling into her face. She stirred a boiling mixture of tubers and rabbit. Another shook out bedding from one of the tents. She could hear a baby cry in the outlying area. Layla's eyes narrowed. What was her next move?

Chapter Thirty-Six

The black falcon circled above Niall, gradually descending to the mews where the young man stood. In a rustle of flapping wings, the bird landed close by. Nan watched Niall and waited, flexing her talons one at a time.

"Find the one with the stag horn."

Nan saw Niall's mouth move, but the voice she heard came from a far-off place, echoing across the land, perfectly clear in meaning.

The falcon launched forward in a dark mass of wings and wind. Nan pumped her wings to gain altitude. From atop Thorncrag she could see every cranny where the enemy might hide.

Niall rejoined the men in the castle.

"Who is good with a longbow?" he asked the assembled group. Three raised their hands confidently; eight more said they were proficient with crossbows. "All right. You shall man the ramparts. You sir, and you," he said, pointing to the oldest of the men, "shall be their support. Keep them in arrows and whatever else they might need. Set up some straw bales for practice in the meantime. The rest of you will use whatever weapon you use best."

"What is your plan?" one of the archers asked. "Surely, it's not a good idea to leave the castle when we are outnumbered? We are protected here."

"Ben is going to villages east of here to try and find more men to join us. In our first battle, we had the element of surprise. I don't think we can count on that again. When the Baldonians retreated, it was not to the open ground in front of the castle as I'd hoped, but to the north where their reinforcements waited. This time, I plan to start a fire on that side, one big enough to force the Baldonians into the open. That's when you archers come into play. Once we have their numbers down, I'll give a signal for the rest of you to come out the gate and finish them off."

Ben and Niall left late in the night. They were silent until they were sure they were safely past any danger from the Baldonians.

"Go to Millfork first," Niall suggested. "If you don't find help there, head straight east to Bitter Creek."

"All right," Ben answered.

"I'll start the fire if the weather turns right, but otherwise, we'll wait for you."

"I'll be back as soon as I can." And with that, Ben was gone.

Instead of going straight back to the castle, Niall made a slow and careful circle of the Baldonian camp. He had to have an idea of numbers. Putting thirteen men on the ramparts left them only a dozen to take on the Baldonians. Niall was sure the Baldonians numbered close to fifty, but he needed to be sure.

Each time he came upon one of the men in uniform, the temptation to pull out an arrow and eliminate one more of the enemy took all of the self-discipline he could muster. He gritted his teeth and moved on. Finding four or five dead guards would alert the enemy of an impending strike, something Niall did not want to do. They needed more time to prepare.

"Sixty-three," he mouthed, sick at heart. It was a good estimate, but the numbers could be higher. How many fighters might Ben be able to find? What else could bring about a shift in his favor? He circled the castle and waited for a band of clouds to obscure the moon before crossing to the falconer's entrance. A tiny breeze blew across his face. He lifted his head to smell as it cooled his brow.

Two days later, Niall slipped down the stairs in the wee hours before dawn, making his way across the open grass to the forest. "You have done well," he had told each man the night before, clasping hands with every one before he left. They were ready. He'd wanted to wait until Ben returned, but the weather and the wind direction had turned in their favor. He wasn't going to miss the opportunity. If he failed, the men were still safely inside, though he knew eventually the castle would run out of food and supplies.

A stout breeze came from the north, rustling the fallen dry leaves. In the light of day, the varied colors of autumn were at their best, but in the dark, a person could not tell them apart. The sharp tang of cold salt air mixed with the damp odor of forest. Niall circled the Baldonian camp. This time, when he encountered a guard, sleeping or otherwise, he loosed an arrow, retrieved it, and quietly moved on.

Nan had brought no news of the woman Niall sought. Not knowing where she was left a niggle of worry in the back of his mind, but routing out their main force was his objective now. Niall took out five guards before reaching his destination on the north side of the Baldonian camp.

He took off his pack and removed the leather bundle at the bottom. Unwrapping the layers, he got to the pitch-soaked cloth, some of which he wrapped tightly around an arrow. He set about building a twenty-foot-long ridge of leaves and twigs, his fingers fumbling in the cold. Finally, he took out his flint and lit the remaining cloth. It flared up instantly. He set it on the pile of dried leaves, then drug it along the ridge. Fire began at once, lighting the area. Niall looked around, aware he was exposed in the eerie light.

All that remained was the signal. He watched the red flames dance higher and higher, then he lit the arrow and sent the blaze high above the forest where anyone awake could see it.

Men nervously watching atop the ramparts saw the signal and passed the word. Niall had set the trap. Dawn was breaking, but already the north wind was fanning flames into a frenzy. Soon pitch from pine trees began to boil, and as each tree exploded, the fire was passed from crown to crown. The wind brought the deadly smell to the Baldonian camp. Utter chaos broke out.

They had three choices. They could escape to the east, the west, or the open ground around the castle to their south. Because Baldonia lay to the west, and he hoped Ben would be on the east side, Niall chose to go to the west. Several Baldonians soon came his way, and he easily took them down.

Layla woke when acrid smoke crept into her tent. She slid the dagger and the horn into their usual places in her belt.

"Tam, wake up."

Tam rolled over. "What?"

"Fire!" With those final words to her companion she was gone. On the outside, men milled around the captain's tent; others ran in various directions away from the fire.

"Stop!" Layla screamed. "Do not run toward the castle. They'll mow you down. We must stick together."

Under any normal circumstance of war, the men would have listened to her words, but the ominous fire strangled their reasoning. She knew that this time they weren't going to heed her. Captain Lodall burst out of his tent, frantically trying to button his pants. He spotted Layla and motioned her to his side.

"What do we do?" he asked, leaning in so others could not hear.

Layla laughed out loud. "Run for your life, captain, unless you have a better idea."

Niall had warned the archers to take care when people burst out of the forest. There were captive women and children who were most likely to run straight to the castle, but daylight made it easy to distinguish those who ran from the forest. Only a few wore the dirty green uniform, and they were easily dispatched by the crossbows from the ramparts. The women and children who had been held as hostages were ushered through the great gates as the Rhyaden men poured out.

Nan circled above Niall, kawing a warning when she detected soldiers moving in his direction. Each time, he was able to stop their escape. Then a contingent of eight moved swiftly toward his position, among them Captain Lodall.

Niall felled three men who ran into the small clearing he guarded before he was spotted. Arrows began to fly in both directions. Thwack!

"Uhhh!" Niall yelped.

Thwangs reverberated among the trees as arrows were embedded deep into trunks or the bodies of men. Swooshing noises passed close to Niall's ears. He loosed no more arrows, holding onto the few that remained in his quiver for sure shots only. An enemy arrow was lodged deep in his left leg. Mustering his strength against the agonizing pain, he pulled the shaft out, the tip ripping open his flesh. Dropping to the ground, he fumbled in his pack for Toeffer to staunch the flow of blood.

"Biscuit!" Niall mouthed. He had removed the herb satchel at the castle when he put the pitch in for the fire.

The crackling roar from the flames grew louder. Screams could be heard in the distance. A loud kaw screamed a warning above him. Niall looked up in time to see a woman with a dagger running at him. She was nimble, and he could see a long, dark braid bouncing behind her as she leaped over a log. The sight was mesmerizing.

Nan dove at the running figure, then veered off at the last possible moment. Her kaw confused the woman for a second's hesitation, giving Niall time to draw his dagger and stand up. On the far side of the woman, the Baldonian captain tripped and fell to the ground as the falcon swept past his head. She landed a few feet away. At the sight of the huge falcon, the two remaining men turned around and fled in the opposite direction.

"Go away, get away from me," the captain screamed. Hearing his voice, her wings rose menacingly higher. She lifted off, and great black talons reached for his head. He managed to

 Barbara Tyner

cover his eyes with his arms, but the talons tore long gashes down the side of his head and one arm. She was not done.

Fire spread to the edge of the camp; only moments remained before everything left behind would be ablaze and lost forever to ash. Small eyes in the corner of the empty tent looked at the pack that held the map of Rhyaden, lost for so long.

Lynmeer had been a great friend, not a master. Ecirp could not help the tears that slipped down his pale, rubbery cheeks. They had enjoyed each other's company for over a century. He reached out and opened the pack, retrieved the map and was gone in the flick of an eye. Never again, as long as he lived, would this map be used against Rhyaden.

Chapter Thirty-Seven

Ben's swordsmanship was self-taught. Most of his practice behind the barn had been defensive moves. He could parry an enemy's thrust but had little practice in offense. The edge of his sword was now razor sharp, however. It would inflict lethal damage. Each of the last two nights, he had sat by a fire and sharpened the blade, worrying as he drew down the stone. Would he return in time?

Unable to sleep in the wee hours of the morning, he took the watch. A cold wind blew out of the north, making him shiver despite his layers of clothing.

"Get some sleep. We'll leave in a few hours," Ben told young Saul sitting at the edge of the sleeping men. An hour later, Ben stood up and yawned. His eyebrows shot up when a blazing arrow lit up the dark sky. It was gone in seconds. He blinked. Had he really seen it? An eerie glow began to appear, not in the west where the sun was rising, but in the north.

"Then it begins," he said.

Ben rousted all the men and led them to a natural rise in the rolling hills beneath Thorncrag, east of the castle. It afforded them good visibility, and they could quickly change positions depending on the direction the enemy took. He posted several men as lookouts. From their high ground, they watched transfixed as the fire turned from a mere glow to a massive inferno fanned by the wind ahead of the storm.

On the east side of the burning camp, those Baldonians who had chosen this direction for escape slowly found each other and their numbers grew to fifteen. They headed toward the Thorncrag Mountains. It would take them several hours of hiking to get around the peaks and back to the longboats.

One Millfork villager besides Ben had a sword; several had daggers. Ben had dared look no further. Eager to rid their kingdom of the scourge from the west, eight who were hardly past boyhood and two old men joined him without hesitation.

Ben held his men back, waiting until the Baldonians had all passed out of the trees to cross the talus slope beneath Thorncrag. At his signal, arrows were loosed by the three who had bows. Cries of pain went up from their targets. Two were hit in the first round. A second volley flew through the morning air, and this time all three found their mark. The arrows were followed by a wave of stampeding men, Ben at the head.

Ben watched young Saul charge the Baldonian closest to him, swinging his father's mace with all his might. The man in uniform crumpled at his feet. Yelling at the top of his lungs, the boy went after another.

A Baldonian carrying a large club turned toward Ben. He saw the man turn and raise his weapon high with both hands, yelling as he charged forward. Ben did not have time to hesitate. He ran the man through, then pulled the sword back. Adrenaline surged through him.

✝ ✝ ✝

Niall stood still, watching as the woman circled around him in the small clearing. Their daggers were of equal length. She had the advantage, since she was not losing blood as Niall was. For the first time in his life, he wondered if being so skilled with the bow was a good thing. He had not practiced often with other weapons.

Screams from the captain and the falcon filled the air. She lifted her head at the sound. Niall held his position, watching her without regard to the battle fought by Nan. Sweat ran down his back. What is she thinking? Niall shifted his stance to give his leg some relief. She looked down at his leg.

"You are bleeding badly. You may ask for mercy, you know," she said.

Niall saw the antler horn at her side. "Why have you invaded my kingdom?"

The question brought a smile to her face. "The DeMont family represents the true monarchy of Rhyaden. Our plan is simply to right that one hundred-year-old mistake."

"You lost that battle once already, and you're about to lose it again," Niall responded. "I think you should consider surrendering. You will be allowed to go home."

"Humph," she snorted. "I don't believe so." She took a step forward. "Admit it, your kingdom has no king. Your people deserve a leader who is brave, unlike King Stephen, little boy that he is. You are smart. I have seen that. Together you and I could rule." She continued her slow, measured steps toward him.

"My mother is Rhyaden's queen," Niall replied, "and she is the one who will rule." A shocked look registered on his adversary's face. "My name is Niall Thoralt and my great-grandfather was Andrew Valdorn," he stated.

"Valdorn's son died in the Great Fire that destroyed the

old castle," the woman countered.

"That was what was told to protect the boy's life. In fact he lived."

"What makes you think I would believe such a story?" she asked. "Even if it mattered." She edged closer. She was near enough for him to see her eyes. They glinted like steel, their intent written plainly for Niall to read. Gunder's last word echoed in his head.

"I'd like to know your name," Niall said softly.

The question took her back, and then she nodded. "I am Layla. Layla DeMont. I suppose that would make us cousins of some sort," she added, with more than a hint of sarcasm.

"Kinship doesn't matter today," he answered. "Your evil deeds have written your destiny. If you refuse to surrender, you will die today."

Layla laughed at him, and then with all of her might, she lunged. Niall side-stepped adeptly, but when he placed weight on his right leg, it buckled. She sensed the falter and swung around hard and fast to slice him through. He ducked and dove for her legs, losing his dagger as they both tumbled to the forest floor. Weak from loss of blood, Niall still outweighed his opponent by more than forty pounds. It was an advantage when they landed, but her skill from years in the wild as a spy was not to be denied. She struggled fiercely with the heavy weight on top of her, then arched her back in order to draw her legs up and send Niall over her head. Anticipating the move, he drove his knee deep into her belly.

"Uumph!" she cried, the air knocked out of her.

Niall shook her dagger hand, his grip cruel. Layla cried out, and the knife slipped to the ground. As she gasped for air, Niall knocked the knife out of her reach.

Taking a shallow breath, Layla rolled hard to her left, against his weak leg, and made a reach for his dagger. Pain shot up his leg as she stretched her fingers to get the knife in her grasp. The agony caused Niall to lose his hold. Black wings suddenly blanketed the two of them. Sharp talons picked up the knife. As suddenly as she came, Nan lifted away.

Niall rolled off and made a dive for Layla's dagger. He jumped up, keeping the weight on his good leg. Layla lay still, the giant bird's action sinking in. Finally, she got to her feet. He watched her chest heave in a long shudder and her head drop in defeat.

For a split second, Niall felt the wrenching pain in his leg and closed his eyes. A nearby tree whispered to him, "Watch."

Niall looked up to see Layla's eyes blazing. She launched herself at him in a desperate last try. He drove her dagger deep into her middle.

"No . . . I . . ." Her voice faltered. She looked at him, her eyes confused. He could see the question she wanted to ask as the life seeped out of her, and then the eyes glazed over and she became dead weight in his arms. He slowly let her body slip to the forest floor.

Moments later, the bitter north wind calmed and a gentle mist descended. To the east of where Niall stood, raindrops sizzled as they hit the glowing embers and put out the fire.

Shouting voices could now be heard coming from the east. Nan rustled a warning from nearby. Niall picked up his bow and limped to a new position, melting behind some trees. He spotted a female running his way. Coming into the open she spied Layla's body. Slowing, she turned towards the body and dropped down. After a moment, she reached out and stroked Layla's face. Her hands shook. With a great sob, she pulled back her wet, tangled hair. A roar of anguish emanated from her. "You killed her! You killed her," she screamed to the trees. "What do I do now?"

"Go home," Niall said, stepping out from behind a tree.

The sobbing stopped abruptly. The woman stood and pulled her knife from her belt.

"Take a message to King DeMont. Tell him a Valdorn sits on the Rhyaden throne," Niall commanded.

Her eyebrows knit together in question.

"Many of us must start again," he continued, "without the people we loved. You too will find a way," he said. "Go home, now, and don't come back."

Tam's chest rose and fell. Seconds ticked by, then she sheathed her knife and ran swiftly past Niall, headed west. Holding his weapon at the ready, he watched her go. Heaving a great sigh, he turned toward Cire. He must get to the castle for help. A small movement stopped him.

Ecirp stepped out from behind a tree. "The war is over, Niall."

Niall nodded in relief, relaxing his stance. After a moment he said, "Your being here makes me fear a great upheaval. What has happened?"

"Lynmeer has died," Ecirp answered.

Tears blurred Niall's vision. He nodded. "I need Toeffer," he managed to say, before crumpling to the forest floor.

† † †

"Your mother was attacked by a Baldonian solder," Ecirp said a few minutes later as he addressed Niall's leg. "He chose to use magic so she would live."

Niall nodded.

"I have Toeffer here. Your leg will heal."

Ecirp cleaned the bloody wound before wrapping it with Toeffer leaves. Niall gritted his teeth and gazed into the distance. He knew the dragon and Ecirp had spent far more years together than what he'd had with Lynmeer.

"Will you be all right, Ecirp?" he asked eventually.

"Yes, Niall, I will be all right. Thank you."

Niall nodded. "Where is my mother? I need to take her home."

"She is recovering at the castle. I believe you will find your father at Cire too."

"Thank you." Niall slowly turned to look directly at Ecirp. "It isn't our gifts that make us powerful, is it, but rather the choices that we make?"

The creature's scales softened, and his pale coloring brightened to a seafoam green, his own sadness lifting the tiniest bit.

"We are all made of the strength that comes from our struggles."

"There is still much for me to learn, isn't there?"

"Yes . . . yes, that is true—for everyone," Ecirp replied. He finished with the leg and looked up into Niall's eyes. "Will you claim your kingdom?"

"I'm... not sure."

"I believe Rhyaden needs you, Niall, more than ever. Even more important than his vow to protect your family, protecting Rhyaden is why Lynmeer came to be your teacher. King Stephen is likely to return to reclaim his throne. He doesn't deserve it, but you will have to fight him for it."

"I ran away, before."

"You are young. Running was a natural reaction to the

horror of your friend's death. What counts in the end is that you chose to come back and finish what needed to be done."

The distant shouts were getting closer. Niall thought then of Lynmeer and the men of Rhyaden who had fought under him and died for Rhyaden's freedom. He struggled to rise. He grabbed his bow and leaned on it to get upright. Straightening his shoulders, he looked around. Ecirp was gone.

Ben burst out of the trees on the other side of the clearing. Seeing Niall, a smile lit Ben's face, and he raised his arms in triumph. "Brothers Forever!"

Then Niall found himself surrounded by men wielding axes and maces and crossbows and knives, his kingdom's men, the lot of them soggy wet and triumphant, raising him up on their proud shoulders.

Barbara K. Tyner

Barbara was born in Colorado and still resides there. A lifelong love for horses and the outdoors led to a life of farming, ranching, and managing a feedlot. She spearheaded a ten-year project in rural eastern Colorado to establish The Grassroots Community Center, park, and health clinic. A board member of the Foundation for nine years, she became the Executive Director of the Center when it opened.

After retiring from ranching, her long dormant love for writing bloomed and she returned to school, earning a BA in English Literature from UCCS. A lifelong love of T.H.White's classic, "*The Once and Future King*" and her granddaughter's love for dragon stories were a major inspiration for "*Rhyaden.*"

Barbara's first novel, "Wait Here, Wait There" was released in 2012. This work deals with the realities of Alzheimer's and pushing one's self through and beyond grief. At the same time, she wrote this first novel, she and her daughter co-wrote a five-book series of children's picture books, **The Badger Books**.

The mother of three children, and grandmother of five, Barbara loves gardening, kayaking, bike riding, snow-shoeing, and visiting National Parks. Through her bi-weekly blog barbaraktyner.wordpress.com she corresponds with people around the globe on all topics of everyday life.